Spenser St. John

Rajah Brooke

The Englishman as Ruler of an Eastern State

Spenser St. John

Rajah Brooke
The Englishman as Ruler of an Eastern State

ISBN/EAN: 9783337141820

Printed in Europe, USA, Canada, Australia, Japan

Cover: Foto ©Raphael Reischuk / pixelio.de

More available books at **www.hansebooks.com**

RAJAH BROOKE

THE ENGLISHMAN AS RULER OF AN EASTERN STATE

BY

SIR SPENSER ST JOHN, G.C.M.G.

AUTHOR OF
'HAYTI; OR, THE BLACK REPUBLIC,'
'LIFE IN THE FORESTS OF THE FAR EAST,'
ETC.

LONDON
T. FISHER UNWIN
PATERNOSTER SQUARE
MDCCCXCIX

PREFACE

I HAVE undertaken to write the life of the old Rajah, Sir James Brooke, my first and only chief, as one of the Builders of Greater Britain. In his case the expression must be used in its widest sense, as, in fact, he added but an inappreciable fragment to the Empire, whilst at the same time he was the cause of large territories being included within our sphere of influence. And if his advice had been followed, we should not now be troubled with the restless ambition of France in the Hindu-Chinese regions, as his policy was to secure, by well defined treaties, the independence of those Asiatic States, subject, however, to the beneficent influence of England as the Paramount Power, an influence to be used for the good of the governed. Sir James thoroughly understood that Eastern princes and chiefs are at first only influenced by fear ; the fear of the consequences which might follow the neglect of the counsels of the protecting State.

The plan which the Rajah endeavoured to persuade the English Government to adopt was to make treaties with all the independent princes of the Eastern Archipelago, including those States whose shores are washed by the China Sea, as Siam, Cambodia and Annam, by which they could cede no territory to any foreign power without the previous consent of England, and to establish at the capitals of the larger States well-chosen diplomatic agents, to encourage the native rulers not only to improve the internal condition of their countries, but to inculcate justice in their treatment of foreigners, and thus avoid complications with other powers.

Sir James Brooke first attempted to carry out this enlightened policy by concluding treaties with the Sultans of Borneo and Sulu, to secure these States from extinction ; the latter treaty was not ratified, however, owing to the timidity of a naval officer, foolishly influenced by a clever Spanish Consul in Singapore, who took advantage of the absence of the Rajah. In the forties and fifties the expansion of Great

Britain, as is well known, was looked upon with genuine alarm by many of our leading statesmen.

Sir James Brooke, however, was not destined to see the fufilment of his ideas, as a ministry came into power in 1853 which cared nothing for the Further East, and in the hope of consolidating their majority in Parliament sacrificed their noble officer to appease the clamour raised by Joseph Hume and his followers, who, like other zealots, pursued their objects regardless of all the evidence which could be brought to refute their unfounded accusations. Joseph Hume may be called a libeller by profession, who began his career by making his fortune in the East India Company's service in a very few years—a remarkable achievement; and who afterwards, when in Parliament, brought himself into notoriety by attacking first Sir Thomas Maitland, secondly Lord Torrington, and ultimately Sir James Brooke, whose shoe latchets he was unworthy to unloose.

Sir James had thus but a short career as an English official. He was named Confidential Agent in 1845, Commissioner and Consul-General in 1846, Governor of Labuan in

1847, and his return to England in 1851 practically closed his active political connection with England, though he did not resign all his offices until 1854.

But the Rajah did not thus conclude his own career; he returned to Sarawak and devoted all his energies to the development of his adopted country, and of the neighbouring districts. I shall have to relate what extraordinary vicissitudes of fortune he had to encounter, and how after many years of conflict he emerged triumphant, to leave to his successor, Sir Charles Brooke, a small kingdom, well organised as far as Sarawak was concerned, with strongly established positions reaching to Bintulu, which have but increased in influence and in power to further the well-being of the natives of every race and class; and to prove to all who care to interest themselves in the subject, what a gain to humanity has resulted from the old Rajah having had the courage and the forethought to found his rule in a wild country, whose inhabitants, with few exceptions, were till then inimical to Europeans, and mostly tainted by piracy. But he argued truly that these people knew very imperfectly what Englishmen were, and he determined to show them that some, at all events, were worthy of their confidence, and could devote themselves without reserve to their welfare.

The peculiarity of the Rajah's system was to treat the natives, as far as possible, as equals; not only equals before the law, but in society. All his followers endeavoured to imitate their chief, and succeeded in a greater or less degree, thus producing a state of good feeling in the country which was probably found nowhere else in the East, except in Perak, one of the Protected States in the Malay Peninsula, into which one of his most able assistants introduced his method of government. I am told that this good feeling, if not the old friendly intimacy between native and European, still exists to a considerable degree throughout the possessions of the present Rajah, which is highly honourable to him and to his officers.

I have not attempted to re-write my account of the Chinese Insurrection (see Chapter VI.). I wrote it when all the events were fresh in my mind, and no subsequent information has rendered it necessary to make any changes. It was a most interesting and important incident in the Rajah's career, and it fixed for ever in the minds of his countrymen how wise and beneficent must have been his rule of the Malays and Dyaks, that they should have stood by him as they did when he appeared before them as a defeated fugitive.

How far-seeing were the Rajah's views and plans is proved by the fact that his successor has found it unnecessary to change any phase of his policy, whether political or commercial, whether financial, agricultural or judicial; with the growth of the country in population and wealth all has been of course considerably augmented, but the lines on which this great advance has been made were laid by the first Rajah, and that this honour is due to him no one should deny.

As there was but one Nelson, so there has been but one Sir James Brooke. How admirable was the simplicity of his character! So kind and gentle was he in manner, that the poorest, most down-trodden native would approach him without fear, confident that his story would be heard with benevolent attention, and that any wrong would, if possible, be righted. And as for the purity of his private life, he was a bright example to all those around him.

It may be thought that I have exaggerated the grandeur of the Rajah's personality, and the great benefits he conferred on the natives, and that I have been influenced in my views by the warm friendship which existed between us. If there be any who hold this opinion, I would refer them to Mr Alfred Wallace's work, *The Malay Archipelago*, in which, after dwelling in a most appreciative manner on the Rajah's rule in Sarawak, he adds these eloquent words, 'Since these lines were written his noble spirit has passed away. But though by those who knew him not he may be sneered at as an enthusiastic adventurer, or abused as a hard-hearted despot, the universal testimony of everyone who came in contact with him in his adopted country, whether European, Malay or Dyak, will be that Rajah Brooke was a great, a wise and a good ruler, a true and faithful friend, a man to be admired for his talents, respected for his honesty and courage, and loved for his genuine hospitality, his kindness of disposition and his tenderness of heart.'

The portrait of Rajah Brooke facing the title page is taken from the picture by Sir Francis Grant, which is one of his best works. It is a most speaking likeness, and I have left it in my will to the Trustees of the National Portrait Gallery, if they will accept it.

SPENSER ST JOHN.

4 Chester Street, S.W.

Note.—I would wish to add a few words to explain why, in the course of this *Life* of Rajah Brooke, I have not dwelt on the controversy which raged for some years about the character of the Seribas and Sakarang Dyaks. The only person who, to a late period, held to his view that these tribes were not piratical was Mr Gladstone; but after reading my first *Life of Rajah Brooke*, in which I defended the policy of my old chief with all the vigour I could command, I received the following note from him, which rendered unnecessary any further discussion of the subject:—

February 25, 1880.

My dear Sir,—I thank you very much for sending me your *Life of Sir James Brooke*, which I shall be anxious to examine with care. I have myself written words about Sir James Brooke which may serve to show that the difference between us is not so wide as might be supposed, and I fully admit that what I have questioned in his acts has been accepted by his legitimate superiors, the Government and the Parliament.—I remain, yours faithfully, W. E. GLADSTONE.

HIS EXCELLENCY SPENSER ST JOHN.

It is as well that I should publish another letter, to show that Mr Gladstone bore me no ill-will on account of the vigorous way I had attacked him whilst defending the policy of my old chief. I had applied to Lord Granville to be sent out as Special Envoy to renew relations with the Republic of Mexico, and the following is his Lordship's reply:—

FOREIGN OFFICE, *May* 28, 1883.

MY DEAR SIR SPENSER,—Many thanks for your note. I have availed myself of your offer, mentioning it to Gladstone, who highly approved (notwithstanding the hard blows you once dealt him), and I have submitted your name to the Queen, who, I feel sure, will sanction the step.—Yours sincerely, GRANVILLE.

It is pleasant to place on record this generosity of feeling in one of our greatest statesmen, whose career has now been closed.

CONTENTS

CHAPTER IV

CHAPTER V

CHAPTER VI

CHAPTER VII

LIST OF ILLUSTRATIONS

Rajah Brooke

CHAPTER I

BROOKE'S ANCESTORS AND FAMILY—HIS EARLY LIFE —APPOINTED ENSIGN IN THE MADRAS NATIVE INFANTRY—CAMPAIGN IN BURMAH—IS WOUNDED AND LEAVES THE SERVICE—MAKES TWO VOYAGES TO CHINA—DEATH OF HIS FATHER—CRUISE IN THE YACHT 'ROYALIST'

JAMES BROOKE was the second son of Mr Thomas Brooke of the Honourable East India Company's Bengal Civil Service, and of Anna Maria Stuart, his wife. Their family consisted of two sons and four daughters. One of the latter, Emma, married the Rev. F. C. Johnson, Vicar of White Lackington; another, Margaret, married the Rev. Anthony Savage; the eldest son, Henry, died unmarried after a short career in the Indian army.

Mr Thomas Brooke was the seventh in descent from Sir Thomas Vyner, who, as Lord Mayor of London, entertained Oliver Cromwell in the Guildhall in 1654; whilst his only son, Sir Robert Vyner, who had taken the opposite side in those civil contests, received Charles II. in the city six years later. On the death of Sir Robert's only son George the baronetcy became extinct, and the family estate of Eastbury, in Essex, reverted to the two daughters of Sir Thomas Vyner, from one of whom, Edith, the Brooke family is derived, as one of her descendants married a Captain Brooke, who was Rajah Brooke's great-grandfather.[1]

Mr Thomas Brooke, though not distinguished by remarkable talent, was a straightforward, honest civilian, and his wife was a most lovable woman, who gained the affections of all those with whom she was brought into contact. She always enjoyed the most perfect confidence of her distinguished son. To her are addressed some of his finest letters, in which he pours forth his generous ideas for the promotion of the welfare of the people whom he had been called upon to govern.

James Brooke was born on the 29th of April 1803 at Secrore, the European suburb of Benares, and he remained in India until he was twelve years old, when he was sent to England to the care of Mrs Brooke, his paternal grandmother, who had established herself in Reigate. He shortly afterwards went to Norwich Grammar School, at that time under Dr Valpy, but he remained there only

[1] These details are taken from Miss Jacob's *Life of the Rajah of Sarawak*, Vol. I., page 1.

a couple of years, as, after the freedom of his life in India, discipline was irksome to him, and he ran away home to his grandmother. I never heard him say much about the master, but he loved and was beloved by many of his schoolfellows, and showed even then, by his influence over the boys, that he was a born leader of men.

About this time his parents returned from India and settled at Combe Grove, near Bath, where they collected their children around them. A private tutor was engaged to educate young Brooke, but it could have been only for a comparatively short time, as in 1819 he received his ensign's commission in the 6th Madras Native Infantry, and soon started for India. He was promoted to his lieutenancy in 1821, and in the following year was made a Sub-Assistant Commissary-General, a post for which, as he used to say, he was eminently unfitted.

When the war with Burmah broke out in 1824 Brooke found himself thoroughly in his element. As the English army advanced into Assam the general in command found himself much hampered in his movements by the want of cavalry. Brooke partly relieved him of this difficulty; his offer to raise a body of horsemen was accepted. By the orders of the general he called for recruits, who could ride, from the different regiments, and soon had under him an efficient body of men, who undertook scouting duties. He found it difficult to keep them in hand, for the moment they saw an enemy they would charge, and then scatter in every direction where they thought a Burmese might be concealed.

During an action in January 1825 he performed very efficient service with his irregular cavalry, charging wherever any body of Burmese collected. He received the thanks of the general, and his conduct was mentioned in despatches as 'most conspicuous.' Two days later occurred an instance of what is almost unknown in our army. A company of native troops had been ordered to attack a stockade manned by Burmese; the English officer in command advanced until, on turning a clump of trees, he came well under fire; then, losing his nerve, he bolted into the jungle. Brooke arrived at that moment, saw the infantry wavering, threw himself from his horse, assumed the command, and thus encouraged they charged the stockade, but Brooke literally 'foremost, fighting fell.' Seeing their leader fall, the men were again about to retreat, when Colonel Richards, advancing with reinforcements, restored the fight, and in a few minutes the place was taken, though with heavy loss. No attempts were ever made to turn these strong stockades, and thus the army suffered severely and to no purpose.

I have often heard Sir James Brooke tell the

story. He had been sent out to reconnoitre; found the enemy strongly posted, and suspecting an ambuscade, galloped back to warn his superior officer, but too late, as firing had already commenced, and the infantry, without a leader, were confused. He placed himself at their head, but as he charged he felt a thud, and fell, losing all consciousness. After the action was over, his colonel, who had seen him fall, inquired about young Brooke, and was told that he was dead; but examining the fallen officer himself, found him still alive and had him removed to hospital. A slug had lodged in his lungs, and for months he lay between life and death. It was not, in fact, until August that he was strong enough to be removed, and then only in a canoe. He was paddled down a branch of the Bramapootra, rarely suffering from pain, but gazing pensively at the fast-running stream and the fine jungle that lined its banks; in after life it seemed to him as a dream.

On the Medical Board at Calcutta reporting that a change of climate was necessary, he was given a long furlough. He returned to England and joined his family at Bath. The voyage did him some good, but the wound continued very troublesome, and at times it appeared as if he could not recover. After the slug had been extracted, however, he gradually got better, so that in July 1829 he was enabled to embark on board the Company's ship

Carn Brae; but fate was against his again joining the Indian army. This vessel was wrecked, and when, in the following March, he sailed for the East on board the *Huntley Castle*, she was so delayed by bad weather, that when she called in at Madras Brooke found that he could not join his regiment before the legal expiration of his leave. He consequently resigned the service and proceeded in the *Huntley Castle* to China.

Brooke never cared much for the East India Company's service, and as he had formed friendships on board the *Huntley Castle* he preferred continuing in her to remaining idle in India awaiting the Directors' decision, which, even if favourable, could scarcely arrive before twelve months had expired. The decision was favourable; but as young Brooke had in the meantime left Madras the matter dropped. The Indiaman first touched at the Island of Penang, one of the Straits Settlements, and here Brooke had an opportunity of seeing what lovely islands there were in the Further East. It is not necessary to dwell on this voyage, as nothing of importance occurred during it; but his stay in China made a deep impression on Brooke's mind. He saw how the Chinese ill-treated and bullied our countrymen, and how the East India Company submitted to every insult in order not to imperil their trade.

After the usual stay in the Canton River, the *Huntley Castle* returned to England, and Brooke found himself at home with no employment whatever.

He formed many projects; the favourite one, which he had discussed with the officers of the *Huntley Castle*, was to purchase a ship, load her with suitable goods, and sail for China or the adjacent markets. But as none of the friends had any capital, Brooke confided their views to his father, and naturally met with the objection that his son was not a trader and never could become one. However, in the end, the young fellow prevailed. The brig *Findlay* was bought, laden with goods, and with his partner, Kennedy, formerly of the *Huntley Castle*, and his friend, Harry Wright, also of the same vessel, he set sail for the Further East. This voyage was not destined to be a success. Brooke wished to introduce on board the easy discipline of a yacht, whilst Kennedy, who was captain, went to the other extreme and would insist upon the severe discipline of the navy, without its safeguards. Differences soon arose, and as they found trade by interlopers was not encouraged, Brooke went to see Mr Jardine, of the firm of Messrs Jardine, Matheson & Company, and laid the case before him. The shrewd man of business could not but smile at the idea of this elegant young soldier managing a trading speculation. He, however, agreed to buy vessel and cargo, and told the partners they had better leave the matter in his hands. No objection was raised, and Mr Jardine so judiciously invested in silks the amount he had arranged to pay, that in the end comparatively little loss accrued, none of which was allowed by Brooke to fall on Kennedy.

On his return to England Brooke wearied of continued leisure, and although he yachted about the Southern Coast and the Channel Islands, he longed for some sphere of action which could bring his great abilities into play. The death of his father, in December 1835, gave him complete independence. The fortune left was sufficient to provide for his wife, and to give to each of his children £30,000. Brooke now decided to carry out the plan he had formed since his first voyage to China, which was to buy a small vessel and start on a voyage of discovery. But this time there were to be no partners and no trade; he intended to be complete master in his own ship. He ultimately fixed his choice on the *Royalist*, a schooner yacht of about 142 tons burden. He was delighted with his purchase, and soon tried her qualifications by starting in the autumn of 1836 for a cruise in the Mediterranean. There he visited most of the principal cities, including Constantinople, which in after years afforded him a constant subject of conversation with the Malays, who interested themselves in every detail of his visit. 'Roum' to them is still the great city where dwells the head of the Mohammedan religion.[1] Among those who accompanied him on this cruise was his nephew, John Brooke

[1] When I first went to live in Brunei, the Sultan of Borneo's capital, there was living there an old haji who was visiting Egypt at the time of Buonaparte's invasion, and who remembered well the Battle of the Nile and the subsequent expulsion of the French by the English.

Johnson, afterwards known as Captain Brooke, and also John Templer, who was then and for many years afterwards one of his warm friends and enthusiastic admirers.

Though determined to make a voyage of discovery in the Eastern Archipelago, Brooke was not able to leave England till December 1838. He employed all his spare time in studying the subject, finding out what was already known, and drawing attention to his plans by a memoir he wrote on Borneo and the neighbouring islands, summaries of which were published in the *Athenæum* and in the *Journal* of the Geographical Society. He felt a great admiration for Sir Stamford Raffles, and ardently desired to carry out his views in dealing with the peoples of the Further East.

How well Brooke sums up the feelings which prompted him to undertake what was in every respect a perilous enterprise! 'Could I carry my vessel to places where the keel of European ship never before ploughed the waters; could I plant my foot where white man's foot had never before been; could I gaze upon scenes which educated eyes had never looked on, see man in the rudest state of nature, I should be content without looking to further rewards.'

It is difficult, even under the most favourable circumstances, to convey to the mind of a reader an exact portrait of the man whose deeds you desire to chronicle; but as I lived for nearly twenty years with James Brooke, I feel I know him well in all his strength and his weakness. Let me try to describe him. He stood about five feet ten inches in height; he had an open, handsome countenance; an active, supple frame; a daring courage that no danger could daunt; a sweet, affectionate disposition which endeared him to all who knew him well. Those whom he attended in sickness could never forget his almost womanly tenderness, and those who attended him, his courageous endurance. His power of attaching both friends and followers was unrivalled, and this extended to nearly every native with whom he came in contact. His few failings were his too great frankness, his readiness to believe that men were what they professed to be, or should have been, and (for a short time in latter years) that the unsophisticated lower classes were more to be trusted and relied on than those above them in birth and education. His only weaknesses were, in truth, such as arose from his great goodness of heart and his confiding nature.

No painter ever succeeded better in conveying a man's self into a portrait than Sir Francis Grant in his picture of Sir James Brooke. I have it now before me, and all I have said of his appearance may be seen at a glance. Although thirty years have passed since we lost him, he remains as much enshrined as ever in the hearts of his few surviving friends.

This brief preliminary chapter ended, I will now describe Brooke's voyage to Borneo, and the events which succeeded that remarkable undertaking.

CHAPTER II

EXPEDITION TO BORNEO—FIRST VISIT TO SARAWAK—VOYAGE TO CELEBES—SECOND VISIT TO SARAWAK—JOINS MUDA HASSIM'S ARMY—BROOKE'S ACCOUNT OF THE PROGRESS OF THE CIVIL WAR—IT IS ENDED UNDER THE INFLUENCE OF HIS ACTIVE INTERFERENCE—HE SAVES THE LIVES OF THE REBEL CHIEFS

BROOKE sailed from Devonport on December 16, 1838, in the *Royalist*, belonging to the Royal Yacht Squadron, which, in foreign ports, admitted her to the same privileges as a ship of war, and enabled her to carry a white ensign. As the *Royalist* is still an historic character in the Eastern Archipelago, I must let the owner describe her as she was in 1838. 'She sails fast; is conveniently fitted up; is armed with six six-pounders, and a number of swords and small arms of all sorts; carries four boats and provisions for four months. Her principal defect is being too sharp in the floor. She is a good sea boat, and as well calculated for the service as could be desired. Most of the hands have been with me for three years, and the rest are highly recommended.'

Whilst the *Royalist* is speeding on prosperously towards Singapore, and calling at Rio Janeiro and the Cape, let me sum up in a few words the object of the voyage.

The memorandum[1] which Brooke drew up on the then state of the Indian Archipelago (1838), shows how carefully he had studied the whole subject. He first expounds the policy which England should follow if she wished to recover the position which she wantonly threw away after the peace of 1815; he then explains what he proposed to do for the furtherance of our knowledge of Borneo and the other great islands to the East. Circumstances, however, as he anticipated might be the case, made him change the direction of his first local voyage.

The *Royalist* arrived in Singapore in May 1839, and remained at that port till the end of July, refitting and preparing for future work. There Brooke received news which induced him to give up for the present the proposed voyage to Marudu Bay, the northernmost district of Borneo, and visit Sarawak instead. Rajah Muda Hassim, uncle to the Sultan of Brunei, was then residing there, and being of a kindly disposition, had taken care of the crew of a shipwrecked English vessel, and sent the men in safety to Singapore. This unlooked-for conduct on the part of a Malay chief roused the interest of the Singapore merchants, and Brooke was requested to

[1] *See* Appendix.

call in at Sarawak and deliver to the Malay prince a letter and presents from the Chamber of Commerce.

This was a fortunate diversion of his voyage, as at that time Marudu was governed by a notorious pirate chief. The bay was a rendezvous for some of the most daring marauders in the Archipelago, and nothing could have been done there to further our knowledge of the interior.

All being ready, and the crew strengthened by eight Singapore Malay seamen,[1] athletic fellows, capital at the oar, and to save the white men the work of wooding and watering, the *Royalist* sailed for Borneo on the 27th of July, and in five days was anchored off the coast of Sambas. All the charts were found to be wrong, so that every care had to be taken whilst working up the coast. A running survey was made, and on the 11th August Brooke found himself at the mouth of the Sarawak river.

When Brooke first arrived in Borneo, the Sultan Omar Ali claimed all the coast from the capital to Tanjong Datu, whilst further south was Sambas, under the influence of the Dutch; but the rule of Omar Ali was little more than nominal, as each chief in the different districts exercised almost unlimited power, and paid little or no tribute to the central Government.

At the time of Brooke's first visit to Sarawak the

[1] I knew one of them, Subu, the favourite of every foreigner in Sarawak.

Malays of the country had broken out into revolt against the oppressive rule of Pangeran Makota, Governor of the district, and fearing that they might call in the aid of the Sambas Malays, and thus place the country under the control of the Dutch, the Sultan sent down Rajah Muda Hassim, his uncle and heir-presumptive, to endeavour to stifle the rebellion; but three years had passed, and he had done nothing. He could prevent the rebels from communicating with the sea, but he was powerless in the interior.

On hearing of the arrival of the *Royalist* at the mouth of the river, Muda Hassim despatched a deputation to welcome the stranger and invite him to the capital—rather a grand name for a small village. Brooke soon got his vessel under weigh, and proceeded up the Sarawak, and after one slight mishap, anchored the next day opposite the rajah's house, and saluted his flag with twenty-one guns.

Muda Hassim received Brooke in state, and the interview is thus described: 'The rajah was seated in his hall of audience, which, outside, is nothing but a large shed, erected on piles, but within decorated with taste. Chairs were arranged on either side of the ruler, who occupied the head seat. Our party were placed on one hand, and on the other sat his brother Mahommed, and Makota and some other of the principal chiefs, whilst immediately behind him his twelve younger brothers were seated. The dress of Muda Hassim was simple, but of rich material, and most of the principal men were well, and even superbly dressed. His countenance is plain, but intelligent and highly pleasing, and his manners perfectly easy. His reception was kind, and, I am given to understand, highly flattering. We sat, however, trammelled by the formalities of state, and our conversation did not extend beyond kind inquiries and professions of friendship.' Brooke's next interview was more informal, and closer relations were established, which encouraged him to send his interpreter, Mr Williamson, to ask permission to visit the Dyaks. This was readily granted, but before commencing his explorations, he received a private visit from Pangeran Makota. He was probably the most intelligent Malay whom we ever met in Borneo, frank and open in manner, but looked upon as the most cunning of the rajah's advisers. He was much puzzled, as were indeed all the nobles, as to the true object of Brooke's visit to Borneo, and confident in his power, determined to find it out. And though Brooke had in reality no object but geographical discovery, he could not convince his guest of that fact, who scented some deep intrigue under the guise of a harmless visit.

Brooke now took advantage of the rajah's permission to explore some of the neighbouring rivers, and he was shown first the fine agricultural district of Samarahan, but only met Malays. His next visit was to the Dyak tribe of Sibuyows, who lived on the river Lundu, which discharged its waters not many miles from Cape Datu, the southern boundary of Borneo proper.

From Tanjong Datu, as far as the river Rejang, the interior populations are called Dyaks — Land or Sea Dyaks—the former, a quiet, agricultural people, living in the far interior, plundered and oppressed by the Malays; they are to be found in Sarawak, Samarahan and Sadong. The Sea Dyaks were much more numerous, and though under the influence of the Malays and Arab adventurers, were too powerful ever to be ill-treated. They occupied the districts of Seribas and Batang Lupar, and those on the left bank of the Rejang, with a few scattered villages in other parts, such as this Sibuyow tribe on the Lundu.

The chief of this branch of the Sea Dyaks, the Orang Kaya Tumangong, was always a great favourite of the English officers in Sarawak. His was the first tribe that Brooke visited, and he then formed a high opinion of the brave man and his gallant sons, who were faithful unto death, and who were always the foremost when any fighting was on hand.

The village they occupied was, in fact, but one huge house, nearly six hundred feet in length, and the inner half divided into fifty separate residences for the fifty families that constituted the tribe. The front half of this long building was an open space, which was used by the inhabitants during the day for every species of work, and at night was occupied by the widowers, bachelors and boys as their bedroom. The Sea Dyaks are much cleaner than the Land Dyaks, and the girls of Sakarang, for instance, looked as well washed as any of their sisters in May Fair.

The distinction of Land and Sea Dyaks was due to the fact that the former never ventured near the salt water, whilst the latter boldly pushed out to sea in their light bangkongs or war boats, and cruised along at least two thousand miles of coast. When the *Royalist* first arrived in Sarawak the majority of the Sea Dyaks were piratically inclined. This practice arose in all probability from their inter-tribal wars—the Seribas against the Lingas and Sibuyows—and from their custom of seeking heads — almost a religious observance. When a party of young men went out to search for the means of marrying, and had failed to secure the heads of enemies, we can easily imagine their not being too particular about killing any weaker party they might meet, even if they were not enemies, and, finding it met with no retaliation, continuing the practice. In this they were encouraged by the Malay chiefs who lived among them, and who obtained, on easy terms, the women and children captives who fell into the hands of the Dyak raiders. Although the Linga and Sibuyow branches of the Sea Dyaks hunted for heads, they were the heads of their enemies, whilst the Seribas, and, in a lesser degree, the Sea Dyaks of the Sakarang and the Rejang spared no one they could overcome.

Brooke's next visit was to the river Sadong, to the north-east of Sarawak, and there he met Sherif Sahib, a great encourager of piracy of every kind. Sometimes he received the Lanuns,[1] the boldest marauders who ever invested the Far Eastern seas, bought their captives and supplied them with food, whilst at others he would aid the Seribas and Sakarangs in their forays on the almost defenceless tribes of the interior, or share their plunder acquired on the coasts of the Dutch possessions.

Finding that the rebellion in the interior of the Sarawak would prevent him from visiting it, Brooke decided to return to Singapore. After a friendly parting with Muda Hassim, whose last words were, 'Do not forget me,' the *Royalist* fell down the river. The night before Brooke had settled to sail he was joined by a small Sarawak boat with a dozen men, who were to pilot him out; but about midnight shouts were heard from the shore of 'Dyak! Dyak'! In an instant a blue light was burnt on board the yacht and a gun fired, and then there came a dead silence. Brooke sprang into a boat and pushed off to the Malay prahu, to find half the crew wounded. It seemed that a cruising party of Seribas Dyaks had no doubt seen the fire lighted on the shore, and had noiselessly floated up with the flood tide and attacked the Malays, not

[1] The Lanuns came from the great island of Mindanau, in the Southern Philippines, which was a nominal possession of Spain, and cruised in well-armed vessels.

observing in the dark night the *Royalist* at anchor. This occurrence showed how necessary it was to be on one's guard at all times.

The news brought by Brooke was well received in Singapore, as it opened up a new country to British commerce, and prevented the Dutch gaining a footing there, with their vexatious trade regulations, which practically debarred native vessels from visiting British ports.

As the Rajah Muda Hassim had assured his English visitor that the rebellion in the interior of Sarawak would collapse before the next fine season, he decided to pass the interval in visiting Celebes, a most attractive island, then but imperfectly known.

No part of Brooke's journals is more interesting than the account of his experiences in Bugis land. They are, however, simple travels, without many personal incidents to be noted ; but here, as elsewhere, he acquired the same ascendency over the natives, and the memory of his visit remained impressed on the minds of the Bugis rulers, who followed his advice in regulating their kingdoms, and especially listened to his counsels when he pointed out the danger of entering into armed conflict with their Dutch neighbours.

The following observations extracted from Brooke's journals are remarkable : 'I must mention the effect of European domination in the Archipelago. The first voyagers from the West found the natives rich and powerful, with strong established governments and a thriving trade. The rapacious European has reduced them to their present position. Their governments have been broken up, the old states decomposed by treachery, bribery and intrigue, their possessions snatched from them under flimsy pretences, their trade restricted, their vices encouraged, their virtues repressed, and their energies paralysed or rendered desperate, till there is every reason to fear the gradual extinction of the Malay. Let these considerations, fairly reflected on and enlarged, be presented to the candid and liberal mind, and I think that, however strong the present prepossessions, they will shake the belief in the advantages to be gained by European ascendency, as it has heretofore been conducted, and will convince the most sceptical of the miseries immediately and prospectively flowing from European rule as generally constituted.'

The above observations naturally apply to the Dutch and Spanish systems, which at that time alone had sway in the Archipelago, as England, with its small trading depots, did not actively interfere with the native princes. Yet it must be confessed that Borneo proper, which had generally escaped interference from their European neighbours, fell from a position fairly important to the most degraded state, entirely owing to the incapacity of its native rulers and not to outside influences.

The visits to Sarawak and Celebes tended to confirm Brooke's convictions that, if England would but act on a settled plan and on a sufficient scale, she could still save and develop the independent native states, without any necessity of occupying them.

In the year 1776 the Sultan of Sulu ceded to England all his possessions in the north of Borneo, and the East India Company formed a small settlement on the Island of Balambangan; this being on a very inefficient scale, was easily surprised by pirates and destroyed. Later on another attempt was made by the Company to establish themselves on the island, but it was soon abandoned.

Brooke, after carefully studying the subject, came to the same conclusion as Sir Stamford Raffles and Colonel Farquhar had done before him, that it was a mistake to take small islands; but that, on the contrary, this country should establish a settlement on the mainland of Borneo. As all the independent states of the Archipelago are filled with a maritime population, islands are not so safe from attack as the mainland, where the interior population is rarely warlike. He recommended that England should take possession of Marudu Bay, establish herself strongly there, be constantly supported by the navy, and from thence the Governor, with diplomatic powers, could visit all the independent chiefs and make such treaties with them as would prevent their being absorbed by other European States. His policy was of the most liberal kind; he would have sought no exclusive trade privileges, but he would have preserved their political independence. He would have established in the more important states carefully-selected English agents, to encourage the chiefs in useful reforms and to prevent restrictions on commerce. On the mainland he would not have instantly established English rule, except in a well-chosen, central spot, and there he would have awaited the invitation of the chiefs to send an English officer to aid them in governing.

Had this great plan been executed on a suitable scale Brooke's name would have been enshrined among the greatest builders of the British Empire. It is not too late even now; but where shall we find another Brooke to carry it out? North Borneo is at present under the protection of Great Britain, but it is owned and administered by a Chartered Company, and in these days cannot, under such conditions, hold the same position as a Crown colony.

The time seems propitious. The Spaniards have lost their hold over the Philippines, and Sulu and the great island of Mindanau will soon be free from their depressing influence; even the Dutch are acting on a more enlightened system, which would be encouraged, if England took an active interest in the Archipelago. The North Borneo Company would scarcely refuse a proposal to place the country under our direct rule, and with another Sir Hugh Low it might be made a valuable possession, and would gradually dominate the whole of the Archipelago.

The Philippines will now be governed by one of the most progressive nations in the world, and the effect of their rule will be far-reaching. It would appear to be advisable that Great Britain should simultaneously take over North Borneo, as the conditions heretofore existing have so completely changed.

From Celebes Brooke returned to Singapore to refit. His plans were to visit Borneo again, then proceed to Manila, and so home by Cape Horn. He arrived at our settlement in May, left it again in August, and reached Sarawak on the 29th, to find himself cordially received by Muda Hassim. The war was not over, nor was the end of it in sight. A few half-starved Dyaks had deserted the Sarawak Malays, and come into the Bornean camp to be fed; but the route to Sambas was still open, and it was suspected that supplies were furnished by the Sultan of Sambas, who coveted the territory.

After considerable discussion and consideration, Brooke thought he would visit the headquarters of the army which was supposed to be besieging the enemy; but he found it seven miles below the principal hostile fort. The spot was called Ledah Tanah, or the tongue of land, where the two branches of the river meet. It was the site of the old capital, and even when I was there some ten years later the iron-wood posts of the houses still existed, untouched by time, though over sixty years in use. As Brooke expected, Makota, at the head of the army, was doing nothing, and as he rejected the advice of his white visitor, and seemed determined not to advance nearer to the enemy, Brooke returned to Sarawak, and even announced his departure, as the North-East monsoon was coming on, and he did not wish to face it on his voyage to Manila. However, Muda Hassim appeared to feel his departure so acutely, that his heart smote him, and he agreed to visit the army once more, particularly as the Land Dyaks were now really leaving the rebels and joining the Bornean forces. He therefore returned to the camp, and by his energy compelled Makota to act. The stockade at Ledah Tanah was pulled down and moved to within a mile of the enemy's chief fort, Balidah, and gradually stockade after stockade was built, until the most commanding one was erected within three hundred yards of the hostile fort. Brooke sent to the yacht for two six-pounders and a sufficient supply of ammunition, and, with the aid of his men, soon battered down the weak defences of the enemy, and then proposed an assault. But this bold advice was looked upon as insanity, and though promises to advance were freely given, when it came to action they all hung back. At length, wearied with this procrastination, Brooke, in spite of the entreaties of all the native chiefs, embarked his guns and returned to the *Royalist*, and sent word to the rajah that his stay was utterly useless; but when Muda Hassim heard the decision, 'his deep regret was so visible that even all the self-command of the native could not disguise it. He begged, he entreated me to stay, and offered me the country, its government and its trade, if I would only stop and not desert him.'

Though Brooke could not accept the grant then, as it would have been extracted from the rajah's deep distress, he agreed to return to the army; and once more the guns were embarked in the boats, and every man who could be spared from the *Royalist* accompanied Brooke to the front. There he met Budrudin, Muda Hassim's favourite brother, with whom he soon contracted a friendship which ended only with the Malay prince's life. He was brave, frank and intelligent; he quickly appreciated the noble character of the white leader of men, and ever after he fully trusted him.

The episodes of the closing campaign of this civil war were so amusing, that although the story has been published several times, I cannot refrain from repeating it again in the words of the English chief.[1]

'On the 10th December we reached the fleet and disembarked our guns, taking up our residence in a house, or rather shed, close to the water. The

[1] *Voyage of the Dido*, Vol. I., page 172, *et seq.*

rajah's brother, Pangeran Budrudin, was with the army, and I found him ready and willing to urge upon the other indolent pangerans the proposals I made for vigorous hostilities. We found the grand army in a state of torpor, eating, drinking and walking up to the forts and back again daily; but having built these imposing structures, and their appearance not driving the enemy away, they were at a loss what to do next, or how to proceed. On my arrival, I once more insisted on mounting the guns in our old forts, and assaulting Balidah under their fire. Makota's timidity and vacillation were too apparent; but in consequence of Budrudin's overawing presence he was obliged, from shame, to yield his assent. The order for the attack was fixed as follows: our party of ten (leaving six to serve the guns) were to be headed by myself. Budrudin, Makota, Subtu and all the lesser chiefs were to lead their followers, from sixty to eighty in number, by the same route, whilst fifty or more Chinese, under their captain, were to assault by another path to their left. Makota was to make the paths as near as possible to Balidah, with his Dyaks, who were to extract the sudas and fill up the holes. The guns having been mounted, and their range ascertained the previous evening, we ascended to the fort about eight a.m., and at ten opened our fire and kept it up for an hour. The effect was severe. Every shot told upon their thin defences of wood, which fell in many places so as to leave storming breaches. Part of the roof was cut away and tumbled down, and the shower of grape and canister rattled so as to prevent their returning our fire, except from a stray rifle. At mid-day the forces reached the fort, and it was then discovered that Makota had neglected to make any road because it rained the night before! It was evident that the rebels had gained information of our intentions as they had erected a fringe of bamboo along their defences on the very spot we had agreed to mount. Makota fancied the want of a road would delay the attack; but I well knew that delay was equivalent to failure, and so it was at once agreed that we should advance without any path. The poor man's cunning and resources were now nearly at an end. He could not refuse to accompany us, but his courage could not be brought to the point, and pale and embarrassed he retired. Everything was ready—Budrudin, the Capitan China and myself, at the head of our men—when he once more appeared, and raised a subtle point of etiquette, which answered his purpose. He represented to Budrudin that the Malays were unanimously of opinion that the rajah's brother could not expose himself in an assault; that the dread of the rajah's indignation far exceeded their dread of death; and in case any accident happened to him, his brother's fury would fall on them. Budrudin was angry, I was angry too, and the doctor most angry of all; but anger was unavailing. It was clear they did not intend to do anything in earnest; and after much discussion, in which Budrudin insisted if I went he should likewise go, and the Malays insisted that if he went they would not go, it was resolved that we should serve the guns, whilst Abong Mia and the Chinese, not under the captain, should proceed to the assault. But its fate was sealed, and Makota had gained his object; for neither he nor Subtu thought of exposing themselves to a single shot. Our artillery opened and was beautifully served. The hostile forces attempted to advance, but our fire completely subdued them, as only three rifles answered us, by one of which a seaman was wounded in the hand, but not seriously. Two-thirds of the way the storming party proceeded without the hostile army being aware of their advance, and they might have reached the very foot of the hill without being discovered, had not Abong Mia, from excess of piety and rashness, began most loudly to say his prayers. The three rifles began then to play on them. One Chinaman was killed, the whole halted, the prayers were more vehement than ever, and after squatting under cover of the jungle for some time they all returned. It was only what I expected, but I was greatly annoyed by their cowardice and treachery—treachery to their own cause. One lesson, however, I learnt, and that was, that had I assaulted with our small party, we should assuredly have been victimised. The very evening of the failure the rajah came up the river. I would not see him, and only heard that the chiefs got severely reprimanded ; but the effects of reprimand are lost where cowardice is stronger than shame. Inactivity followed, two or three useless forts were built, and Budrudin, much to my regret and to the detriment of the cause, was recalled.

'Amongst the straggling arrivals I may mention Pangeran Dallam, with a number of men, consisting of the Orang Bintulu, Meri, Muka and Kayan Dyaks from the interior. Our house, or, as it originally stood, our shed, deserves a brief record. It was about twenty feet long, with a loose floor of reeds and an attap or palm-leaf roof. It served us for some time, but the attempts at theft obliged us to fence it in and divide it into apartments—one at the end served for Middleton, Williamson and myself. Adjoining it was the storeroom and hospital, and the other extreme belonged to the seamen. Our improvements kept pace with our necessities. Theft induced us to shut in our house at the sides, and the unevenness of the reeds suggested the advantage of laying a floor of the bark of trees over them, which, with mats over all, rendered our domicile far from uncomfortable. Our forts gradually extended to the back of the enemy's town, on a ridge of swelling ground, whilst they kept pace with us on the same side of the river on the low ground. The inactivity of our troops had long become a by-word amongst us. It was, indeed, truly vexatious, but it was in vain to urge them on, in vain to offer assistance, in vain to propose a joint attack, or even to seek support at their hands; promises were to be had in plenty, but performances never.

'At length our leaders resolved on building a fort at Sekundis, thus outflanking the enemy and gaining the command of the upper course of the river. The post was certainly an important one, and in consequence they set about it with the happy indifference which characterises their proceedings. Pangeran Illudin (the most active amongst them) had the building of the fort, assisted by the Orang Kaya Tumangong of Lundu. Makota, Subtu and others were at the next fort, and by chance I was there likewise; for it seemed to be little apprehended that any interruption would take place, as the Chinese and the greater part of the Malays had been left in the boats. When the fort commenced, however, the enemy crossed the river and divided into two bodies, the one keeping in check the party at Pangeran Gapoor's fort, whilst the other made an attack on the works. The ground was not unfavourable for their purpose, for Pangeran Gapoor's fort was separated from Sekundis by a belt of thick wood which reached down to the river's edge. Sekundis itself, however, stood on clear ground, as did Gapoor's fort. I was with Makota at the latter when the enemy approached through the jungle. The two parties were within easy speaking distance, challenging and threatening each other, but the thickness of the jungle prevented our seeing or penetrating to them. When this body had advanced, the real attack commenced on Sekundis with a fire of musketry, and I was about to proceed to the scene, but was detained by Makota, who assured me there were plenty of men, and that it was nothing at all. As the musketry became thicker, I had my doubts when a Dyak came running through the jungle, and with gestures of impatience and anxiety begged me to assist the party attacked. He had been sent by my old friend the Tumangong of Lundu, to say they could not hold the post unless supported. In spite of Makota's remonstrances, I struck into the jungle, winded through the narrow path, and, after crossing an ugly stream, emerged on the clear ground. The sight was a pretty one. To the right was the unfinished stockade, defended by the Tumangong ; to the left, at the edge of the forest, about twelve or fifteen of our party, commanded by Illudin, whilst the enemy were stretched along between the points, and kept up a sharp-shooting from the hollow ground on the bank of the river. They fired and loaded and fired, and had gradually advanced on the stockade, as the ammunition of our party failed ; and as we emerged from the jungle, they were within twenty or five-and-twenty yards of the defence. A glance immediately showed me the advantage of our position, and I charged with my Englishmen across the padi field, and the instant we appeared on the ridge above the river, in the hollows of which the rebels were seeking protection, their rout was complete. They scampered off in every direction, whilst the Dyaks and Malays pushed them into the river. Our victory was decisive and bloodless; the scene was changed in an instant, and the defeated foe lost arms and ammunition either on the field of battle or in the river, and our exulting conquerors set no bounds to their triumph.

'I cannot omit to mention the name of Si Tundu, a Lanun, the only native who charged with us. His appearance and dress were most striking, the latter being entirely of red, bound round the waist, arms, forehead, etc., with gold ornaments, and in his hand his formidable Bajuk sword. He danced, or rather galloped, across the field close to me, and, mixing with the enemy, was about to despatch a haji, or priest, who was prostrate before him, when one of our people interposed, and saved him by stating that he was a companion of our own. The Lundu Dyaks were very thankful for our support, our praises were loudly sung, and the stockade was concluded. After the rout, Makota, Subtu and Abong Mia arrived on the field; the last, with forty followers, had ventured half way before the firing ceased, but the detachment, under a paltry subterfuge, halted so as not to be in time. The enemy might have had fifty men at the attack. The defending party consisted of about the same number, but the Dyaks had very few muskets. I had a dozen Englishmen, Subu, one of our Singapore boatmen, and Si Tundu. Sekundis was a great point gained, as it hindered the enemy from ascending the river and seeking supplies.

'Makota, Subtu and the whole tribe arrived as soon as their safety from danger allowed, and none were louder in their own praise, but, nevertheless, their countenances evinced some sense of shame, which they endeavoured to disguise by the use of their tongues. The Chinese came really to afford assistance, but too late. We remained until the stockade of Sekundis was finished, while the enemy kept up a wasteful fire from the opposite side of the river, which did no harm.

'The next great object was to follow up the advantage by crossing the stream, but day after day some fresh excuse brought on fresh delay, and Makota built a new fort and made a new road within a hundred yards of our old position. I cannot detail further our proceedings for many days, which consisted, on my part, in efforts to get something done, and on the others, a close adherence to the old system of promising everything and doing nothing. The Chinese, like the Malays, refused to act; but on their part it was not fear, but disinclination. By degrees, however, the preparations for the new fort were complete, and I had gradually gained over a party of the natives to my views; and, indeed, amongst the Malays, the bravest of them had joined themselves to us, and what was better, we had Datu Pangerang and thirteen Illanuns, and the Capitan China allowed me to take his men whenever I wanted them. My weight and consequence was increased, and I rarely moved now without a long train of followers. The next step, whilst crossing the river was uncertain, was to take my guns up to Gapoor's fort, which was about six or seven hundred yards from the town, and half the distance from a rebel fort on the river's bank.

'Panglima Rajah, the day after our guns were in battery, took it into his head to build a fort on the river's side, close to the town in front, and between two of the enemy's forts. It was a bold undertaking for the old man after six weeks of uninterrupted repose. At night, the wood being prepared, the party moved down, and worked so silently that they were not discovered till their defence was nearly finished, when the enemy commenced a general firing from all their forts, returned by a similar firing from all ours, none of the parties being quite clear what they were firing at or about, and the hottest from either party being equally harmless. We were at the time about going to bed in our habitation, but expecting some reverse I set off to the stockade where our guns were placed, and opened a fire upon the town and the stockade near us, till the enemy's fire gradually slackened and died away. We then returned, and in the morning were greeted with the pleasing news that they had burned and deserted five of their forts, and left us sole occupants of the left bank of the river. The same day, going through the jungle to see one of these deserted forts, we came upon a party of the enemy, and had a brief skirmish with them before they took to flight. Nothing can be more unpleasant to a European than this bush-fighting, where he scarce sees a foe, whilst he is well aware that their eyesight is far superior to his own. To proceed with this narrative, I may say that four or five forts were built on the edge of the river opposite the enemy's town, and distant not above fifty or sixty yards. Here our guns were removed, and a fresh battery formed ready for a bombardment, and fire-balls essayed to ignite the houses.

'At this time Sherif Jaffer, from Linga, arrived with about seventy men, Malays and Dyaks of Balow. The river Linga, being situated close to Scribas, and incessant hostilities being waged between the two places, he and his followers were both more active and warlike than the Borneans; but their warfare consists of closing hand to hand with spear and sword. They scarcely understood the proper use of firearms, and were of little use in attacking stockades. As a negotiator, however, the Sherif bore a distinguished part; and on his arrival a parley ensued, much against Makota's will, and some meetings took place between Jaffer and a brother

Sherif at Siniawan, named Moksain. After ten days' delay nothing came of it, though the enemy betrayed great desire to yield. This negotiation being at an end, we had a day's bombardment, and a fresh treaty brought about thus: Makota being absent in Sarawak, I received a message from Sherif Jaffer and Pangeran Subtu to say that they wished to meet me; and on my consenting they stated that Sherif Jaffer felt confident the war might be brought to an end, though alone he dared not treat with the rebels; but, in case I felt inclined to join him, we could bring it to a favourable conclusion. I replied that our habits of treating were very unlike their own, as we allowed no delays to interpose; but that I would unite with him for one interview, and if that interview was favourable we might meet the chiefs at once and settle it, or put an end to all further treating. Pangeran Subtu was delighted with the proposition, urged its great advantages, and the meeting, by my desire, was fixed for that very night, the place Pangeran Illudin's fort at Sekundis. The evening arrived, and at dark we were at the appointed place and a message was despatched for Sherif Moksain. In the meantime, however, came a man from Pangeran Subtu to beg us to hold no intercourse; that the rebels were false, meant to deceive us, and if they did come we had better make them prisoners. Sherif Jaffer, after arguing the point some time, rose to depart, remarking that with such proceedings he would not consent to treat. I urged him to stay, but finding him bent on going I ordered my gig (which had some time before been brought overland) to be put into the water—my intention being to proceed to the enemy's kampong and hear what they had to say. I added that it was folly to leave undone what we had agreed to do in the morning because Pangeran Subtu changed his mind; that I had come to treat, and treat I would. I would not go away now without giving the enemy a fair hearing. For the good of all parties I would do it—and if the Sherif liked to join me, as we proposed before, and wait for Sherif Moksain, good; if not, I would go in the boat to the kampong. My Europeans, on being ordered, jumped up, ran out and brought the boat to the water's edge and in a few minutes oars, rudder and rowlocks were in her. My companions, seeing this, came to terms, and we waited for Sherif Moksain, during which, however, I overheard a whispering conversation from Subtu's messenger, proposing to seize him, and my temper was ruffled to such a degree, that I drew out a pistol, and told him I would shoot him dead if he dared to seize, or talk of seizing, any man who trusted himself from the enemy to meet me. The scoundrel slunk off, and we were no more troubled with him. This past, Sherif Moksain arrived, and was introduced into our fortress alone—alone and unarmed in an enemy's stockade, manned with two hundred men. His bearing was firm; he advanced with ease and took his seat, and during the interview the only sign of uneasiness was the quick glance of his eye from side to side. The object he aimed at was to gain my guarantee that the lives of all the rebels should be spared, but this I had not in my power to grant. He returned to his kampong, and came again towards morning, when it was agreed that Sherif Jaffer and myself should meet the Patingis and the Tumangong, and arrange terms with them. By the time our conference was over the day broke, and we descended to our boats to have a little rest.

'On the 20th December we met the chiefs on the river, and they expressed themselves ready to yield, without conditions, to the rajah, if I would promise that they should not be put to death. My reply was that I could give no such promise; but if they surrendered, it must be for life or death, according to the rajah's pleasure, and all I could do was to use my influence to save their lives. To this they assented after a while; but then there arose the more difficult question, how they were to be protected until the rajah's orders arrived. They dreaded both Chinese and Malays, especially the former, who had just cause for angry feelings, and who, it was feared, would make an attack on them directly their surrender had taken from them their means of defence. The Malays would not assail them in a body, but would individually plunder them, and give occasion for disputes and bloodshed. Their apprehensions were almost sufficient to break off the hitherto favourable negotiations, had I not proposed to them myself to undertake their defence, and to become responsible for their safety until the orders of their sovereign arrived. On my pledging myself to this they yielded up their strong fort of Balidah, the key of their position. I immediately made it known to our own party that no boats were to ascend or descend the river, and that any person attacking or pillaging the rebels were my enemies, and that I should fire upon them without hesitation.

'Both Chinese and Malays agreed to the propriety of the measure, and gave me the strongest assurances of restraining their respective followers; the former with good faith, the latter with the intention of involving matters, if possible, to the destruction of the rebels. By the evening we were in possession of Balidah, and certainly found it a formidable fortress, situated on a steep mound, with dense defences of wood, triple deep, and surrounded by two enclosures, thickly studded on the outside with *ranjaus*. The effect of our fire had shaken it completely, now much to our discomfort, for the walls were tottering and the roof as leaky as a sieve. On the 20th December, then, the war closed. The very next day, contrary to stipulation, the Malay pangerans tried to ascend the river, and when stopped began to expostulate. After preventing many, the attempt was made by Subtu and Pangeran Hassim in three large boats, boldly pulling towards us.

Three hails did not check them, and they came on, in spite of a blank cartridge and a wide ball to turn them back. But I was resolved, and when a dozen musket balls whistled over and fell close around them, they took to an ignominious flight. I subsequently upbraided them for this breach of promise, and Makota loudly declared they had been greatly to blame, but I discovered that he himself had set them on.

'I may now briefly conclude these details. I ordered the rebels to burn all their stockades, which they did at once, and deliver up the greater part of their arms, and I proceeded to the rajah to request from him their lives. Those who know the Malay character will appreciate the difficulty of the attempt to stand between the monarch and his victims. I only succeeded when, at the end of a long debate—I soliciting, he denying—I rose to bid him farewell, as it was my intention to sail directly, since, after all my exertions in his cause he would not grant me the lives of the people, I could only consider that his friendship for me was at an end. On this he yielded. I must own that during the discussion he had much the best of it; for he urged that they had forfeited their lives by the law, as a necessary sacrifice to the future peace of the country; and argued that in a similar case in my own native land no leniency would be shown. On the contrary, my reasoning, though personal, was, on the whole, the best for the rajah and the people. I explained my extreme reluctance to have the blood of conquered foes shed; the shame I should experience in being a party, however involuntarily, to their execution, and the general advantage of a merciful line of policy. At the same time I told him that their lives were forfeited, their crimes had been of a heinous and unpardonable nature, and that it was only from so humane a man as himself, one with so kind a heart, that I could ask for their pardon; but, I added, he well knew that it was only my previous knowledge of his benevolent disposition, and the great friendship I felt for him, which had induced me to take any part in the struggle. Other stronger reasons might have been brought forward, which I forbore to employ, as being repugnant to his princely pride, viz., that severity in this case would arm many against him, raise powerful enemies in Borneo proper, as well as here, and greatly impede the future right government of the country. However, having gained my point, I was satisfied.

'Having fulfilled this engagement, and being, moreover, with many of my Europeans, attacked with ague, I left the scene with all the dignity of complete success. Subsequently the rebels were ordered to deliver up all their arms, ammunition and property; and last, the wives and children of the principal people were demanded as hostages and obtained. The women and children were treated with kindness and preserved from injury or wrong. Siniawan thus dwindled away. The poorer men stole off in canoes, and were scattered about, most of them coming to Kuching. The better class pulled down the houses, abandoned the town and lived in boats for a month when, alarmed by the delay in settling terms and impelled by hunger, they also fled—Patingi Gapoor, it was said, to Sambas, and Patingi Ali and the Tumangong amongst the Dyaks. After a time it was supposed they would return and receive their wives and children. The army gradually dispersed to seek food, and the Chinese were left in possession of the once renowned Siniawan, the ruin of which they completed by burning all that remained and erecting a village for themselves in the immediate neighbourhood. Sherif Jaffer and many others departed to their respective homes, and the pinching of famine succeeded to the horrors of war. Fruit, being in season, helped to support the wretched people, and the near approach of the rice harvest kept up their spirits.'

Thus ended the great civil war, which is so renowned in local history. The three chiefs mentioned —Patingi Gapoor, Patingi Ali and the Tumangong— with their sons and relatives, will appear again as some of the principal actors in the history of Sarawak. All except Patingi Gapoor remained faithful to the end, or are still among the main supports of the present Government. I knew them all, with the exception of Patingi Ali, who was killed whilst gallantly heading an attack on the Sakarang pirates during Captain Keppel's expedition in 1844.

CHAPTER III

THIRD VISIT TO SARAWAK — MAKOTA INTRIGUES AGAINST BROOKE — VISIT OF THE STEAMER 'DIANA'—HE IS GRANTED THE GOVERNMENT OF SARAWAK—HIS PALACE—CAPTAIN KEPPEL OF H.M.S. 'DIDO' VISITS SARAWAK—EXPEDITION AGAINST THE SERIBAS PIRATES—VISIT OF SIR EDWARD BELCHER—RAJAH BROOKE'S INCREASED INFLUENCE — VISIT TO THE STRAITS SETTLEMENTS—IS WOUNDED IN SUMATRA—THE 'DIDO' RETURNS TO SARAWAK—FURTHER OPERATIONS—NEGOTIATIONS WITH BRITISH GOVERNMENT—CAPTAIN BETHUNE AND MR WISE ARRIVE IN SARAWAK

PEACE being again restored to the country, Brooke was enabled to study the position. Muda Hassim occasionally mentioned his intention of rewarding his English ally for his great services by giving him the government of Sarawak ; but nothing came of it, as when the document for submission to the Sultan was duly prepared it proved to be nothing but 'permission to trade.' However unsatisfactory this might be,

Brooke accepted it for the moment, and it was agreed that he should proceed to Singapore, load a schooner with merchandise, and return to open up the resources of the place. In the meantime the rajah was to build a house for his friend, and prepare a shipload of antimony ore as a return cargo for the schooner.

While in Singapore Brooke wrote to his mother concerning his plans, and he now added, 'I really have excellent hopes that this effort of mine will succeed; and while it ameliorates the condition of the unhappy natives, and tends to the promotion of the highest philanthropy, it will secure to me some better means of carrying through these grand objects. I call them grand objects, for they are so, when we reflect that civilisation, commerce and religion may through them be spread over so vast an island as Borneo. They are so grand, that self is quite lost when I consider them; and even the failure would be so much better than the non-attempt, that I could willingly sacrifice myself as nearly as the barest prudence will permit.'

Many, perhaps, could write such words, but Brooke really felt them, and fully intended to carry out his views, whatever obstacles might stand in his way; and they were many, for on his return to Sarawak in the *Royalist*, with the schooner *Swift* laden with goods for the market, he found no house built and no cargo of antimony ready. A house in Sarawak could be built in ten days or a fortnight, as the materials are all found in the jungle and the natives are expert at the work.

The antimony was procurable, but, as Brooke afterwards found, it was the product of forced labour, almost always unpaid. One cannot but smile at Brooke's first attempt at trade. Without sending up to see whether the antimony was ready, he accepted Muda Hassim's word, and then handed over to him the whole of the cargo of the *Swift*. What might have been expected followed. No sooner had the Malay rajah secured the goods than the most profound apathy was shown as to the return cargo. The same system was followed with regard to the government of the country; every attempt to discuss it was evaded, and I believe that Makota did his best to persuade Muda Hassim that the Englishman was but a bird of passage, who would soon get tired of waiting, and would sail away without the return cargo, and drop all thoughts of governing the country.

Pangeran Makota, who had been Brooke's enemy throughout all these proceedings, was now ready to act. He knew that the Land Dyaks in the interior, as well as the Malays of Siniawan whom the Englishman had aided to subdue, now looked to him as their protector; he therefore determined to destroy his prestige. He invited the Seribas Sea Dyaks and Malays to come to Sarawak; they came in a hundred bangkongs, or long war boats, with at least three thousand men, with the ostensible object of attacking a tribe living near the Sambas frontier, who had not been submissive enough to Bornean exactions; but every violent act they committed would have been overlooked if they only gave a sufficient percentage of their captives to the nobles. Already these wild devils had received the rajah's permission to proceed up the river; the Land Dyaks, the Malays, the Chinese were full of fear, as all are treated as enemies by the Seribas when out on the warpath. As soon as Brooke received notice of what Muda Hassim, instigated by Makota, had done, he retired to the *Royalist* and prepared both his vessels for action. The Malay rulers, hearing how angry he was, and uncertain what steps he might take, recalled the expedition, which returned, furious at being baulked of their prey, and would have liked to have tried conclusions with the English ships, but found them too well on their guard.

This very act which Makota expected would lower the Englishman's prestige, naturally greatly enhanced it, as it was soon known, even into the far interior, that the white stranger had but to say the word and this fearful scourge had been stayed.

Another event soon followed which greatly raised Brooke's influence among the natives. He received notice that an English vessel had been wrecked on the north coast of Borneo, and that the crew were detained as hostages by the Sultan of Borneo for the payment of a ransom. He now sent the *Royalist* to try and release them, whilst he despatched the *Swift* to Singapore for provisions, and remained with three companions in his new house in Sarawak. Could anything better prove his cool courage? The *Royalist* failed in its mission, but almost immediately after its return, an East India Company's steamer came up the river to inquire as to its success, and finding the captive crew still at Brunei, proceeded there and quickly effected their release. The appearance of the *Diana* twice in the river had its effect on the population, as it was probably the first steamer they had ever seen.

Makota had been greatly disappointed that his intrigues had failed to force the white strangers to quit the country, but his fertile invention now thought of more sure and criminal means. 'Why not poison them?' He tried, but failed; his confederates confessed, and then Brooke resolved to act. Either Makota or himself must fall. By a judicious display of force, quite justified under the circumstances, he freed the rajah from the baneful influence of Makota, who from that time forward ceased to act as chief adviser, and regained his former ascendency. Muda Hassim immediately carried out his original promise, and in a formal document handed over the government of the district of Sarawak to Brooke. The news was received with rejoicing by the Land Dyaks, the Sarawak Malays and the Chinese, but with some misgivings by the rascally followers of the Bornean rajahs. This event took place in September 1841.

Brooke's first act was to request Muda Hassim to return to their families the women and children who had been given as hostages after the close of the civil war. He succeeded in most cases, but as the younger brothers of Muda Hassim had honoured with their notice some of the unmarried girls, he was forced to leave ten of them in the harems of the rajahs.

Being now Governor of Sarawak, he determined to effect some reforms. One of the greatest difficulties he encountered was the introduction of impartial justice; to teach the various classes that all were equal before the law. He opened a court, at which he himself provided, aided moreover, by some of the rajah's brothers and the chiefs of the Siniawan Malays, and dispensed justice according to the native laws, which in most cases are milder than those of European countries. When absent himself his chief officer acted for him. As long as these laws were only applied to Dyaks, Chinese or inferior Malays, there was no resistance, but when the privileged class and their unscrupulous followers were touched, there arose some murmurings.

Brooke saw at once that to ensure stability to his rule he must govern the people through, and with the aid of, the chiefs to whom they were accustomed. He therefore proposed to Muda Hassim to restore to their former positions the men who had been at the head of the late rebellion, and who certainly had been

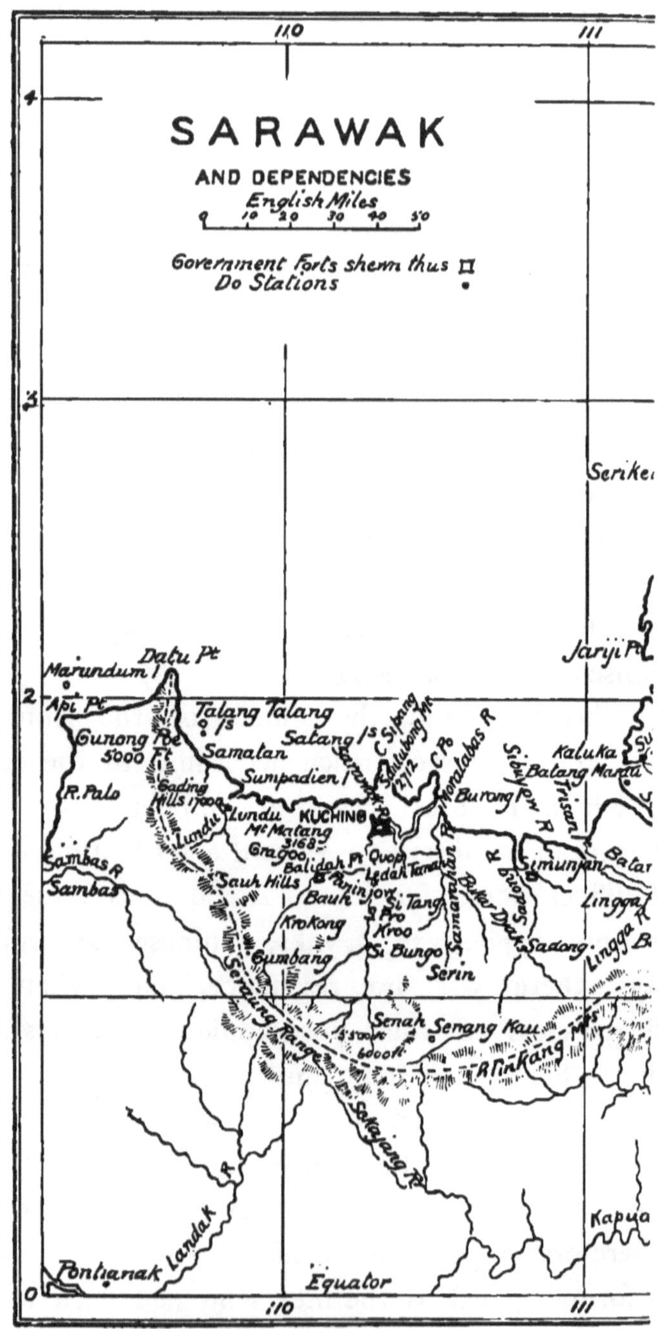

MAP OF SARAWAK AND ITS DEPEND

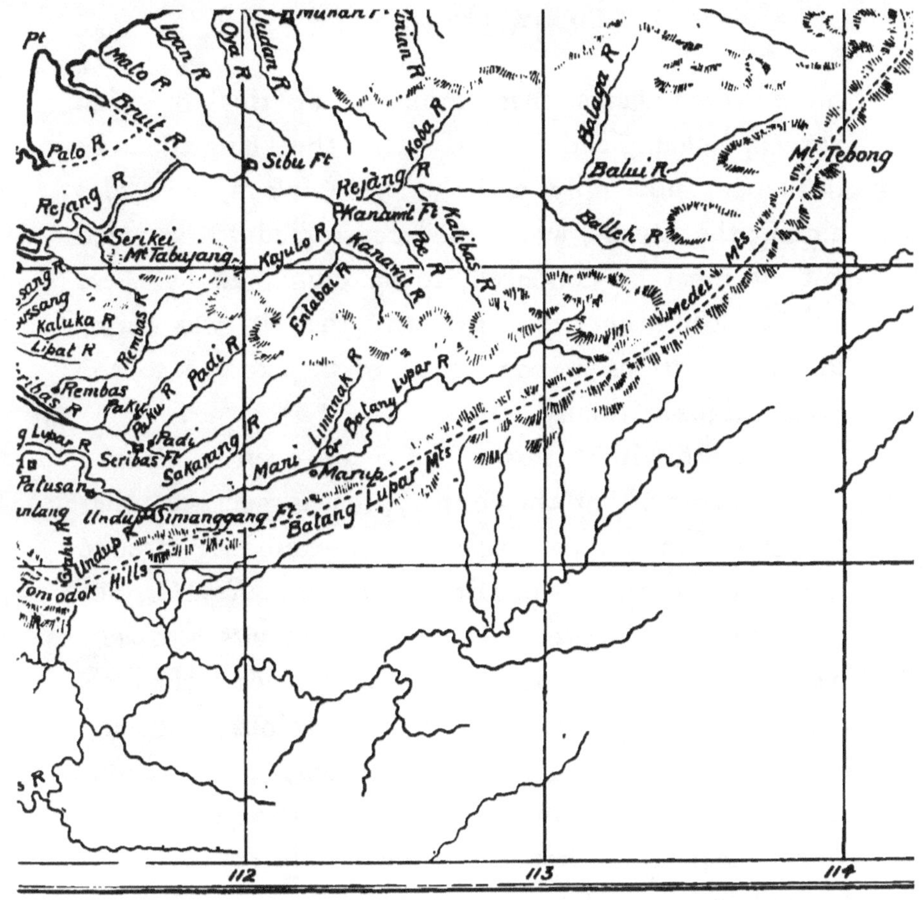

ENCIES AT THE CLOSE OF SIR JAMES BROOKE'S GOVERNMENT.

more sinned against than sinning. To this the rajah agreed, which added much to the Englishman's influence, not only among the Malays, but also among the Dyaks, who were accustomed to be ruled and, it must be confessed, to be plundered by these chiefs. But the tribes thought that it was better to pay exactions to one than to be exposed to the persecutions of many.

Although Muda Hassim had made over to Brooke the government of the country, it was necessary that this grant should be ratified by the Sultan. Brooke therefore proceeded to Brunei in the *Royalist*, accompanied by Pangeran Budrudin. It was also very necessary to pave the way for Muda Hassim's return to the capital, with his rapacious followers, before Sarawak could really prosper. Everything succeeded; the Sultan not only ratified the grant, but sent a strong invitation to his uncle to return to his old position of being the prime minister, whose absence they all deplored. His Highness sent letters to that effect, and when the *Royalist* arrived at Sarawak there was very general rejoicing.

The greatest state was observed when the Sultan's letters were taken on shore. 'They were received and brought up to the reception hall amid large wax torches. The person who was to read them was stationed on a raised platform. Standing near him was the Rajah Muda Hassim, with a sabre in his hand; in front was his brother Jaffer with a tremendous Lanun sword drawn; and around were the other brothers and myself, all standing, the rest of the company being seated. The letters were then read—the last one appointing me to hold the government of Sarawak—after which the rajah descended from the platform and said aloud, "If anyone present disowns or contests the Sultan's appointment, let him now declare it." All were silent. "Is there any pangeran or young rajah that contests the question? Pangeran Der Makota, what do you say?" Makota expressed his willingness to obey. One or two other obnoxious pangerans, who had always opposed themselves to me, were each in turn challenged, and forced to promise obedience. The rajah then waved his sword, and with a loud voice exclaimed, "Whoever he may be that disobeys the Sultan's mandate now received, I will cleave his skull." And at the moment some ten of his younger brothers jumped from the verandah, and drawing their long krises, began to flourish and dance about, thrusting close to Makota, striking the pillar above his head, and pointing their weapons at his breast. A motion on his part would have been fatal, but he kept his eyes on the ground and stirred not. I too remained quiet, and cared nothing about this demonstration, for one gets accustomed to these things. It all passed off, and in ten minutes the men who had been leaping frantically about, with drawn weapons and inflamed countenances, were seated, quiet and demure as usual. This scene is a custom with them, the only exception being that it was pointed so directly at Makota.'

This unworthy chief was now ordered to leave the country, as his presence was not only distasteful to the Tuan Besar, as Brooke was called, but to all those whom he had driven, by his oppressions, into the rebellion which had lately been quelled. The Bornean rajahs also looked upon him as an interloper, and he found no support from them; he was said, in fact, to be a stranger from the Dutch 'sphere of influence,' as it is now the fashion to call possession without occupation.

A new era was about to dawn on Sarawak by the advent of the British navy. Before dwelling on the change which took place in consequence, let me glance briefly at Brooke's position. He had been granted the government of the country by Rajah Muda Hassim, a grant confirmed by the Sultan; he had gained the confidence of the former, who leaned on him for support, and who hoped through his influence to recover his former paramount position in the capital; he was cordially supported by the Siniawan Malays, and was fully trusted by the Land Dyaks. He was also aided to a certain extent by those useful but troublesome subjects the Chinese, who then only dreamt of making themselves supreme in the interior. He was supported by three English followers, and the occasional presence of his yacht, the *Royalist*. How was it possible for anyone, therefore, to declare that he had seized the country by force, and held it by force, as was afterwards affirmed by a small English faction? His only enemies were Pangeran Makota and a few discontented Borneans, who dreaded the reign of justice and order. Though secure of the support of the inhabitants of Sarawak, he was opposed by his neighbour the Sultan of Sambas, backed by the Dutch, and he had the mouths of his rivers almost blockaded during eight months of the year by the fleets of Lanun and Balignini pirates who cruised along the coast during the fine season. His people were also in constant peril from the expeditions organised by Sherif Sahib, the chief of the neighbouring district of Sadong, the rendezvous of every species of pirate; and all coast trade was stopped by the constant presence of the Seribas and Sakarang Dyaks, led by their warlike Malays, who foraged along the whole western coast of Borneo. He was saved simply by his great prestige, as he had in reality no force with which he could cope with a large pirate fleet--a prestige acquired by his bravery, his tact, his great kindness, and the just and benevolent rule which he was striving with all his energy to introduce into his adopted country.

And what were his chief objects? How well the following lines express them: 'It is a grand experiment, which, if it succeeds, will bestow a blessing on those poor people, and their children's children will bless my name.' Again, 'If it please God to permit me to give a stamp to this country which shall last after I am no more, I shall have lived a life which emperors might envy. If by dedicating myself to the task I am able to introduce better customs and settled laws, and to raise the feeling of the people, so that their rights can never in future he wantonly infringed, I shall indeed be content and happy.'

This is how the Rajah describes his residence and mode of life at Kuching: 'I may now mention our house, or, as I fondly call it, our palace. It is an edifice fifty-four feet square, mounted on numerous posts of the nibong palm, with nine windows in each front. The roof is of nipa leaves, and the floors and partitions are all of planks. Furnished with couches, table, chairs, books, etc., the whole is as comfortable as man could wish for in this out-of-the-way country; and we have besides bathing-house, cook-house and servants' apartments detached. The view from the house to the eastward comprises a reach of the river, and to the westward looks towards the blue mountains of Matang; the north fronts the river and the south the jungle. Our abode, however, though spacious, cool and comfortable, can only be considered a temporary residence, for the best of all reasons, that in the course of a year it will tumble down, from the weight of the superstructure being placed on weak posts.

'The time here passes monotonously, but not unpleasantly. Writing, reading, chart-making employ my time between meals. My companions are equally engaged—Mackenzie[1] with copying logs, learning navigation and stuffing specimens of natural history; Crymble is teaching our young Bugis and Dyak boys their letters for an hour every morning, copying my vocabularies of languages, ruling charts and the like; whilst my servant Peter learns reading and writing daily, with very poor success, however. Our meals are about nine in the morning and four in the afternoon, with a cup of tea at eight. The evening is employed in walking never less than a mile and a half measured distance, and, after tea, reading and a cigar. Wine and grog we have none, and all appear better for it, or, at least, I can say so much for myself. Our bed-time is about eleven.'

In 1843, after an almost unbroken stay of nearly two years in Borneo, Brooke again visited Singapore, and found welcome news. The British Government had decided to inquire into the Bornean question, and it was stated that Sir Edward Belcher had been ordered to visit Sarawak in H.M.S. *Samarang;* but what was of much greater importance, and proved of incalculable benefit to Sarawak and to British interests in Borneo, was that Brooke made the acquaintance of Captain the Hon. Henry Keppel, who was in command of H.M.S. *Dido.* As I have elsewhere remarked, Keppel, with the instincts of a gentleman, at once recognised that he had no adventurer but a true man before him, and henceforward exerted all his energy

[1] He was afterwards killed by Chinese pirates.

and influence to further his friend's beneficent projects. They were indeed genuine Englishmen, and looked to what would advance the veritable interests of their own country—to increase its prestige in Borneo and clear the seas of the pirates who destroyed native commerce on its way to our settlements.

The *Dido* in the first days of May 1843 sailed from Singapore for Sarawak, and on the 13th anchored off the Moratabus entrance of the river. When the natives heard that their Governor had arrived, they swarmed down to the ship in their boats, delighted at his return among them; and the sight of the beautiful frigate, so powerful in their eyes, assured them that she would not leave before some measures had been taken against the pirates. Rajah Muda Hassim eagerly seized on this opportunity to obtain some security for native trade, and earnestly entreated Captain Keppel to attack the pirates of Seribas and Sakarang, who were especially dangerous to the coast traffic. Having satisfied himself of the truth of the allegations against the marauders, Keppel determined to act, and, having announced his intention, he was soon assured of the support of a native contingent, who decided to follow their English chief wherever he went, although with many misgivings as to the result of an attack on these much-feared corsairs, who had plundered their coasts with impunity for several generations.

I need not describe this expedition against the pirates, as the details have been often published; and as Admiral Keppel is now engaged in writing his memoirs, we shall have full particulars at first hand.[1] The *Dido* anchored off the Scribas river, and being joined by a native force of five hundred men, the English boats put off with crews of about eighty seamen and marines, and carried in the most dashing style every fort or obstruction placed in their way. No obstacles daunted them, and their enemies, numbering many thousands on each branch of the river, were so astonished by this novel mode of fighting in the open that they fled on every occasion, abandoning their towns and forts, which were promptly destroyed by our native allies, now trebled in number. The Scribas considered themselves invincible, and had collected their means of resistance in well-chosen spots, their guns covering the booms across the river, but to no purpose, and the towns of Paku, Padi and Rembas all shared the same fate.

It is a very remarkable circumstance that as soon as each section recognised the hopelessness of resistance, they entered freely into communication with their assailants, and under cover of the white flag, and often unarmed, approached their English conquerors with perfect trust and confidence. They all agreed to visit Sarawak, and promised amendment for the future.

The complete collapse of the defence astonished everyone, and those natives who had taken part in this memorable campaign began to acquire confidence

[1] Sir Henry Keppel's Memoirs have lately been published.

in themselves, and were ever ready to follow their white leaders in all future expeditions.

Captain Keppel, in his *Voyage of the Dido*, has given us a very good account of the house in which Mr Brooke lived in 1843, and of which I have already introduced its occupant's own description. Captain Keppel says that the English Rajah's residence, although equally rude in structure with the abodes of the natives, was not without its English comforts of sofas, chairs and bedsteads. It was larger than any other house in the place, but, like them, was built on nibong piles, and to enter it it was necessary to make use of a ladder. The house consisted of but one floor; a large room in the centre, neatly ornamented with every description of firearms in admirable order and ready for use, served as audience hall and mess room, and the various apartments around it as bedrooms, most of them comfortably furnished with matted floors, easy-chairs, pictures and books, with much more taste and attention to comfort than bachelors usually display. But, the fact is, you could never enter any place where Brooke had passed a few days without being struck by the artistic arrangement of everything. His good taste was shown even in trifles, though comfort was never sacrificed to show. The house was surrounded by palisades and a ditch, forming an enclosure, in which were to be found sheep, goats, pigeons, cats, poultry, geese, ducks, monkeys, dogs, and occasionally a cow or two.

Then, as later, the great hour of meeting was sunset, when, after the preliminary cold bath to brace the nerves, relaxed by the heat of the day, all the party met to dine. When Keppel was at Kuching all the officers of the *Dido* were welcome, and many a merry evening was passed at Brooke's house. I have often heard him speak of that glorious time. Then the future was all hope, no disappointments had depressed the mind, and the cheerfulness of the host was infectious. I have never met anyone who in his playful mood was more charming. He told a story well, he was animated in discussion, fertile in resource, and, when beaten in argument, would shift his ground with great dexterity, and keep up the discussion to the entertainment of us all. An appreciative observer once wrote, 'The Rajah has certainly a most uncommon gift of fluency of language. Every subject derives an additional interest from his mode of discussing it, and his ideas are so original that to hear him speak is like opening out a new world before one. His views about Sarawak are so grand that it is with real pain one thinks how very little has been done to aid him in his noble efforts.' Captain Keppel was also a capital storyteller, so that between the two, with occasional assistance from the others, the time passed gaily, and it was often well on in the small hours before the party broke up.

It was a great disappointment to all that Captain Keppel now received orders to proceed to China, as he had intended before his departure to complete his work by attacking the Sakarangs, who lived in the interior of the Batang Lupar river, and who were powerfully supported by Arab and Malay chiefs.

The next event of importance was the arrival of Sir Edward Belcher in H.M.S. *Samarang*. He had been sent to report on Sarawak and on Bornean affairs in general. He was a clever but very unpopular man, and made his ship the most uncomfortable in the service. After a short stay in Sarawak, visiting the interior and making inquiries, he decided to proceed to Brunei and enter into communication with the Sultan. Brooke was to have accompanied him, but the *Samarang* had but just started to descend the river when she touched on a rock, and as the tide fell, she turned over on her side and filled with water. It was a misfortune to the ship, but a blessing to Sarawak, as it drew general attention to Brooke's settlement. By dint of the greatest exertion on the part of officers and crew, and the aid afforded by the native population, within eleven days the vessel was again afloat. In the meantime the *Royalist* had been sent to Singapore for provisions and aid, and before twelve days had elapsed she returned with a ship of war. Others soon followed, to find the *Samarang* out of all danger. As soon as her refit was completed, she sailed for Brunei with Brooke on board. His friends had pointed out to him that, to render his work in Sarawak permanent, he must obtain a grant in perpetuity from the Government of Brunei, and this he readily secured. Moreover, His Highness the Sultan wrote to Sir Edward Belcher expressing the strong desire of his Government to trade and their wish to co-operate in the suppression of piracy.

Whilst all was proceeding favourably in Borneo, Brooke was much disturbed by the news of the proceedings of Mr Wise, his agent in London. There was no doubt of the talent and earnestness of this man, but those who knew him well felt that he was rather working for his own benefit than for that of his employer. He knew that a true account of the actual state of Sarawak would fail to draw the attention of the mercantile community; he therefore raised false expectations as to the value of the trade which would arise as soon as Borneo was thrown open to British commerce. When Brooke was made aware of this he wrote to his friend Templer, 'It does appear to me, judging from Mr Wise's letters and the steps he has taken, that some exaggerated hopes are entertained, and hopes as unreasonable as exaggerated. . . . In fact, I will become no party to a bubble; or gain, or accept any negotiation from Government upon false grounds' (*sic*).

Brooke's views on the management of a wild country and the only way to develop commerce among savage, and even among half-civilised peoples, were so wise and trustworthy that they would merit being quoted in full did space permit. He was indeed a most sagacious ruler, with a positive instinct as to the manner in which native races should be treated, and he always insisted that progress to be permanent must be slow, and that throwing capital *en masse* into an undeveloped country would only produce disappointment and loss.

How true is the following: 'Good temper, good sense and conciliatory manners are essential to the good government of natives, and on this point it is that most Europeans are so grossly wanting. They always take [with them] their own customs, feelings and manners, and in a way force the natives to conform to them, and never give themselves the trouble of ascertaining how far these manners are repugnant to the natives.' In my long experience I could scarcely name a dozen men whom I have seen treat native races as they should be treated, and most of these were among the devoted followers of Rajah Brooke. His own manners were perfect.

One result of the defeat of the Seribas was the increased influence of the English ruler. Sherif Sahib of Sadong now thought it prudent to return to the Sow tribe of Dyaks fifty of the women and children whom his people had seized, and although this was but an instalment it was something gained.

In a few lines written on November 14, 1843, Brooke sketched the policy which he wished the English Government to pursue. 'If we act, we ought to act without unnecessary delay. Take Sarawak and Labuan, or Labuan alone, and push our interest along the coast to Sulu, and from Sulu towards New Guinea, gaining an influence with such states (and acquiring dormant rights) as are clear of the Dutch on the one hand and of the Spaniards on the other.' But this policy was neglected, and to some extent it is now too late to carry it out.

In December 1843 Brooke again visited Singapore, and there he shortly afterwards received news of his mother's death. Though affectionate to all his relations, his love and tenderness centred in his mother, and her loss was the more acutely felt, as, from a mistaken feeling, the seriousness of her illness had not been reported to him.

Whilst visiting Penang Brooke joined in an expedition to punish some piratical communities on the coast of Sumatra; and as a guest on board H.M.S. *Wanderer*, he went with the boats that were sent to attack the town of Murdoo. A strong current swept the captain's gig under an enemy's stockade. There was no help for it, so Brooke sprang out and led a rush upon the fort, during which he received a gash in the forehead and a shot in the arm. Reinforcements coming up, the place was soon captured. On the return of the expedition to Penang the ship's crew begged the captain's permission to man yards and give three cheers for their gallant guest. Here he met Captain Keppel on his way to Calcutta, who promised to pick him up at Singapore on his return and visit Sarawak again, and chastise the pirates of Sakarang.

Brooke therefore waited, but was again disappointed, as the *Dido* was ordered to China, and he had therefore to remain in the Straits until the end of May, when Captain Hastings gave him a passage over to Borneo in the *Harlequin.*

This long absence had encouraged his enemies, who now hoped that they were free from their troublesome neighbour. Sherif Sahib, however, though boasting as loudly as ever, did not feel secure in Sadong, and therefore prepared his vessels to remove himself and all his immediate following to the interior of the Batang Lupar river, where he would be in touch with the other Arab adventurers who commanded the different districts of that mighty stream. As a defiance to Sarawak, he invited all the Sakarang Dyaks to meet him at the entrance of the Sadong river, and there they rendezvoused to the number of two hundred Dyak bangkongs and Malay war boats. Some mischief was done along the coast, but Brooke surprised one of their expeditions and captured several of their war vessels.

During Brooke's absence from Sarawak, his new house on the left bank of the river had been built on a rising knoll between two running streams, with the broad river flowing below. It was a pretty spot, and now he could write, 'I like couches, and flowers, and easy-chairs, and newspapers, and clear streams, and sunny walks.' Here and there were planted and tended with uncommon care some rose plants, the

Rajah's favourite flower. 'All breathes of peace and repose, and the very mid-day heat adds to the stillness around me. I love to allow my imagination to wander, and my senses to enjoy such a scene, for it is attended with a pleasing consciousness that the quiet and the peace are my own doing.'

At length, however, the *Dido* came, accompanied by the Company's steamer *Phlegethon*, and it was decided to begin operations by attacking the Arab sherifs in their strongholds on the Batang Lupar river.

The Batang Lupar for the first twenty miles looks a noble stream. About that distance from the mouth occurs the Linga, the first branch of the river which leads to the Balow villages, inhabited by Dyaks under the influence of Sherif Jaffer—the same Dyaks who had joined Keppel's expedition against the Seribas pirates; they were warlike but not piratical. The next branch on the left bank of the river was the Undup, and then on the right bank the Sakarang, a stream inhabited by a dense population of piratical Dyaks; and about fifteen miles below the mouth of that branch was built the town of Patusin, strongly defended by forts and stockades.

As the arrival of the *Dido* had been fully expected, the Sarawak preparations for the expedition were well advanced, and in view of Keppel's triumphs in the previous year, there was no holding back, but all were eager for the fray. Even Pangeran Budrudin was permitted to join the Sarawak contingent—something quite new in the annals of the royal family.

On the 5th of August 1844 the expedition started, and on the 6th was well within the river Batang Lupar. By the 8th all was ready for the attack, and on the rising flood tide the steamer and boats were carried up stream at a bewildering pace, and soon found themselves in face of the town and forts of Patusin. The English boats formed up alongside of the steamer, and pulled to the shore under a very hot fire; but nothing could daunt their crews, and they carried the forts by assault, with the loss of only one English sailor killed and a few wounded. Nor were the natives behindhand; they vied with their white comrades, and were soon in full pursuit of the flying enemy.

In the afternoon the force marched to the attack of a neighbouring town where the chief Sherif Sahib had his residence; but there was no resistance, and the place was soon plundered and destroyed by our native allies. Amongst the spoil captured at Patusin were sixty-four brass guns and a smaller number of iron ones; the latter were thrown into the river. Having completely destroyed these Malay pirate settlements, not forgetting that which had been formed by Pangeran Makota, and handed over to the natives those war boats which would be useful to them, while the remainder were hacked to pieces and burnt, the force prepared for an assault on the Sakarang pirates.

The attack on the Sakarangs was similar in its incidents to that on the Seribas. The river was staked, but nothing could stop the onset of the invaders. The town was taken without much opposition; but the greatest loss on the British side was incurred from the imprudence of a scouting party. Brave old Patingi Ali had been sent ahead to reconnoitre, when, probably urged on by a Mr Stewart, who had been concealed in his boat, he proceeded too far; and when a large force rowed down the river to attack him, he found his retreat cut off by long rafts which had been pushed off from the banks and completely closed the river. He and his party were overwhelmed, and out of seventeen men only one escaped; Mr Stewart was among the killed.

Having completed their work, Captain Keppel and Brooke pulled back to Patusin, where they were joined by Sir Edward Belcher and the boats of the *Samarang*. They now all returned to Sarawak, but within a few days after their arrival the news came that the Arab chiefs and their followers were collecting at Banting on the Linga, the chief village of the Balow Dyaks, under the protection of Sherif Jaffer. The expedition immediately returned, and drove off the intruders; and Pangeran Budrudin, in the name of the Bornean Government, deposed Sherif Jaffer, and so settled the country, under the advice of Brooke, that comparative peace reigned there for nearly five years.

At this time it was calculated that Sarawak had received an increase of five thousand families, or, more probably, individuals; it was a genuine proof of the confidence of the people of the coast in the only spot where peace and security could be obtained, but it was also a sign of the terror inspired by the piratical fleets, and the general bad government of the districts under the rule of the native chiefs.

The greatest service Sir Edward Belcher ever did for Sarawak was the removal of Muda Hassim to Brunei. He had been long anxious to leave, but he would not do so, except in state. So Sir Edward arranged that not only the rajah and his immense family should be received on board the Company's steamer the *Phlegethon*, but as many of his rascally followers as possible; and then, with Brooke on board, the *Samarang* set sail for Brunei. The expedition was received with some suspicion, but ultimately Muda Hassim and the Sultan were to all appearance reconciled, and the former was restored to his position as prime minister. An offer was made by the Sultan to cede Labuan to England as a British settlement, and that offer was transmitted to the English Government. Labuan is an island off the mouth of the Brunei and neighbouring rivers, which appeared admirably adapted for a commercial and naval post, and the discovery of coal there settled the point.

As soon as Muda Hassim had departed from Sarawak, and Brooke was left, *de facto* as well as *de jure*, the only governor, confidence in his remaining in the country grew rapidly, and trade improved. But the negotiations which his friends were carrying on with the British Government moved slowly and drew forth some impatient remarks from him. Henceforth I may occasionally call him the Rajah, *par excellence*, as he now was in truth the only rajah in Sarawak.

Hearing that some members of Sir Robert Peel's Government had stated that they did not understand Brooke's intentions, the Rajah wrote rather indignantly—'December 31, 1844. . . . I am surprised, however, that they say they do not understand my intentions. Independently of my published letter, I thought they had had my intentions and wishes dinned into them. My intention, my wish, is to develop the island of Borneo. How to develop Borneo is not for me to say, but for them to judge. I have, both by precept and example, shown what can be done; but it is for the Government to judge what means, if any, they will place at my disposal. My intention, my wish, is to extirpate piracy by attacking and breaking up the pirate towns; not only pirates direct, but pirates indirect. Here again the Government must judge. I wish to correct the native character, to gain and hold an influence in Borneo proper, to introduce gradually a better system of government, to open the interior, to encourage the poorer natives, to remove the clogs on trade, to develop new sources of commerce. I wish to make Borneo a second Java. I intend to influence and amend the entire Archipelago, if the Government will afford me means and power. I wish to prevent any foreign nation coming on this field; but I might as well war against France individually, as to attempt all I wish without any means.'

Was this policy not clear enough? Had it been followed, the independent portion of the Eastern Archipelago would have been completely under our influence, and would have ended by becoming practically ours. We should have had New Guinea and the islands adjacent, and thus given the Australians a free hand to develop what certainly should be considered as within their sphere of influence. How the English Rajah's policy was wrecked, I must explain later on; at this time (1845) all seemed advancing to its fulfilment.

In the meantime the British Government were acting in their usual cautious, half-hearted way. They did not really care a rush about Borneo or the Eastern Archipelago, and I have no doubt that the subordinate members of the Government offices looked with disgust on those who were urging them to intervene in Borneo. They hated any new thing, as it forced them to study and find out what it was all about. But as they could not stand still, they sent out Captain Bethune to inquire. He arrived in February, in H.M.S. *Driver*, and brought with him the temporary appointment of Brooke as Her Majesty's confidential agent. This was a distinct advance, as he had now to proceed to the capital to deliver officially a letter from the Queen to the Sultan and the Government of Brunei. With Captain Bethune came Mr Wise, the Rajah's agent in England.

In Brunei they did not find Muda Hassim's Government very firmly established, as they were threatened not only by Pangeran Usop, a connection of the Sultan's and a pretender to the throne, but by the pirates of the north, with whom Usop was in league. During their stay in Brunei, both Brooke and Captain Bethune examined the coal seams near the capital, but they do not appear to have been considered workable, as no one has ever attempted to open a mine there. The quality of the coal has been pronounced good, and as the seams crop out of rather lofty hills it cannot be considered as surface coal.

CHAPTER IV

SIR THOMAS COCHRANE IN BRUNEI — ATTACK ON SHERIF OSMAN — MUDA HASSIM IN POWER — LINGIRE'S ATTEMPT TO TAKE RAJAH BROOKE'S HEAD—MASSACRE OF MUDA HASSIM AND BUDRUDIN—THE ADMIRAL PROCEEDS TO BRUNEI—TREATY WITH BRUNEI—ACTION WITH PIRATE SQUADRON—RAJAH BROOKE IN ENGLAND—IS KNIGHTED ON HIS RETURN TO THE EAST—VISITS THE SULU ISLANDS—EXPEDITION AGAINST SERIBAS PIRATES

HEARING that Admiral Sir Thomas Cochrane was expected in Singapore, the English Rajah determined to proceed there to explain to him the true position of affairs on the north-west coast of Borneo. He found the admiral ready to take measures to suppress piracy, and the Rajah left with the impression that he would act against the great pirate chief, Sherif Osman. In the meantime, he returned himself to Brunei in the *Phlegethon* to find his Bornean friends very despondent. However, in August the admiral appeared, and at the invitation of the Sultan attacked Pangeran Usop for holding two British subjects in slavery. This noble and his followers fled to the hills. Sir Thomas then proceeded to Marudu Bay to chastise Sherif Osman, the most notorious pirate chief in the Archipelago. His place of residence, up a narrow river, was carefully fortified with an extra strong boom across the stream. A very powerful expedition was sent up from the fleet. In attempting to force their way through the well-prepared obstructions our men were exposed to a murderous fire from the forts, and we lost heavily; but the town was taken and burnt. I visited the place afterwards, and was somewhat surprised that a detachment was not landed below the boom and the position turned; but we always like to take the bull by the horns. The pirates suffered severely. Sherif Osman was mortally wounded and died shortly afterwards, and Marudu ceased for a time to be a pirate rendezvous.

Returning to Brunei with the good news, Brooke was delighted to hear that his friend Budrudin had defeated Usop, who, with a force from the hills, had come down to surprise the town, and had driven him away from the neighbourhood of the capital. He was some time afterwards taken at a place called Kimanis, and by order of the Sultan was strangled with all the formalities due to a person who had royal blood in his veins. Thus Muda Hassim's power appeared securely established. His enemies without and within had been defeated, and his warlike brother, Lanun, on the mother's side—which accounted for his unusual daring — was at the head of a strong party. The English Rajah felt that they were comparatively safe; yet he had his secret misgivings, and tried in vain to persuade the admiral to station a brig on the coast.

Captain Bethune now returned to England to make his report to the British Government, and Brooke was left to a welcome repose—doubly welcome after all the exertions of the previous months.

It was during the summer of this year that a very curious episode occurred. Whilst the Rajah was at dinner with his English followers in the new house to which I have already referred, and which had been constructed some distance below the Malay town, Lingire, the well-known pirate chief, walked into the dining-hall, followed by a large party of his warriors. As they were all fully armed, the Rajah saw at once that mischief was meant. He received the chief most courteously. A chair was given him, and all the other Dyaks squatted down on the floor round the table. Cigars were handed round, and then the Rajah asked what was the news. Lingire answered that they had just pulled up the river to pay him a visit.

The Rajah called up a very intelligent native servant and said to him in English, 'Bring me another bottle of sherry,' and then added in a careless voice, 'Let the Malay chiefs know who are here.' The servant duly brought in the wine and then retired.

Whilst the Seribas chief was drinking his sherry, the Rajah exerted himself to the utmost to entertain him—told him story after story, got the Dyak to relate instances of his own prowess. His vanity was so tickled that, forgetting the object of his visit, he dilated on his forays into the Dutch territories, where he had surprised the Chinese settlers. 'They won't fight, those cowards,' he said. 'They run away from an armed man, or drop on their knees and beg for mercy.' The Rajah encouraged him to continue, but time and the Datus moved slowly, and he could see the Dyaks exchanging glances, as if to say the moment had arrived for action. In another minute they would have been on their feet and the unarmed Englishmen slain, when footsteps were heard on the gravel walk. Lingire looked anxious as the powerful form of the Datu Patingi appeared in the verandah, which was soon crowded with armed Malays. The Datu Tumangong soon followed, and the Dyaks were surrounded. They did not move — a move would have sealed their fate. The Datus threatened and scolded them to their hearts' content, asked how they had dared to enter the Rajah's house with arms in their hands, and had not the white chief interfered the Malays would have executed summary justice on the rascals.

The Rajah then spoke. He said he knew very well that Lingire had come to surprise them, but he would not have it said that anyone who came to his country should be in fear of death, however much he merited it, that he would forgive him, and he might go. At a sign from the Rajah the Malays opened their serried ranks, and Lingire and his followers crept out like whipped curs and disappeared from the river. Years after, I saw Lingire sitting on a chair beside the Rajah, but I do not think he ever confessed to us that his design had been to kill the white men, though it was well known that he came for no other purpose. He had, in fact, boasted that he would take the Rajah's head and hang it up in a basket which he had already prepared and placed in a tree near his village. Had he attacked the Rajah the moment he entered the room nothing could have saved the Englishmen, as they were quite defenceless; and he could have done it with impunity, as no Malay war boat could have overtaken a Dyak bangkong. This is but a specimen of the Rajah's marvellous escapes. I had the above account from his cousin, Arthur Crookshank.

The year 1846 opened satisfactorily. The attack on the pirate haunts at Marudu, the punishment and the subsequent death of Pangeran Usop, rendered the position of Muda Hassim stronger, and the strict watch kept on the Seribas and Sakarangs during 1845 had prevented any marauding on their part. Whilst peace appeared now to be established both at home and abroad, the Rajah was again troubled by the action of his agent Wise. This clever but unscrupulous man kept writing that he would make Brooke the richest commoner in England if he would give him a free hand; and, in fact, without waiting for any permission, he began to project large associations which were to take over the country of Sarawak and rival the old East India Company in wealth and power. When Brooke understood what his agent was doing, he wrote that he would be no party to such schemes, and that he would not surrender Sarawak to the tender mercies of a mercantile association.

I first made the acquaintance of Mr Wise in 1846, and I well remember how lavish he was in the praise of Brooke, and what hopes he entertained of the success of an all-absorbing company. But as time passed his enthusiasm for his friend and employer gradually lessened, till the result was an open rupture. To this I must refer hereafter.

1846, which opened under the finest auspices, soon however changed its aspect. News came of marauding on the part of the Sakarang Dyaks; but this was trifling to what followed. H.M.S. *Hazard*, Commander Egerton, had been sent by the admiral to Brunei to communicate with Rajah Muda Hassim. As soon as the ship anchored at the mouth of the Brunei river, a native hurried on board, and by signs made the officers understand that some great calamity had occurred at the capital, while he appeared to warn Egerton not to proceed up the river. Fortunately his warning was attended to; and as he kept repeating in

Malay, 'Tuan Brooke' and 'Sarawak,' the *Hazard* weighed anchor and proceeded to that place. The Malay brought serious news indeed. The Sultan had ordered the murder of Muda Hassim, Budrudin and the rest of the legitimate royal family, and had succeeded in destroying the most important chiefs. These were his own uncles and cousins.

A conspiracy seems to have been hatched among the Sultan's followers, who were the friends and associates of the late Pangeran Usop, to kill Muda Hassim and his family, not only for the sake of revenge, but to prevent them gaining a preponderating influence in the country. Already the people were looking to them as the rising power, and the Sultan's prestige was visibly declining. Besides, with their increasing influence they were acquiring too many of the profits which used to accrue to the Sultan's *entourage*. As the representatives of the party which preferred the old methods of government, the latter disliked the alliance which was springing up between this branch of the royal family and the Rajah of Sarawak, as the representative of the English, and therefore they found no difficulty in persuading the half-imbecile Sultan that his immediate deposition was meditated. He therefore gave the order that Muda Hassim and his family should be attacked and killed. Though warned that some conspiracy was brewing, they took no heed, lulled in fancied security, and were easily surprised. Muda Hassim defended his home with a few followers, but finding that they would soon be overpowered, shot himself so as not to fall into the hands of his enemies.

Pangeran Budrudin was attacked at the same time. Brooke wrote to Keppel, on April 5th 1846, 'After fighting desperately and cutting down several of the Sultan's hired assassins, he was shot in his left wrist, his shoulder and chest were cut open so as to disable his right arm. A woman, by name Nur Salum, fought and was wounded by his side. His sister and a slave boy called Jaffir, though both wounded, remained by him, the rest of his few followers having been cut down or having fled. The four retired into the house and barred the door. Budrudin, wounded and bleeding, ordered the boy to get down a cask of powder, break in the head and scatter it in a small circle. He then told Jaffir to escape, gave him my signet ring, of which I had made him a present, and told him to beg me not to forget him and to tell the Queen of England of his fate. He then called the women to him, and when the boy had dropped through the flooring into the water, fired the powder, and all three were blown into the air.' No hero could have died more nobly, and what fine creatures must those women have been!

No natives ever appear to consider or to care for the consequences of their acts until the acts are done. They are blinded by their hate; but no sooner had the conspirators murdered the principal members of the royal family than they began to tremble for the future. They knew the friendship which united the English Rajah to Pangeran Budrudin, and began to reflect that he would spare no pains to punish them. With the death of this brave pangeran all hopes of regenerating the Government of Brunei vanished.

At that time we had in the East an admiral who dared to act—Sir Thomas Cochrane. When he heard of the massacre he determined to proceed to Brunei to inquire what was the meaning of these violent measures. He rightly argued that the massacre did not directly concern England, unless the Sultan was about to repudiate all his engagements with us. On his way he called in at Sarawak to see Brooke, and to ask him, as the British Government's confidential agent, to accompany the expedition.

The squadron arrived off the Brunei river on the 6th June, and Sir Thomas immediately sent a message to the Sultan, saying he was about to visit the capital and desired an interview with His Highness. Some messengers of inferior rank brought down the reply that the admiral might ascend the river in two small boats. No notice was taken of this restriction, and the steamers, with the smaller vessels in tow, and accompanied by the boats of the squadron, began to ascend the river. As they neared the capital they were received with volleys from every battery; but the marines and blue-jackets were soon on shore, and the defenders fled in haste. On entering the central canal of Brunei, a battery at the Sultan's Palace opened fire, which did considerable damage to the *Phlegethon*. There was no serious resistance, however, and when the force took possession of the town they found it completely deserted. The Sultan escaped to the interior, and the party sent to capture him naturally failed in their object.

A provisional government was established under Pangeran Mumein, a respectable noble, not of royal descent, and Pangeran Mahomed, a brother of Muda Hassim, but not of much intelligence; then a proclamation was issued, saying that the Sultan might return to his capital if he were prepared to fulfil his engagements.

Nothing ever raised the prestige of the English so much as the capture of Brunei. As a military feat of arms it was of no importance, but to the tribes of the interior it was looked upon as a marvel of heroism. They naturally thought Brunei to be the only great power on earth, so that when they heard that the English had taken their capital, they rejoiced that their oppressors had received such a lesson. Cautiously looking around to see that no Malay was present, they would laughingly tell how they had seen the Sultan and his nobles flying through the jungle with the English at their heels, and ask why having once taken the country we did not keep it. These or similar inquiries were made wherever I travelled in the interior.

Sir Thomas Cochrane, having seen the establishment of the provisional government, sailed for China; but during his passage up the north-west coast of Borneo destroyed several pirate communities, and, leaving Captain Mundy of H.M.S. *Iris* to complete the work, proceeded to Hong Kong.

When Brooke returned to Sarawak he was indeed received as the 'Conquering Hero.' The Malays there were very much like the tribes of the interior, thoroughly imbued with the idea that the Sultan of Brunei was a great monarch, second to none; and therefore the news that the capital had been taken and that the Sultan had fled to the woods was a complete surprise; but the surprise was only equalled by the pleasure it gave, as the Brunei Government was unpopular to the last degree, indeed hated for its oppression.

While in Brunei Brooke collected those of the families of Muda Hassim and his brothers who wished to be removed from the capital, and brought them down to Sarawak, where for years they were supported by him.

1846 closed, as it had begun, with every sign of prosperity. There was peace in all the neighbouring districts, and the native trade on the coast was considered to be very flourishing. Kuching, the capital of Sarawak, was continually increasing, as the natives removed to it from the less secure rivers, and there was every hope that the British Government would now really make an effort to develop the coast. They had decided to occupy the island of Labuan and establish a commercial settlement there, and this, it was expected, would lead to a more forward policy.

Having received instructions from Her Majesty's Government, Brooke, in May 1847, proceeded to Brunei to negotiate a treaty with the Sultan, which should not only regulate the trade relations between the two countries, but should contain a clause declaring that British subjects committing offences within His Highness's dominions might only be tried by Her Majesty's representative. The treaty was signed, and then Brooke left on board the Company's steamer *Nemesis*, Captain Wallace, who was on his way to Singapore. When they arrived near the mouth of the Brunei river they were hailed by a native prahu and were informed that a Balignini pirate squadron was outside, capturing fishing and trading boats. As soon as the *Nemesis* rounded the sandy point of the island of Muara they saw eleven Balignini prahus in full chase of a native vessel, but as soon as the steamer appeared the pirates turned towards the shore, and finding escape hopeless, pulled into a shallow bay, anchored their vessels, bows seaward, and all kept in position by hawsers connecting the prahus to each other. The steamer arrived, when the pirates immediately opened fire on her, and after rather a prolonged action they cut their cables. Some prahus pulled away to the north, others to the south, while the remainder were deserted by their crews. It is needless to enter into details, but it may be mentioned that in all the vessels taken were found crowds of captives, principally from the Dutch possessions. None of the prahus made the Balignini Islands, as the three that escaped the steamer were so riddled with shot that the crews had to take to their boats, and after a painful voyage at last reached home. The pirates of the eight other prahus were forced to seek refuge on shore, and after committing some murders and other excesses, were surrounded, and then they surrendered to the Sultan, who had them all put to death.

Peace being established along the north-west coast by the energetic action of Sir Thomas Cochrane and the wise policy of Brooke, the latter decided to visit England after an absence of nearly nine years. He knew that the action with the Balignini would deter those pirates from visiting the coast for some time; he was satisfied that the Brunei Government could do no mischief; the Dyak pirates were still under the influence of the punishment they had received, and Sarawak was prosperous and safe. So leaving his cousin, Arthur Crookshank, in charge, he started for England, where he was sure to be well received, as Captain Keppel's successful *Voyage of the Dido* had made the ruler of Sarawak well known to all Englishmen.

After a tedious voyage Brooke landed in England

on October 2nd, and was soon surrounded by friends and relations. The Queen received him at Windsor Castle, and he was so fêted by all that he had but little time left to transact business. Brooke could not but feel that his countrymen fully appreciated the services he had rendered to England. He was presented with the freedom of the City of London, many clubs elected him a member by special vote, Oxford honoured him with her distinctions. The undergraduates went wild with enthusiasm at the mention of his name, for he was pre-eminently a leader to create that feeling among young men. He made friendships, which were lifelong, with Earl Grey and the Earl of Ellesmere.

Mr Wise gave him a grand dinner, and there delivered a speech which was an unqualified eulogium on his employer ; it was not only eulogistic, it was fulsome in his praise. I remember well all the circumstances, and they are important ; they impressed themselves deeply in my mind. My father, who was present at this dinner, when he came home, said to me, 'I cannot understand Wise. He has just made a speech in which he has declared that Brooke is one of the greatest and best of men, whilst privately he tells me he is a robber and a murderer.' On my father asking for an explanation, Mr Wise excused himself, saying that it was the necessity of his position which forced him to dissemble.

Brooke, who before he left Borneo had been named

Commissioner and Consul-General, was now called upon to accept the position of Governor of the new settlement of Labuan, and was placed at the head of an efficient staff. I was appointed secretary to the Rajah, as Commissioner, and was thus brought into the closest relations to him. We were all ordered to hold ourselves in readiness to proceed to Borneo in H.M.'s frigate *Meander*, Captain Keppel, on the 1st February 1848.

How high were our hopes when we sailed from Portsmouth! They nearly made us forget the discomforts of our position on board—discomforts almost inseparable from an attempt to turn a ship of war into a passenger vessel. Our progress appeared to us slow, first from very stormy weather, and then from incessant calms.

The *Meander*, though of forty-four guns, was but a second-rate frigate; she had, however, a picked crew, whom the fame of her captain had induced to join; she was fitted with special boats for river service, as she was intended to act against the pirate communities. I need not dwell on the details of this voyage, but I must introduce an anecdote related by Sir Hugh Low of his great chief. 'No circumstances, however unexpected, flurried him. . . . I was once a passenger with him in a large man-of-war. His cabin was on the port side of the vessel, and he was sitting in an arm-chair which leant against the bulkhead. I was stretched on a locker on the opposite side of the cabin, and there being a fresh breeze the ship was heeling over to starboard, when we felt a sudden increase in the lurch, which threw me headlong against the lee bulkhead, the Rajah's chair being tilted up so that his feet were in the air. I attempted to crawl towards the door, when the Rajah, who had been reading, asked me where I was going. I said, "I am going to see what is the matter; the vessel is capsizing." He replied, "You have nothing to do with it; you are only a passenger. Stay where you are." The danger was averted by the promptness of the carpenter, who with one stroke of his sharp axe severed the main brace, and the vessel immediately righted itself.'

We were all glad to reach Singapore, for although the officers did their utmost to make us comfortable, it was not possible that much success could attend their efforts. I daresay they were as pleased to see us land as we were to find ourselves on shore. One thing I may mention, however; the gun-room officers pressed me to remain with them instead of facing the expense and discomforts of a Singapore hotel; but I could not avail myself of their kindness as I had my secretary's duties to perform.

About three weeks after our arrival, the surveyor, the late Mr Scott, afterwards Sir John Scott, and Captain Hoskins, harbour-master, were sent ahead to prepare the necessary buildings for the officers that were to follow. This was our first mistake. Neither of these gentlemen knew anything about tropical countries, nor even the language of Borneo, and fixed the site of the settlement on a grassy plain, that turned into a swamp as soon as the rainy season commenced. Had the Lieutenant-Governor, Mr Napier, been sent ahead, or had Mr Low (now Sir Hugh Low), the Colonial Secretary, accompanied the advance party, their special knowledge of the Tropics would have saved us the consequences of this disastrous error. After a long and apparently unnecessary delay of three months and a half at Singapore, we sailed in the *Meander* for Sarawak. Before our departure, however, news arrived that Her Majesty had been pleased to name Mr Brooke a K.C.B., and he was duly installed before we left that British settlement.

On September 4, 1848, the *Meander* anchored off the Muaratabas entrance of the Sarawak river, and the reception accorded to their Rajah by the native inhabitants made a deep impression, not only on me, but on all who witnessed it. The whole population turned out to meet him, and the river, as far as the eye could reach, was thronged with boats. Everything that could float was put into requisition—the trading vessels, the war boats carrying their crews of a hundred, a few unwieldy Chinese junks, and every canoe in the capital. All were gaily dressed, and the chiefs crowded on board the frigate. At 1 p.m. we left under a royal salute, with yards manned and hearty cheers from the crew, and started for a six hours' pull to the capital. We arrived after sunset and found every house brilliantly illuminated. The Rajah's reception at Government House, where all the English were assembled, was naturally very hearty, and soon the whole place was crowded with natives.

Finding that during his absence the piratical tribes had recommenced their raids on the neighbouring towns, the Rajah thought of forming a league of the well-disposed districts, and therefore introduced a flag, which was not only a Sarawak flag, but might be used by any member of the league. This flag was hoisted, with great ceremony, on the staff in front of the Government House, and it is now used along the whole coast as far as, and in a place or two beyond, the Sultan's capital.

About this time a mission, under the auspices of the Church of England, was established in Sarawak, and great hopes were entertained of its success.

I may as well mention who were the members of the Rajah's staff. While we were at Kuching, his nephew, Captain Brooke of the 88th, joined him as A.D.C., but as he was to be the Rajah's heir in Sarawak it was thought he would soon retire from the army; then Arthur Crookshank, who had hitherto represented him in Borneo; Charles Grant, his private secretary; Brereton, at that moment unattached; and myself, secretary to the Commissioner.

In the first days of October we embarked on board the *Meander* and sailed for Labuan, where we arrived on the 7th. Labuan lies, as I have stated, off a large bay, into which flow the Brunei, the Limbang, the Trusan, and many other rivers, and seemed well adapted for a commercial and naval station. It has a fine harbour and plenty of coal, and as we arrived on a bright day, the place looked very attractive. A broad grassy plain, which skirted the harbour, was about three quarters of a mile deep, then it met the low hills and thick jungle. Our houses had all been constructed near the sea, with the plain behind us, and their neat appearance, although only of native materials, quite delighted us. Keppel soon sailed to tow down to Singapore H.M.S. *Royalist*, which had been dismasted by a sudden squall, and we were left to the care of a few marines and blue-jackets.

The south-west monsoon was now blowing fiercely, and brought up with it heavy clouds and drenching rain, and our plain speedily became a fetid swamp, which laid many low with fever and ague. In an interval of fine weather we proceeded to Brunei in the *Jolly Bachelor*, a vessel belonging to the Rajah, but manned by blue-jackets, the steam tender *Ranee* and some other boats, to ratify our treaty with the Sultan, and found prepared for us a long, low shed of a house, in which we all took up our quarters. Brunei was in truth a Venice of hovels, or rather huts, perched on posts driven into the mud banks found in the broad river. Everything looked as though it were falling to decay—the palace, the mosque, the houses of the pangerans, in fact, the whole city of perhaps 20,000 inhabitants.

The wretched Sultan was even then suffering from a disease—cancer on the lip—which carried him off a few years subsequently. He was a mean-looking creature, and his previous atrocities had earned for him the description, 'the head of an idiot and the heart of a pirate.' After finishing our business we returned to Labuan.

I never spent such a wretched month as that of November 1848. After a short respite the south-west monsoon began to blow again, the rain fell in torrents, the sea was driven up to such a height that the waves washed under all our houses, which were built on piles, and destroyed many of our stores. The Rajah's English servant attributed the diminution of the wine and brandy to the same cause. Fever was soon upon us. First the marines and blue-jackets fell ill and many died; then all our Chinese workmen and Kling servants; then Sir James Brooke, the Lieutenant-Governor, the Colonial Secretary, the Colonial Doctor, Captain Brooke, Mr Grant, and many others were down with this weakening disease. The only ones to escape were Mr Scott and myself. Admiral Collier arrived during this period, and fled, panic-stricken, from the place, and ever after did all in his power to injure the colony, and certainly did what he could to keep Her Majesty's vessels away, though those on board ship scarcely ever suffered. There was gloom in every house; even the Chinese would not stay, and went over to establish themselves in the capital.

Fortunately the barracks for the Madras garrison had been built on the swelling ground at the back of the plain, and to this place the Governor sent all those he could. While there they quickly recovered, and it was decided to have fresh houses built for the whole staff near the military quarters.

At the end of November the weather began to improve, as the north-east monsoon made itself felt, and the *Meander* fortunately arrived, and Keppel insisting, Sir James and some of his staff were embarked on board, and we sailed along the north-west coast on the way to Balambangan Island, where an English vessel had been wrecked. Finding her burnt to the water's edge, Sir James decided to proceed to Sulu and visit the Sultan.

At Sugh, the capital, we found both coolness and hesitation. Some Dutch vessels had lately bombarded the town, and the Sultan had not forgotten our attack on Sherif Osman of Marudu Bay. This chief had married a relative of his, and his death after the engagement with the English was still remembered. Besides, there were some survivors and many relatives of those killed in the engagement in May 1847, against whom it was necessary to take every precaution.

Whatever was the motive, the Sultan got over his

soreness of heart, and determined to see the great white chief whose fame had long since reached his ears. He and the people were soon assured that the English had no hostile intentions, and shortly after our arrival a reception was arranged.

The Sulu Islands were claimed by the Spaniards, but they had never made good their claim, for although they had sent several expeditions against the Sultan, which were followed by treaties, these were seldom observed by either side. The islands themselves are as beautiful as, perhaps more beautiful than, any others I have ever seen, well cultivated and producing all the food the natives required, but their commerce appeared very limited. They were the principal rendezvous of the Balignini and Lanun pirates, and consequently a slave emporium. The products of the sea, such as pearls and mother-of-pearl—*bêche de mer*—so prized by the Chinese, were the most valued articles of trade, a large portion of which, however, came from the islands further east. The proceeds of the plunder sold by the pirates were too often invested in guns and powder.

Sulu is nominally governed by a Sultan and a council of nobles, who, however, possess but limited authority over the population of the thousand and one isles.

The Sultan and his nobles received us in such state as they could manage in a hurry, since after the late attack on them by the Dutch their valuables had been sent to the mountains. Their reception of the English envoy was most kind. As Sir James did not wish to introduce business during this visit, our intercourse was purely formal, and after mutual inquiries as to the state of our health, and a curious reference made by the Sultan to the recent revolution in France, we took our leave. The Sultan was a young man, pale and emaciated, the result, it was said, of too much indulgence in opium.

The *Meander* soon sailed from Sulu, and after calling at Samboangan, the Spanish penal settlement in the island of Mindanau, we returned to our colony of Labuan, where we were pleased to find that all the officers were well, and that they had removed from the swampy plain to the higher land behind it. There was, however, but little progress visible, as the fever panic still prevailed. We did not stay long here, as the Rajah was anxious to begin operations against the Seribas and Sakarang pirates, who had again commenced to ravage the coast. We reached Sarawak on the 16th February. A daring attack of the Seribas Dyaks on the Sadong district, when they captured over a hundred heads, made us move out with our native fleet to pursue them, but a return of the north-east monsoon drove us to shelter. Later on, accompanied by the boats of the steamer *Nemesis*, we destroyed some of their inland villages, and thus kept them quiet for a time.

To crush these pirates, however, we required a

stronger force, and had to wait for the arrival of one of Her Majesty's ships. In the meantime, in order to save the independence of Sulu, threatened both by the Dutch and the Spaniards, Sir James determined to proceed there in the steamer *Nemesis* and negotiate a treaty. After calling in at Labuan, we continued our course to the Sulu seas. We were received by the Sultan and nobles in the most friendly manner, and Sir James had no difficulty in negotiating a treaty which, had it been ratified and supported, would have effectually preserved the independence of the Sultan. Our intercourse with these people was most interesting. Preceded by his fame, Sir James soon made himself trusted by the brave islanders, and one proof was that the Sultan asked him to visit him in a small cottage, where he was then staying with a young bride. I was among those who accompanied our Rajah, and on the darkest of dark nights we groped our way there. The Sultan was almost alone, and he soon began to converse about his troublesome neighbours, the Dutch and the Spaniards, expressing a strong hope that the English would support him.

Sir James explained to him our position in Labuan, and cordially invited his people to come and trade there, assuring him that the English had no designs on the independence of their neighbours, but that they only wanted peace and the cessation of piracy. One or two nobles dropped in, and the conversation turned on the subject of hunting, and our hosts proved themselves eager sportsmen, and invited us to return when the rice crop was over and they would show us how they hunted the deer, both on horseback and on foot. The Sultan, during the evening, took a few whiffs of opium, whilst the rest of the company smoked tobacco in various forms. The women were not rigidly excluded, as they came and looked at us whenever they pleased; but we could not see much of them, and it is a form of politeness to pretend not to notice their presence. After a very enjoyable evening, we bade farewell to the Sultan, as we were to sail the following day.

Sir James Brooke had intended to return there, establish himself on shore for a month, and join the nobles in their sports, and thus acquire a personal influence over them. He thought he could wean them from intercourse with the pirates and turn them into honest traders. It must be confessed that when we were there we had abundant evidence that the Balignini and Lanun pirates did frequent the port to sell their slaves and booty and lay in a stock of arms and ammunition. Sir James was, however, persuaded that if British war steamers showed themselves every now and then in Sulu waters, the pirates would abandon these seas. The moment was propitious; the Spaniards had just destroyed the haunts of Balignini, capturing many and dispersing the rest. The sanguinary defeat of eleven of their vessels in

1847, by the *Nemesis*, was not forgotten, and it required but a little steady patrolling to disgust the nobles with this pursuit; in fact, many had sold their war vessels and guns, saying, that now the English steamers were after them, it was no longer the profession of a gentleman. I never met natives who pleased me more; the young chiefs were frank, manly fellows, fond of riding and hunting, and our intercourse with them was very pleasant. It was always a matter of regret with me that I never had an opportunity of visiting them again.

Leaving Sulu, we called in at Samboangan, and had a very agreeable time with the acquaintances we had previously made there. We saw how little the Spaniards had done to develop the immense island of Mindanau. Here and there on the coast were some small settlements, with cultivation extending but a few miles inland, but there was a great air of neatness about the places dotted along the coast.

On our return voyage we touched at Labuan, and then went on to Sarawak, where we found H.M.'s brig *Albatross*, Commander Farquhar, and the *Royalist*, Lieutenant-Commander Everest. The *Nemesis* proceeded on to Singapore, but soon rejoined us.

The expedition which was now organised was the largest that ever left the non-piratical districts for the punishment of the marauders. Besides the steamer *Nemesis*, we had the boats of the *Albatross* and *Royalist*, and about one hundred native prahus,

MAP OF BORNEO AND PART OF THE EASTERN ARCHIPELAGO, SHE
AND FEDERATED MALA

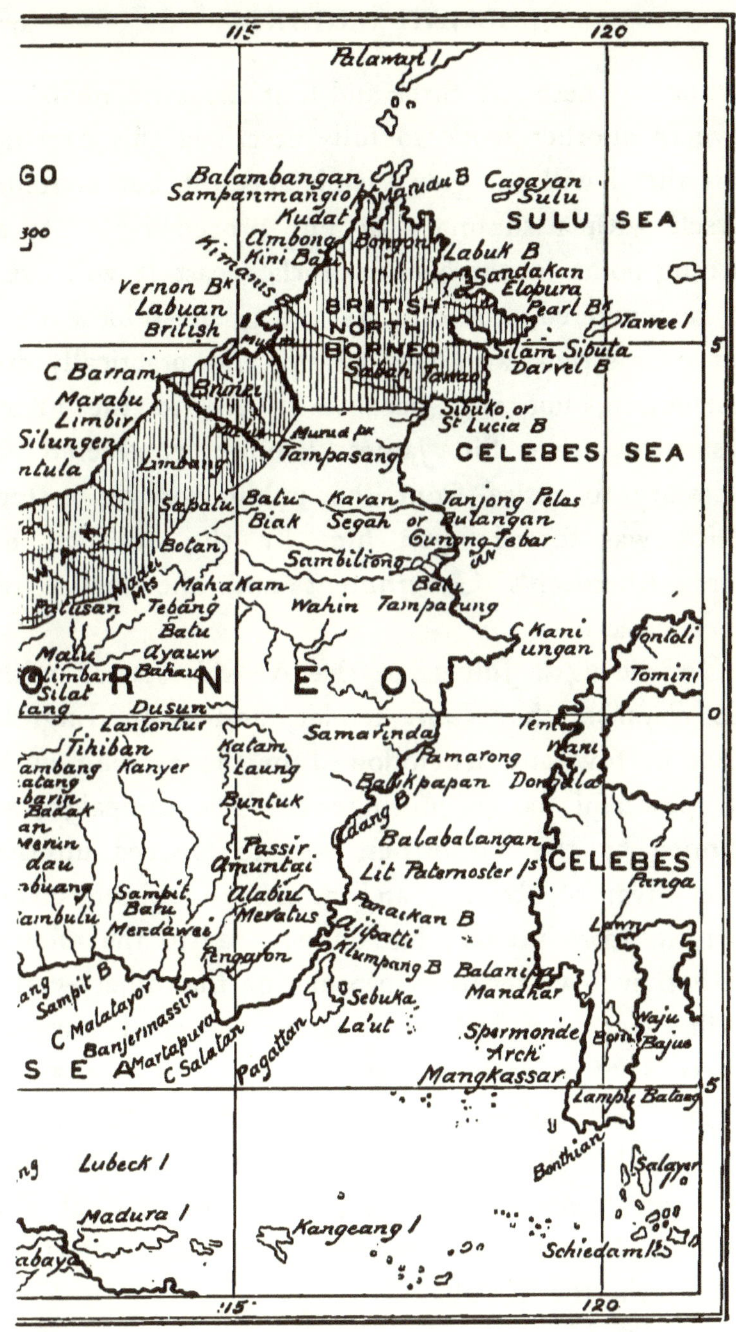

WING BRITISH TERRITORIES, BRITISH PROTECTORATES,

Y STATES.

manned by between three and four thousand men. I have in another work so fully described this expedition that I will not give a fresh account, but content myself with a summary of our proceedings. As a turning point in the history of the coast it will ever be remembered, not only as the greatest blow that was ever struck at Dyak piracy, and practically its destruction, but also because it led to the great misfortune that Sir James Brooke considered it necessary to retire from the public service, a step which was forced upon him by the weakness of Lord Aberdeen's Government and the malice of his enemies.

On the 24th July 1849 the *Nemesis* started with the *Royalist*, the *Ranee* tender, and seven English boats in tow, and we followed in the evening with our powerful native contingent. The campaign, as planned by the authorities, was to proceed up the great river of Rejang, and attack the pirate communities from inland; but on our way to the mouth of that river we received information that ninety-eight Seribas war boats had pulled along the coast towards our point of rendezvous, the Rejang. It was instantly decided that on its return we should attempt to intercept this fleet, and our force was divided into two squadrons, one to guard the entrance of the Seribas, the other the mouth of the next river to the north, the Kaluka.

After two days' waiting, our spy boats, at sunset on

the 31st, brought intelligence of the approach of the pirate fleet. When they saw us at the mouth of the Kaluka, they gave an exultant shout and dashed away for home, but their hopes soon vanished as they were met by the *Nemesis*, the English boats, and the mass of our native fleet. Some turned to escape by the Kaluka, but were driven back and pursued by our light division. They now lost all hope of being able to get away in their heavy bangkongs; they therefore ran them on shore and escaped into the jungle.

In the morning the Rajah received a note from Farquhar to say that he had gone up the Seribas with the steamer to prevent any of the pirate boats escaping, but the few who had forced their way through the blockading squadron were already far beyond his reach. Our division then proceeded to the mouth of the Seribas. What a sight it was! Seventy-five of their war boats were lying on the sands, eighteen had been sunk at sea, and twelve alone escaped up the river. Such a defeat had never before been known.

These war boats were very different from what have been described by certain critics. I measured one. It was eighty feet in length, nine in breadth, and its pulling crew must have consisted of at least seventy men. The pirates murdered all their girl captives, and, after shocking mutilations, cut off their heads and escaped. We soon had ample proof of the piracies committed by this fleet. Not only had they attacked villages on shore, but they had captured two large native vessels on their way to and from Singapore. It would have been easy to have destroyed the fugitive pirates by occupying a narrow isthmus over which they must pass, but Sir James Brooke, convinced that this great defeat would have full effect, called off his excited native followers to the attack of the interior strongholds.

During our stay on the districts of Paku, we lost some men from the over-confidence of the sons of the Orang Kaya Tumangong of Lundu, who advanced to clear the path by which we were to march on the town. They were stooping to pull out the *ranjaus* when the Seribas, headed by Lingire, sprang upon them, and cut down two, while the third son escaped, as a party of our Malays poured a volley into the enemy and killed several of them. However, we advanced next day and laid their country waste, our native contingent loading themselves with plunder. Having showed the pirates that no defences could prevent our punishing them, it was decided to carry out the original plan and attack those Sakarang and Seribas Dyaks who lived on the Kanowit, a branch of the great Rejang river, about a hundred miles from the mouth of the latter. These men were most feared by the inhabitants of the Sago districts, which were situated near the western entrances of the mighty stream.

Many of our native allies now left us, as they were

loaded with plunder and were not provisioned for so long a voyage ; so we proceeded with the *Nemesis*, the English boats, and our principal Malay war prahus, and as soon as we appeared on the Rejang fresh bodies of natives began to join us, eager to retaliate upon those who had so often attacked them and captured their trading vessels. The Rejang is a splendid river, destined some day to be an important highway of commerce, as its various branches open out a large extent of country, and it penetrates further into the great island of Borneo than any other stream on the north-west coast.

The *Nemesis* towed many of the boats up to the entrance of the Kanowit branch, and anchored there whilst the expedition pushed up to attack the great pirate chief Buah Ryah, who had established his quarters in the interior of this broad river. We advanced rapidly, and were within one day's pull of his forts, while Captain Brooke, with the light division of fast-pulling boats had reconnoitred some miles ahead, and found that the pirates were beginning to show in great numbers, which made us feel assured that we should soon be in touch with the main body. We landed to inspect a large village house, which was surrounded by a cotton plantation, and found it well built, and full of baskets of the skulls of the unfortunates who had been surprised by these marauders. I counted three hundred heads in one village. We then fell down the river to join Sir James Brooke and the English force, in great spirits at the prospect of coming in contact with the enemy next day. We were therefore astonished to hear, on our arrival, that it had been decided to give up the object of our expedition and return. As dinner was over, we removed to a short distance from our chiefs to have our meal in quiet, and to express to each other our indignation at the decision to which our naval commander had come. Some others joined us, equally disappointed. Towards the end of the meal, I could not help raising my glass and saying aloud, 'Oh, for one hour of bonnie Keppel!' Captain Farquhar sprang up and came over to us to inquire what I meant. We told him why we considered his determination very detrimental to the cause, as we were approaching Buah Ryah's stronghold. He urged, however, the fatigue of his men, who had been pulling many days in succession against a strong current. We proposed a day's rest, but on a hint from Sir James I gave up the discussion. He thought as I did, that Buah Ryah would, with some reason, proclaim that we were afraid to attack him, and would be thus encouraged to hold out. This actually happened, and thus the pacification of these districts was delayed for many years. There is no doubt that the English sailors were really tired, and possibly also dissatisfied, as all the skirmishing was done by our native contingent, who forged ahead of the slow-pulling men-of-war's boats. How we missed the special boats of the *Meander!* The sailors, however, might have been sure that had there been any real fighting ahead, all would have waited for them.

As we gloomily fell down the river we met thousands of natives who were coming to join our expedition, and who were desperately disappointed that Buah Ryah had not been punished. When near the mouth of the Kanowit we were hailed by the inhabitants of the villages we had destroyed. A conference ensued; they showed their faith in the white man by boldly pulling out to our prahus. They did not attempt to deny their piracies, but promised amendment; and most of these chiefs kept their word.

As we returned towards Sarawak the native chiefs of all the trading towns on the coast came to express their unbounded thanks to the English Rajah and to the Queen's forces for the punishment they had inflicted on the pirates, and the prospect it held out of trade being carried on free from danger of pillage and death.

CHAPTER V

ATTACKS ON THE RAJAH'S POLICY—VISITS TO LABUAN, SINGAPORE AND PENANG—MISSION TO SIAM—THE RAJAH'S RETURN TO ENGLAND—DINNER TO HIM IN LONDON—HIS REMARKABLE SPEECH—LORD ABERDEEN'S GOVERNMENT APPOINTS A HOSTILE COMMISSION—THE RAJAH'S RETURN TO SARAWAK—COMMISSION AT SINGAPORE—ITS FINDINGS.

WE were fairly contented with the results of the recent expedition, and thought that all would be satisfied with our efforts to put down piracy and protect trade. We were therefore greatly surprised on our arrival in Sarawak to find that two English papers had commenced violent attacks on our proceedings, founded at first on some reports of excesses by our native allies during our expedition in the spring, when we punished the pirates at the Kaluka river. At the time we suspected, and it was clearly proved afterwards, that the originator of this campaign against the Rajah was Mr Henry Wise, Sir James's discarded agent.

I have already mentioned that Mr Wise had been

accidentally entrusted with a mass of the Rajah's private correspondence with his mother and with Mr John Templer; in the former Mr Wise found the expression, 'A friend was worth a dozen agents'; and in the latter such words as, 'If Wise does not obey my instructions I will kick him to the devil.' Mr Wise was by nature vindictive, and it was not surprising that he was somewhat roused by such freedom of expression, though it occurred in confidential letters to the Rajah's most intimate friends. The reason why these energetic remarks had been made was Sir James's discovery that Wise was trading on his great name, and (as already stated) endeavouring to form companies with very large capital to develop the resources of Sarawak. The Rajah tried in vain to stem this current by pointing out that there could be no employment for a large capital in a new country, and that everything must advance gradually. This would not have suited Wise's views, which were to gain for himself a large fortune, careless as to who suffered in the process.

Mr Wise succeeded in floating the Eastern Archipelago Company, with a nominal capital of £100,000, and managed so to mystify the directors that they agreed to accept his own terms, by which he would have monopolised nearly all the profits. But notwithstanding that there were some respectable names among the directors the public did not come forward, and all, or nearly all, of the shares remained in the hands of the company. The City would not help, as it soon became known that capitalists of undoubted strength had been ready to find the money, but were suspicious of Mr Wise's refusal to state his terms before the company was formed.

Having secured, as he thought, three thousand a year for certain, with other great advantages in prospect, Mr Wise threw off the mask, and now declared to Government that he could no longer associate himself in any way with Sir James's sanguinary policy. He forgot entirely that his company had been formed to take advantage of the English Rajah's unique position in Borneo, so as to develop its resources and to work the coal in Labuan, of which colony Sir James Brooke was Governor.

Mr Wise was soon in communication with the press, but the majority saw through the discarded agent, and would have nothing to do with his pretended disclosures. He succeeded, however, in gaining the ear of Joseph Hume, who promised to bring the case before Parliament, and managed to win over to his side Mr Cobden, and, to a lesser degree, Mr Bright. I must here observe that because Mr Cobden advocated Free Trade with great ability and success, his followers appear to consider that words must not be applied to him which he was ready enough to apply to others. Many pretended to be shocked that Sir James Brooke answered these attacks with his characteristic energy; and I remember meeting one of the foremost statesmen of the present day at a dinner on my return from Borneo in 1860, who, in reply to a question of mine, said that the language which Sir James Brooke had employed when speaking of ministers had prevented them from restoring him to his position in the public service or showing their appreciation of the great good he had done. It took my breath away. After they had heaped on him every humiliation which was possible, he was to sit quiet and bear it. It was not, however, in his nature to sit quiet when calumny after calumny was propagated by his enemies. I will allow that his language was strong and occasionally injudicious, but we must remember the provocation, and that his heart was set on the safety of Sarawak. I must add that not one of those around him ever attempted to increase his indignation; on the contrary, we urged him to treat these attacks with contempt.

After having spent one hundred and sixty days in ships and boats during the first eight months of 1849, we were, indeed, glad of a little rest. The squadron now dispersed, Her Majesty's ships sailed for Singapore; Captain Brooke, suffering from fever, went to China for a change; and Grant and I remained with the Rajah. Though quiet, we were busy, as deputation after deputation arrived from the pirate rivers to express their firm determination to give up piracy, and messengers came from the distant inland tribes to interview the Rajah, 'for the Dyaks had heard, the whole world had heard, that the Son of Europe was the friend of the Dyak.'

We also visited several of the interior tribes, and the manifold proofs that the Rajah witnessed of the great advance made by those poor and humble subjects of his raj must have been pleasing to him.

It was during these quiet months that we gave ourselves up to the library. The Rajah was a good reader, and it was a treat to hear him read Miss Austen's novels, which were great favourites of his. He was also very fond of religious discussions, and I think we listened to the whole of the long controversy between Huxley and Priestley, and heard all Channing's Essays. Whatever the Rajah touched appeared to gain an additional brightness. He was always gay and full of fun, and dearly loved an argument.

Every evening the native chiefs came in to talk to the Rajah, who supplied them with cigars, and it was from these conversations that he gained that minute knowledge of the local politics of every district, which served him so admirably when he had to deal with the chiefs along the coast. The Rajah had the rare gift of never forgetting a name or a face. One evening a poor Milanau came in, and after touching the Rajah's hand, squatted on the floor, and remained silent, as many chiefs were present. 'I have seen that man before,' said Sir James; and presently he turned round and addressed the native by name, and said, 'Bujang, what is the news from Bintulu?' This man had piloted a steamer into that river ten years previously, and the Rajah had never seen him since.

Finding he could not shake off the fever and ague contracted during our expeditions, Sir James decided to proceed to the island of Penang, one of the Straits Settlements, where he had been offered the use of Governor Butterworth's bungalow on a hill more than two thousand feet above the sea level. Hearing, however, that his officers in Labuan were at loggerheads, he decided first to proceed to that colony and investigate the cause of these dissensions. We left Sarawak on the 11th December, reaching our destination on the 14th; and it was time indeed that the Governor should arrive. Our few days were prolonged to over ten weeks, as an inquiry had to be instituted into the conduct of the Lieutenant-Governor. Though I do not think that anything was proved against his personal honour, it was clearly established that his violent temper and quarrelsome disposition rendered him unsuited for the position, and Sir James Brooke suspended him from his functions.

While this inquiry was going on, we proceeded to Brunei to see the Sultan, and heard, whilst we were in the capital, that the Chinese traders were most anxious to remove to our colony, but I do not believe they ever really intended to do so. They had built houses for themselves in the capital, and were doing a thriving trade on a small scale; and unless they all agreed to move at the same time, none would move. The Bornean Malay traders also talked of migrating from the capital to a spot opposite the colony. The slave question would prevent their establishing themselves within its boundaries; but it is always a difficult thing for men to abandon their homes, and in this case, as the power of the Brunei Government was broken, they no longer feared oppression. So the colony remained stagnant.

We left Labuan at the end of February, and after calling in at Sarawak, proceeded to Singapore, where a budget of news awaited us. The English Governor had appointed Sir James as Special Envoy to proceed to Siam and Cochin China to form treaties with those states; at the same time we heard of the renewal of virulent attacks on the Rajah's policy by certain journals and Members of Parliament. After a pleasant stay of a fortnight, we proceeded to Penang in the hope that we should all shake off the fever and ague contracted during our exhausting expeditions.

No man loved nature more than did the Rajah, and he enjoyed his stay on this lofty hill. He could ride, or wander among the lovely flowers and plants of the Governor's garden, or he could gaze on the beautiful scenery which unfolded itself around us. Those six weeks were indeed delightful, and we often looked back on our quiet sojourn there and its refreshing rest. We busied ourselves also in preparing for our missions to Siam and Annam, to which I had been appointed secretary.

As the ship of war which was to have taken us to Siam was soon expected, we would not wait for the mail steamer, but left Penang in a sailing vessel, and took seventeen days to reach Singapore, a distance of only four hundred miles; in our case it was the greater haste the less speed.

On our arrival in Singapore we found that there was no vessel ready for us, and we had to wait weary months there before one was placed at our disposal. At first we were to have had the *Hastings* battleship; then, from some personal reason, it was decided by Admiral Austen, brother to Jane Austen, no doubt the 'William' of *Mansfield Park*, that we were to have H.M.'s steamer *Sphynx*, Captain Shadwell. It was quite useless to show ourselves in Siam without a commanding force, if we wished to secure a favourable treaty. It was known that the King of Siam had become hostile to Europeans, and nothing but fear would work on his prejudiced mind. Had we appeared off the Menam River with a strong squadron, our mission would have been respected.

Early in August we left Singapore for Siam in the *Sphynx*, attended by the Company's steamer *Nemesis*, and were soon at our destination. Captain Brooke and I were sent in to the forts at the mouth of the river to make arrangements for the Envoy's suitable reception. We found the people on shore in great alarm, and we heard that a heavy boom had been placed across the river to prevent the steamers proceeding to the capital. When we had settled our business we returned to Sir James, and it was arranged that he should enter the river next morning in the larger ship. It appeared to a landsman that no sufficient precautions were taken to mark the deepest passage, but we trusted to a native pilot, who speedily ran us on a sandbank. There was no help for it, as the *Sphynx* could not be moved, but to be transferred to the *Nemesis*, and we then steamed on to the forts.

The minister charged with foreign affairs had come down to receive us, so the first meeting between him and the English Envoy took place at the village close to the mouth of the river.

It was an amusing scene. The arrogance of this half-civilised people was extreme, and the minister, to show his disdain, had the seats intended for the English Envoy and his suite placed in a position of marked inferiority. He himself was seated on a divan, with soft cushions, and surrounded by his gold betel boxes and tea service, whilst his followers crouched behind him, and no native approached, except on his hands and knees, crawling like an insect along the floor. The minister rose as we entered, and pointing to some chairs, motioned us to be seated, but Sir James passed them by. He approached the minister and shook hands, and sat down opposite to him; we all followed suit, and did the same, placing our chairs beside that of our chief. The minister was breathless with astonishment, but he resumed his seat, and in a short time recovered his composure, and the usual routine of questions and answers followed. He said that the Government had built a house for the reception of the mission, and that state barges were being prepared to convey the Envoy and his suite to the capital. Had the *Sphynx* been able to enter the river, we might have insisted on going to the capital in the *Nemesis*, but it was settled that we should proceed in the state barges. Captain Brooke and I went first to inspect the temporary house allotted to us, but finding it unsuitable, we accepted the offer of an English merchant to take his house for the mission, and use the other for our escort and for visitors from the ships.

Sir James Brooke was soon satisfied that, under the then reigning king, success was hopeless, as he had imbibed a strong prejudice against foreigners through the unjustifiable conduct of an English merchant, who had nearly ruined the prospects of our trade by an attempt to coerce the King into buying a steamer at four times its value. But what proved of importance was the confidential intercourse which took place with Chaufa Mungkut, the legal heir to the throne. This prince had retired to a monastery to avoid the persecution of the King, who was an illegitimate elder brother.

We readily gathered sufficient information as to the King's ill-treatment of various British subjects to warrant our Government acting against him; but all our present advances were rejected. I may again repeat that had we arrived with a strong squadron, with ships which could have entered the river, and decided to proceed to Bangkok in a war vessel, there would have been little opposition to signing a treaty; but Sir James thought that not much would be gained by forcing a convention on the Siamese.

Satisfied that nothing could be done, Sir James sent to the Foreign Minister the value of all presents received, and we started for the mouth of the river in the state barges, and soon found ourselves on board the *Sphynx* on our way to Singapore. Our only success had been the discovery that Chaufa Mungkut was favourable to the English, that he was an educated prince, who could converse and correspond in our language, and that when he came to the throne he would be ready to negotiate.

On our arrival in Singapore we received the particulars of the debate of July 12, 1850, which had taken place in the House of Commons concerning our proceedings against the Seribas pirates. Though Mr Hume's motion had been rejected by a great majority, Sir James justly complained that no minister had stood up to express their approval of his policy.

However, though these attacks might irritate, they could not do away with the pleasure afforded by the good news from Sarawak. The civil war which had broken out in Sambas between the Chinese gold-working companies and the Sultan, backed by the Dutch, had caused about 4000 Chinese agriculturists to fly from that country and take refuge in Sarawak. This was a welcome addition, for wherever Chinese settle there are trade and cultivation, and revenue follows in their footsteps.

As soon as we could send off the papers connected with the Siam Mission we proceeded to Sarawak to find great activity there. The Chinese were spreading about the town and in the interior, and the Rajah was soon busy regulating the affairs of the country, preventing the encroachments of the Chinese on the Dyaks, to which they were very prone, and visiting various inland tribes to mark their progress. At one of those villages we were struck by the intelligent questions put by several of the Dyaks regarding Siam and the neighbouring states, and on inquiry we found that before the advent of the white Rajah the rulers of the country were accustomed to send them to pull an oar in the pirate fleets which then cruised throughout these seas. They had evidently used their eyes to some purpose whilst thus employed.

A very severe attack of fever and ague interrupted the Rajah's activity, and he was at length persuaded to listen to the voice of his medical man, and to return to England for the benefit of his health. But he first visited Labuan, which he found still making but slow progress; and, though it appeared at one time that there was really about to be an influx of Chinese and Malays from the capital, when it was found that the Governor was returning to England they made up their minds not to move until he came back. Some of the latter had had their prahus towed over by the *Nemesis*, but they soon went away again, and the contemplated movement never took place. The fact was that at that time they trusted only the English Rajah, and if he were not in Labuan to protect them they would not risk exciting the hostility of the Brunei Government.

We soon started again for Sarawak, and on the 17th of January the Rajah left us for Singapore on his way to England. His three offices were thus filled—Mr Scott, afterwards Sir John Scott, was in charge of the Colony of Labuan; Captain Brooke of the Principality of Sarawak; and I remained as acting Commissioner.

I should mention that whilst we were away attending to Siamese affairs, Mr Balestier, Special Envoy from the United States, went to Sarawak in a frigate, the bearer of a letter from the President to Sir James Brooke, as ruler of the State of Sarawak, proposing a convention between the two countries. As a British official, Sir James thought it right to submit the subject to Lord Palmerston, who found nothing objectionable in the proposed arrangement; however, amid the heated controversy that was in progress, the question was unfortunately neglected.

We had all hoped that this visit to Europe was for health's sake; but the requisite rest could not be obtained, as Sir James found himself at once pursued by the malignity of his enemies—Mr Wise and the Eastern Archipelago Company—who had found channels to diffuse their false accusations, as I have before noticed, in Mr Hume and Mr Cobden. In the debates in the House, Lord Palmerston spoke out strongly and clearly, and the majority was absolutely crushing; but Joseph Hume did not know when he was beaten, and brought the question again and again before Parliament.

Sir James now turned on his enemies; dragged the Eastern Archipelago Company into court, and the case ended by it being declared that 'The directors had signed a false certificate, knowing it to be false.' This was in regard to their capital. Their charter was therefore abrogated and the seal torn off that document. These directors must have bitterly regretted having joined Wise in his campaign against the Rajah.

Sir James was also busy in answering hostile attacks, and his letters addressed to Mr Drummond, M.P., on Mr Hume's assertions, were considered masterly compositions, completely establishing his case—the view entertained by all reasonable men. Mr Sidney

Herbert also determined to break a lance with the Rajah, but soon repented of his temerity and retired discomfited from the field. Sir James had this advantage over his adversaries, that his conduct in Borneo had been marked by so much courage, and was so straightforward and honourable, that they could find no weak point in his armour.

A great dinner was given to Sir James Brooke at the London Tavern, on the 30th April 1852, attended by over two hundred men of distinction, and among the many speeches that were made, one by Baron Alderson was especially remarkable. He observed, 'that the greatest benefactors of the human race have been most abused in their own lifetime,' but notwithstanding this, 'he promised him the approbation of his own conscience, the approbation of all good and reasonable men, and of Almighty God, who does justice and who will reward.'

The speech of the evening, however, was that of the guest. Those who had never heard him before were surprised and delighted. His noble presence, his refined manner, the charm of his voice, quite captivated them, whilst his words carried conviction. He wound up by saying, 'Do not disgrace your public servants by inquiries generated in the fogs of base suspicions; for, remember, a wrong done is like a wound received—the scar is ineffaceable. It may be covered by glittering decorations, but there it remains to the end.' Prophetic words!

Lord Derby's Government was now in office, and Lord Malmesbury settled with Sir James Brooke that he should be appointed Her Majesty's representative in the Further East, to enable him to negotiate treaties with foreign powers. He was to begin with Siam and Cochin China. A General Election, however, took place in the autumn of 1852, which sealed the fate of the Conservative Ministry. Sir James had already been named Envoy to Siam, and would have proceeded at once to that country by the special wish of Chaufa Mungkut, the new king, when the Mission was suddenly and unexpectedly put off, owing to His Majesty's desire to have further time to complete the elaborate funeral ceremonies required by custom for his brother, the late king. Ever since our mission to Siam in 1850, Chaufa Mungkut had kept up a private correspondence with the Rajah of Sarawak, in whose doings he showed great interest.

So closed the year 1852, and on the 1st January 1853 appeared the list of the new ministers—the Coalition Ministry of Lord Aberdeen. 'England loves not coalitions,' said D'Israeli; and we certainly did not love this one. Probably to strengthen their parliamentary majority, and yielding to the influence of Mr Cobden, the new Government decided to grant Mr Hume's demand and issue a Commission to inquire into the conduct of Sir James Brooke. Sir James himself had always courted inquiry, and therefore the Ministry might have communicated their intention to him before he left England, which he had decided to do during the first week in April. But instead of consulting with him, they tried to keep the whole affair dark, and it was only accidentally that Sir James heard of it. I never could understand how a frank, loyal man like Lord Clarendon could lend himself to such proceedings, but I suppose he was overruled by Lord Aberdeen and Mr Sidney Herbert.

Finding that their determination to issue a Commission of Inquiry could no longer be concealed from Sir James Brooke, they wrote to him officially on the subject, and stated that they would call on the Governor-General of India to choose Commissioners. They further assured Sir James that 'the inquiry should be full, fair and complete.' But the whole transaction had been so underhand, so humiliating to him personally, so derogatory to him as ruler of Sarawak, that he felt it bitterly, and he closed his despatch to Lord Clarendon, April 4, 1853, the day he left England, with these words: 'It is with sorrow unmixed with anger that I leave the world to judge the services I have rendered and the treatment I have received.'

On Sir James Brooke's arrival in Singapore he found that while the Government had been reticent with him, they had been confidential with Mr Hume, who repaid that confidence by divulging all the details of the proposed Commission to the editor of a hostile paper in Singapore. This personage made the most of it, and indulged in violent tirades, in which he gloated over the disgrace which had fallen upon Sir James. But this abuse affected none of the Rajah's friends, who were the flower of Singapore society.

No ships of war were now at his disposal, and I doubt whether in his then state of mind he would have accepted their services. He returned to Sarawak in a small merchant brig, the *Weeraff*, commanded by a cheerful little Frenchman.

His reception in his adopted country might have consoled him for the injustice of his own Government, for never had he received a more sincere welcome. The whole population was astir, and the hill on which Government House stood, as well as the house itself, was crammed with his joyous subjects; but he soon complained of being tired. We noticed that the Rajah's face looked swollen, and I heard a native say he had *purunasi*, but none of us understood the word, which meant smallpox in the language of the north. Fever came on, and I used to sit for hours with him. At last it was manifest to everyone that it was small-pox. No sooner did he hear this than he insisted that all those who had not suffered from that disease should leave the room, and he chose his attendants among the Malays and submitted to native treatment. His cousin, Arthur Crookshank, watched over him, and all would have braved the danger of contagion, but he would have none of us with him. A Mr Horsburgh, a missionary, who thought he had passed through the ordeal, joined those who were nursing him.

By the Rajah's express order our hill was tabooed, and all were forbidden to approach for fear the disease might spread; but this rule was afterwards relaxed in favour of those who had already suffered from it, and as most of the Malays were in that case, they came every day to inquire. There was no doubt of the intense feeling of anxiety that oppressed the people. There were prayers in the mosques, votive offerings by Klings and Chinese, and as for the Dyaks, they were in despair. However, the crisis passed, and then the Rajah was overwhelmed with presents. Scented water was brought for his bath; delicate dishes, to tempt his appetite, came from the native ladies; and the rejoicing was true and heartfelt. We all remained near the Rajah, and as soon as we were permitted eagerly joined in nursing him. The attack had been most severe, and it would have been difficult for a casual acquaintance to have recognised the same man in our chief, who had just escaped from the very jaws of death.

As soon as the Rajah was sufficiently recovered, he decided to visit the capital. The Sultan Omar Ali was dead, and Pangeran Mumein had been chosen to fill that office, although he did not belong to the royal family. We started in the same little merchant brig *Weeraff*, and were soon at the capital. The Rajah knew that every kind of intrigue had been going on during his long absence. The Eastern Archipelago Company had sent their agent to try and induce the late Sultan to complain of the conduct of Her Majesty's Commissioner; and the Ex-Lieutenant-Governor of Labuan had also written to the Brunei Government to tell them of the Commission, and to insinuate that Sir James was no longer the powerful personage that he had been. The Queen had decided to inquire into his conduct; so now was the time to act. However, these intrigues completely failed.

The Rajah had not been a week in the capital when his influence was as completely re-established as when he had an admiral and a squadron at his back. The grant of Sarawak was confirmed, and a new deed was made out, giving him the government of the rivers, as far as the Rejang, on the payment of £1000 a year. Not even Mr Hume could say that he obtained these concessions by the use of force.

While we were in Brunei, we lodged in the Sultan's palace, and were fed from the royal kitchen; we found the cuisine excellent. The Sultan and pangerans were constant visitors, and we enjoyed our stay among them. Not only did the Brunei Government confirm public grants, but they handed over to the Rajah the originals of the letters addressed to them by Mr Napier and others, showing how active his enemies had been as soon as it was known that a Commission of Inquiry had been granted by our vacillating ministers.

Nothing could better illustrate the conduct and character of the Rajah than the results of this visit. Here was this man, under the ban of the British Government, exposed to every insult from a reptile press—fortunately among English papers a very small minority—and apparently in deep disgrace. Yet in his own adopted country he was respected, loved and trusted beyond any other man by all races and creeds.

Upon our return to Sarawak we heard of Lord Clarendon's instructions to the Commission which was to inquire into Sir James Brooke's conduct and position. As I propose to devote a few pages to it later on, I need not dwell upon them now.

The Rajah had long meditated a scheme to bring the Land Dyaks of Sarawak, Samarahan and Sadong under the direct rule of the Government. Up to the year 1853 the Dyak tribes had been apportioned among the three Datus or Malay chiefs, which was the immemorial custom; but it was found in practice to work badly, particularly in the hands of the Datu Patingi. He was an ambitious man, fond of parade, and kept up two large establishments for his principal wives. To support the expense, he not only exacted all that was legally due to him, but carried on a system of forced trade, preventing the Dyaks from buying, except of him and his agents—a truck trade on an extended system and in its worst form. The complaints which reached headquarters were numerous. After he had married his daughter to one of the Arab adventurers on the coast, who pretended to be a descendant of the Prophet, his extortions knew no bounds.

The Rajah determined to pay the Datus fixed salaries, fifty per cent. beyond their legal dues, and to insist on the trade with the Dyaks being as free in practice as it was in theory. The Malay chiefs were pleased with the arrangement ; but gradually the old abuses of forced trade were reintroduced by the Patingi, and the Rajah was often obliged to interfere to protect the Dyaks.

The Patingi became dissatisfied when he found his evil courses checked, and began to conspire against his benefactor, who had saved his life after the civil war was ended ; and when he heard that a Commission had been appointed by the English Government to try the Rajah, he became very active in his intrigues, and proposed to the other chiefs to expel the English from Sarawak. None joined him, and though they kept a watch on his proceedings, they never breathed a word of the nascent conspiracy either to the Rajah or to any of his officers. When the whole executive Government, English as well as Malay, were away on an expedition, a brave young chief, Abong Patah, came to me (I was then Her Majesty's acting Commissioner) and revealed all the details of the plot. I instantly sent off the news to the Rajah, who did not doubt its truth for a moment. He had himself observed very suspicious movements of the Patingi's armed vessels, and had also noticed that whenever that chief anchored near the English war prahu, where all the Rajah's officers assembled every evening, the other chiefs would, apparently by accident, allow their prahus to drop alongside. The Rajah communicated the discovery to some of his most trustworthy followers, both English and Malay, but left the Patingi in ignorance, though judicious precautions were taken to frustrate his machinations.

As soon, however, as the Rajah returned to the capital, he summoned a meeting of all the chiefs and principal men of the country, and in open court accused the Patingi of all his crimes and misdemeanours. He told him that on account of the respect he had for his family he would not try him for high treason; but that all his arms and ammunition must be handed over to abide the decision of the Government. The Patingi was too surprised to deny his guilt; in fact, he knew that every chief present was aware of his criminal intentions. It ended by his being permitted to make the pilgrimage to Mecca. The Rajah's leniency, though judging by subsequent events misplaced, was so natural that it met with general approval, except among the more far-seeing of the Malays, who predicted that this ungrateful chief would yet do the English an ill turn.

The Rajah then tried an experiment, of which some doubted the wisdom, of supplying the place of the deposed Datu by appointing the head of the Mohammedan priesthood in Sarawak to become the third ruling Malay chief. He was brother to the Datu Bandhar—a quiet, honest, good Malay. How well the Rajah judged has been shown by the subsequent history of Sarawak. The Datu Imaun has always proved the mainstay of the English in all their troubles and difficulties; and, although much over eighty, I heard of his being well and active until quite recently.

The Rajah had intended to adopt no warlike measures against the pirate Dyaks, headed by the notorious chief Rentab, until the Commission was over, but after waiting fifteen months, and finding no signs of its assembling, he determined to lead an expedition against them. Previous attempts by his officers had failed, but this expedition was so well organised that its success was assured.

Eight thousand Malays and Dyaks answered to the summons of their chief, whilst an expedition of fifteen hundred men threatened the enemy in the interior of the Rejang, and well-armed war prahus anchored in the Seribas. We pushed up the great Batang Lupar river, then ascended the Sakarang as far as our big war boats would go, built a fort for their protection, left a garrison—and there the Rajah was persuaded to remain, as his state of health did not permit him to expose himself to the further hardships of the advance.

We proceeded in our light boats, or pushed through the jungle. I never saw such a go-as-you-please expedition. An enterprising enemy might have cut us off as we scattered through the woods, but fortunately they were over-awed by the reports of our numbers and of our arms. Captain Brooke, who was in command, saw the danger of this method of advance, and decided to continue the expedition in boats. Our people had found a large number of these in the jungle, hidden there by the enemy, so we soon had enough for the Malays. At first most of the Dyaks preferred to walk, but gradually they secured sufficient canoes to enable all to advance by the river.

The object of the expedition was to attack Sungei Lang—a large fortified village held by Rentab and his followers, and, if possible, a stronghold he had constructed on the summit of the Sadok Mountain. After much skirmishing and firing, the fort was gallantly stormed, and before sunset was completely in our hands. And glad we were that there had been no delay, as scarcely were we housed, when a violent tempest burst, that would have effectually drenched us had we remained in the open. We stayed in this village whilst our men were employed punishing the followers of Rentab; but no attempt was made to attack his fortified post on the summit of the Sadok mountain. Natives seldom care to continue a campaign after its announced object has been accomplished, and our object was to take Sungei Lang. Sadok defied successive expeditions for eight years more. The Sakarang river was now in flood, so that on our return we passed over all natural obstructions in safety. We were heartily received by the Rajah and congratulated on our success, as the storming of Rentab's stronghold was no mean achievement with only native followers.

On our arrival at Sarawak we had news of the Commissioners being expected at Singapore, and H.M.'s. brig *Lily* arrived to convey Sir James Brooke and his followers to our Straits Settlements, but the Rajah had to go alone, as Grant, Brereton and myself were down with fever, the result of over-exposure to sun and rain and the cold watches of the night. Brereton did not recover, and in him the Rajah lost a most efficient and devoted officer.

No one now cares for the Commission sent to inquire into the position and conduct of Sir James Brooke, Rajah of Sarawak, and Commissioner and Consul-General in Borneo; but as its results were so disastrous I must devote a few pages to it.

As I have before mentioned—and here I am obliged to repeat some observations I have previously made—when Sir James Brooke found that his agent in England, Mr Wise, was trying to involve him in schemes which he considered doubtful, he endeavoured to check him, and used strong language about his projects, looking upon them as designs to defraud the public by false representations. Mr Wise accidentally came to know the energetic expressions used by his employer, and decided to have his revenge, but he held his hand until the right moment had arrived. He still continued to press Sir James to join his gigantic companies, but failed in his attempts. Other events occurred which excited him still more, such as the Rajah's handing over to the British Government, instead of directly to himself, the grant of the coal seams in certain portions of the Sultan's dominions which Sir James had received whilst Her Majesty's Agent. At length, when his employer called upon him to produce his accounts, as a very large balance was due to him, Mr Wise began to denounce him publicly. The Farquhar expedition furnished him with the opportunity, and he now posed as a humanitarian, and furnished certain members of the press with garbled information. We may imagine how unscrupulous he was when Lord Clarendon stated, 'It had been detected in the Foreign Office that Mr Wise's "*Papers printed for use in the Government Offices*" could not be relied on, and that some were "simple forgeries."'

Mr Wise, however, managed, as I have said, to persuade Mr Joseph Hume to enter into his projects, who found an ally in Mr Cobden, and they both commenced a campaign in the House of Commons against the Rajah. This continued until the Coalition Ministry, under Lord Aberdeen, came into power in 1853. To secure the Parliamentary support of the Free Trade party, Lord Aberdeen weakly consented to issue a Commission on the lines suggested by Mr Hume, Sir James's vindictive adversary.

The Commission might have been issued with the concurrence of both parties, as Sir James was anxious for a full inquiry; but the Government, whilst informing Mr Hume of their intention to accede to his demand, thought it becoming to keep Sir James ignorant of it, and he found it out by accident.

Forty-five years have passed since this event occurred, and yet I cannot write of it without a flush of indignation. Mr Gladstone made this observation: 'His (Sir James's) language respecting Mr Hume and Mr Cobden, two men of the very highest integrity . . . is for the most part quite unjustifiable.' Mr Hume's integrity, by his own confession, was not above suspicion, and Mr Cobden may be judged by the following extract: 'Sir James Brooke seized on a territory as large as Yorkshire, and then drove out the natives, and subsequently sent for our fleet and men to massacre them.' The insolence and ignorance displayed in the latter statement, as I have elsewhere observed, are about equal.

Grant and I soon followed the Rajah to Singapore, and found the Commission sitting. It was composed of Mr Prinsep and Mr Devereux, the former suffering from a malady which was beginning to show itself at intervals, and quite incapable of conducting the inquiry with dignity; the latter everything which could be desired—a man of marked ability, impartial and painstaking.

When the Commission opened its sittings, only two complainants came forward—the ex-Lieutenant-Governor of Labuan, and an editor of a newspaper. Both of these were informed that their cases were beyond the scope of the Commission. As, however, above fifty inhabitants of Singapore had signed an address to Mr Hume, supporting his demand for an inquiry into the character of the tribes of Seribas and Sakarang, the Commissioners naturally thought that they would be prepared with some evidence of their assertion that these tribes were not piratical, and that they had been massacred under false pretences; but all the memorialists who were called by the Commissioners denied having any knowledge on the subject, and many had signed under the impression that they were aiding the cause of Sir James Brooke. The Commissioners waited day after day for hostile witnesses, but none came.

While we were all waiting for that testimony which was not forthcoming, a gentleman who was sitting next me said, 'I should like to give evidence.' I mentioned his wish to the Commissioners. He was then called forward, and stated that his name was Boudriot; that he was in the Civil Service of the Dutch Government; that he had resided four and a half years in Borneo. He knew of the Seribas and Sakarang Dyaks; he had always known them as pirates, killing and murdering all along the coast. They came down in large, armed boats, holding each a crew of from eighty to ninety, killing the men they met and carrying off the women and children as slaves. In one excursion they killed about four hundred men. This happened in the Dutch possessions. They had ravaged the Dutch settlements; probably the recorded instances would number one hundred. 'As every one in Borneo knows them (as pirates), I am surprised that anyone should question their existence.'

When it is remembered that this evidence was given unsolicited by a high and experienced Dutch official, who, on his way home on furlough, happened to be passing through Singapore, and that the Netherlands Government had shown itself exceedingly jealous of Sir James Brooke's position in Borneo, no further evidence would seem to have been required. Mr Boudriot's coming forward to bear testimony in favour of a political opponent was as honourable to the Dutch official as to his Government, which he knew would not object to his testifying in favour of the truth.

The witnesses called by the hostile memorialists came to curse, but remained to bless. Reluctant as they were to tell all they knew, enough was dragged out of them to show the true character of the Seribas and Sakarang Dyaks. One was the dismissed Lieutenant-

Governor of Labuan, the second a man of German extraction, who had lived on Sir James Brooke's bounty for many years, and the third the banished Patingi of Sarawak; but he showed no animus against Sir James Brooke. In point of fact, they did not prove hostile witnesses, as the testimony of the first two, apart from the feeling displayed, was quite satisfactory. Mr Devereux and Mr Prinsep observe in their reports that the memorialists or their agent did what they could to prevent the native witnesses from appearing, but enough came forward to prove to both Commissioners the piratical character of these Dyaks, and Mr Devereux pointedly remarks that no undue severity was exercised.

In spite of the instructions to the Commissioners, which were remarkable for their hostile spirit, these gentlemen reported favourably on all those points on which the public felt any interest; the Seribas and Sakarang Dyaks were declared pirates, and it was found and placed on record that Sir James had not been a trader whilst in the service of the Crown. On matters of opinion they differed, and did not accept Sir James's claim of the complete independence of Sarawak *de jure*, though it was so *de facto*. The other questions were of no practical importance.

Although we did not receive the report of the Commissioners until the end of the following year, I may now notice the findings, and then close this unfortunate story of ministerial weakness and bad faith.

There were four heads of inquiry.

First—Whether the position of Sir James Brooke at Sarawak was compatible with his duties as Commissioner and Consul-General?

It was decided to be incompatible; but Mr Devereux added, 'It may be stated as regards the past that the junction of the two positions has had beneficial results.' As the British Government had appointed Sir James to the post without any solicitation on his part, with a full knowledge of his position at Sarawak, any blame would be theirs and not his. As, however, he had resigned his posts, this point had only an academic interest.

Second—Whether the interests of Sir James Brooke as a holder of territory, and as a trader in the produce of that territory, were compatible?

It was found that Sir James was not a trader in the true sense of the term any more than the Governor-General of India.

Third—Personal complaints against Sir James Brooke.

Two were made, but not entertained by the Commissioners.

Fourth—What were the relations of Sir James Brooke with and towards the native tribes on the north-west coast of Borneo, with a view to ascertain whether it was necessary that he should be entrusted with a discretion to determine which of these tribes were piratical, or, taking into account the recent operations on the coast, to call for the aid of Her Majesty's forces for the punishment of such tribes.

Mr Devereux remarked, 'It appears most desirable that there should be an authority empowered to call for the aid of Her Majesty's naval forces for the suppression of piracy.'

'I have already declared my opinion that the Seribas and Sakarang Dyaks are piratical tribes; it was therefore most just and expedient, and in conformity with the obligations of treaty, that punishment should be inflicted on them with the view to the suppression of their atrocious outrages. The exact measure of punishment which should have been inflicted is a question which does not belong to me to decide, but I may say that it was essential that the thing should be done, and done effectually. So far as regards the loss of life inflicted on them, there does not appear any reasonable ground for sympathy for a race of indiscriminate murderers.'

I have thus shortly summed up the proceedings and findings of the Commission. I have not thought it necessary to enter into any details, as the questions are dead, and no one feels any interest in the mendacious statements of a W. N. or a Chameroozow.[1] The Seribas and Sakarang Dyaks are now

[1] *Remarks on a Recent Naval Execution.* By W. N. *Borneo Facts versus Borneo Fallacies.* By Louis A. Chameroozow.

some of the best subjects of Sarawak, so faithful that they are enlisted as soldiers and garrison the principal forts.

The Commission closed, and we returned to Sarawak towards the end of November with a feeling of great relief. As a ship of war had fetched the Rajah from Sarawak, so a ship of war took him back, and Captain Blaine of H.M.S. *Rapid* showed him every courtesy, and treated him officially as a prince in his own country.

Our next six months were passed quietly. The Rajah was anxious about the report of the Commission, but he felt that in all essential points it must be in his favour. During this peaceful time he busied himself with the interior affairs of the country, or retired for recreation to his charming cottage among the hills.

No one who had not lived in close intimacy with the Rajah could form any idea of the charm of his society. His conversation was always attractive, whether he was treating of political or religious questions, and when he was in good spirits, his ordinary talk was enlivened by playful humour. His affectionate disposition endeared him to all, and although subsequently differences arose with some of his followers and relatives, no one among them but preserved a kindly feeling towards their old chief. Our visits to the hill cottage left so pleasant an impression on my mind that they can never be forgotten.

At this time, on the advice of Earl Grey, the Rajah

created a 'Council of Sarawak,' the first members of which were himself and his two nephews, to represent the English element, and four Malay chiefs to represent the native inhabitants of Sarawak. It proved a most useful measure, and the native members showed themselves highly efficient.

In October 1855 Captain Brooke and Charles Grant left us for a visit home, and Arthur Crookshank was still absent in England, so that much work fell on the Rajah. We had scarcely settled down to a quiet life when we were disturbed by the arrival of despatches from Lord Clarendon, enclosing the Blue Book containing all the documents relating to the Commission, and expressing a cold approval of Sir James Brooke's conduct. I also received despatches, one appointing me Consul-General in Borneo, and the other containing an Order in Council directing me to send to the nearest English colony all British subjects accused of crimes and misdemeanours within the Sultan's dominions, including Sarawak. The absurdity of such an Order in Council appears never to have struck the Foreign Office. In the first place, it was in direct opposition to our Treaty with the Brunei Government; secondly, the sending for trial to Singapore of a prisoner and all the witnesses would have entailed an expenditure of hundreds of pounds, possibly on account of a thief who had stolen the value of a shilling. It was no difficult matter to point out to our Government that it was wiser to let well alone; that the courts of Sarawak had always exercised jurisdiction over British subjects, and that no complaints of injustice had ever been made. I consequently suggested that the system then at work should be continued.

Any other solution would have been felt to be intolerable, both by the Rajah and by the native chiefs. Fortunately wise counsels prevailed in England, and the proposed arrangement, which was founded on ignorance, was reversed. I was authorised to inform the Sarawak Council that Her Majesty's Government had no desire whatever to interfere with them, or to prevent them choosing what form of government they pleased; and I added that the British Government accepted the plan suggested for settling the question of jurisdiction. In fact, the Sarawak courts were authorised to continue to try British subjects as before.

The Rajah was deeply mortified by Lord Clarendon's despatches. After all the promises the latter had made to the late Lord Ellesmere, that if the Commission reported in Sir James Brooke's favour the Government would be prepared to do all that he desired, to receive a bare statement of approval of his conduct was very disheartening. After all the mischief which arose from the mere appointment of the Commission, the loss of prestige which produced the Patingi's abortive plot, and later on the Chinese insurrection, such treatment was inexplicable to him. He was sore and indignant. He only asked for a steamer to be placed on the coast to check piracy. Even this was refused.

However, when Lord Clarendon agreed to recognise the jurisdiction of the Sarawak courts, the Rajah was greatly mollified. He wrote, 'The Government has done far more than I expected, and our misunderstanding is at an end.' The strong expressions of good-will contained in the same despatch had a very tranquillising effect upon him, and he almost thought he had forgiven the Government their great injustice.

As the British Government would not allow me to ask for an *exequatur* from the Sarawak authorities, I left Kuching for Brunei in August 1856. It was severing very precious ties. Before I sailed, Arthur Crookshank had returned to his post and brought with him, as his bride, a 'vision of beauty,' to use the Rajah's own phrase.

During this year some capitalists in London formed the Borneo Company, to develop the resources of the territories under Sarawak rule. Coal had been discovered in various places, and there were valuable products to be collected, principally sago, guttapercha and india-rubber; there was also the produce of the antimony mines, and subsequently cinnabar, or the metal containing quicksilver.

A short time before Mr Macdougall, the head of

the Borneo Mission, had been raised in rank, and was named Bishop of Labuan and Sarawak.

As slight returns of fever and ague had weakened the Rajah, he accepted Sir William Hoste's offer of a passage to Singapore in H.M.S. *Spartan*, where he passed a few months recruiting his health. Towards the end of January 1857 he returned to Sarawak in the *Sir James Brooke*, a steamer sent out by the Borneo Company to aid in their commercial work. The Rajah found the country greatly excited by persistent rumours of a Chinese conspiracy. His valuable officer, Mr Arthur Crookshank, fully believed in the hostile intentions of the Chinese Kungsi or Gold Working Company, and had therefore manned the forts with sufficient garrisons. But Sir James Brooke, having summoned the Chinese chiefs before him, and punished them for their illegal acts, was satisfied with their submission, and believed they would not be so insensate as to endeavour to carry out their previous threats. He therefore dismissed the extra men from the forts, and wrote to me on February 14th, 'Congratulate me on being free from all my troubles.'

CHAPTER VI

THE CHINESE SURPRISE THE TOWN OF KUCHING—THE RAJAH AND HIS OFFICERS ESCAPE—THE CHINESE PROCLAIM THEMSELVES SUPREME RULERS—THEY ARE ATTACKED BY THE MALAYS—ARRIVAL OF THE 'SIR JAMES BROOKE'—THE CHINESE, DRIVEN FROM KUCHING, ABANDON THE INTERIOR AND RETREAT TO SAMBAS—DISARMED BY THE DUTCH

CHINESE colonists are the mainstay of every country in the Further East; but they carry with them an institution which may have its value in ill-governed countries, but which in our colonies is an unmitigated evil. I refer to their secret societies. A secret society is ostensibly instituted under the form of a benevolent association, but actually its members are banded together to obey no laws but their own, to carry out the behests of their leaders without question, and to afford protection to each other under all circumstances. If a member of the secret society commit a crime he is to be protected or hidden away; if he be taken by the police, the society is bound to secure him the ablest legal assistance, furnish as many false witnesses as may be required, and if he be convicted, pay his fine, or do all in its power to alleviate the discomforts of a prison. Therefore, flogging is the most deterrent form of punishment, as it cannot be shared. Should the society suspect any member of revealing its secrets, or from any cause desire to be rid of an obnoxious person, it condemns the individual to death, and sentence is carried out by its members, who, through fear of the last penalty, always obey their oath. On these occasions the mark of the society is put on the victim to show who has ordered the deed. In our colonies we have not been altogether successful in putting down these pernicious associations.

For many years the Chinese living in Kuching, the capital of Sarawak, had attempted to form secret societies, but the Rajah's vigorous hand had crushed every attempt, and it appeared as if success had attended his policy. This was the case so far as the Chinese of the capital were concerned; but in the interior, among the gold workers, the Kungsi performed the functions of a secret society, and its chiefs carried on extensive correspondence with their fellow-countrymen in Sambas and Pontianak, the neighbouring Dutch possessions, and with the Tien-Ti-Hué (Heaven and Earth Secret Society) in Singapore.

When Mr Fox and I made a long tour, in July 1856, among the Chinese settlements of the interior, we became convinced that opium smuggling was being carried on to a great extent, as however numerous might be the newcomers, the revenue from that source had a tendency to decrease.

At last it was discovered that opium was sent from Singapore to the Natuna Islands, and from thence it was smuggled into Sarawak and the Dutch possessions of Sambas and Pontianak. It was proved that the Kungsi had been engaged in this contraband trade, and it was fined £150, a very trifling amount, considering the thousands it had gained by defrauding the revenue, and measures were immediately taken to suppress the traffic. This, and the punishment of three of its members for a gross assault on another Chinaman, were the only grounds of complaint which could be alleged against the Sarawak Government.

But these trivial cases were not the real cause of the Chinese insurrection in Sarawak. Before that date all the Celestials in the East had been greatly excited by the announcement that the English had retired from before Canton, and that the Viceroy of the province had offered a reward of £25 for every Englishman slain. The news had been greatly exaggerated. It was said we had been utterly defeated by the Chinese forces, and now was the time, the Gold Company thought, to expel the English from Sarawak and assume the government themselves. The secret societies were everywhere in great excitement, and the Tien-Ti-Hué sent emissaries over from Singapore and Malacca to incite the gold workers to rebellion, and used the subtle, but unfortunately cogent argument, that not only were the English crushed at Canton, but that the British Government was so discontented with the Rajah that it would not interfere, if the Kungsi only destroyed him and his officers, and did not meddle with private English interests or obstruct trade. Here we see another disastrous effect of the Commission.

It was also currently reported that the Sultan of Sambas and his Malay nobles offered every encouragement to the enterprise; and the Chinese listened much to their advice, as these noblemen can speak to the Celestials in their own language, and are themselves greatly imbued with Chinese ideas. To explain this curious state of things, it may be mentioned that the children of these nobles are always nursed by girls chosen from among the healthiest of the daughters of the Chinese gold workers. Further, about that time there was a very active intercourse carried on between the Malay nobles of Sambas and Pangeran Makota, the Rajah's old enemy and the Sultan of Brunei's favourite minister, and the latter was constantly closeted with an emissary of the Tien-Ti-Hué of Singapore, to whom I am about to refer.

To show that this was not a mere conjecture I may state that on the 14th of February 1857, four days before the insurrection in Sarawak, a Chinese named Achang, who had arrived at Brunei from Singapore a few days previously, and had a year before been expelled from Sarawak for joining a secret society, came to my house to try and induce my four Chinese servants to enter the Hué, adding as a sufficient reason that the Gold Company of Sarawak would by that time have killed all the white men in that country.

At Bau, the chief town of the Chinese in Sarawak, the secretary of the Kungsi showed a letter from the Straits Branch of the Tien-Ti-Hué to a Malay trader named Jeludin, urging them to act against the foreigner. I mention these facts to show the extraordinary ramifications of these secret societies, which in every country where they exist are the source of endless trouble and disorder.

During the month of November 1856 rumours were abroad that the Chinese Gold Company intended to surprise the small stockades which constituted the only defences of the town of Kuching, and which, as no enemy was suspected to exist in the country, were seldom guarded by more than four men each. Mr Crookshank, who was then administering the government, took the precaution (as has been stated) to man them with a sufficient garrison, for it was said that during one of their periodical religious feasts several hundred men were to collect quietly, and make a rush for the arsenal. On the Rajah's return from Singapore he instituted some inquiries into the affair, but could obtain no further information than such as vague rumour afforded. He consequently reduced the garrisons, after punishing the Chinese chiefs; but such experienced officers as Mr Crookshank and the chief constable, Mr Middleton, were not satisfied, feeling that there was mischief in the air; and Mr Charles Johnson wrote to me that if their high tone was not lowered the Chinese would certainly do the country a mischief.

I was sitting one day reading in my verandah, in the Consulate at Brunei, when a Malay hastily entered and said, 'I have just arrived from Singapore. Whilst detained by very light winds we approached a schooner coming from Sarawak, and one of the crew called out to us, "The Chinese have risen against the Rajah and killed all the white men." He knew no more. This, coupled with what I had previously heard of the conversations of the Hué leader, made me feel very uncomfortable. I would have left for Sarawak at once, but there was no means of direct communication. In a few days a hurried note from a friend who had escaped to Singapore told me part of the catastrophe, but it was not for two months that I had the full particulars in a letter from the Rajah himself.

It appears that when the Kungsi saw their professions of loyalty accepted, they began to prepare for hostile operations, and on the morning of the

18th of February 1857 the chiefs assembled about six hundred of their followers at Bau, their most important station, and placing all the available weapons in their hands, marched them down to their principal wharf at Tundong, where a squadron of their large cargo boats was collected. It is now known that until they actually began to descend the river none but the heads of the movement were aware of its true object, so well had the secret been kept. To account for the preparations, it was given out that an attack was meditated on a Dyak village in Sambas, whose fighting men had in reality killed some Chinese.

During their slow passage down the river, a Malay, who was accustomed to trade with the Chinese, overtook them in a canoe, and actually induced them to permit him to pass under the plea that his wife and children lived in a place called Batu Kawa, eight miles above the town, and would be frightened if they heard so many men passing, and he was not there to reassure them. Instead of returning home, he pulled down as fast as he could till he reached the town of Kuching, and going straight to his relative, a Malay trader of the name of Gapur, a trustworthy and brave man, told him what he had seen; but Gapur said, 'Don't go and tell the chiefs or the Rajah such a tissue of absurdities;' yet he went himself over to the Datu Bandhar and informed him. The chief's answer was, 'The Rajah is unwell; we have heard similar reports for the last twenty years; don't go and bother him about it. In the morning I will tell him what your relative says.' This great security was caused by the universal belief that the Chinese could not commit so egregious a folly as to attempt to seize the Government of the country, considering that, with agriculturists included, they did not number above four thousand, while at that time the Malays and Dyaks within the Sarawak territory amounted to two hundred thousand at least. It was strange, however, and unpardonably negligent on the part of the Datu Bandhar not to have sent a fast boat up the river to ascertain what was really going on. Had he done so, the town and numerous lives would have been saved, and punishment would only have fallen on the guilty.

Shortly after midnight the squadron of Chinese barges pulled silently through the capital, and dividing into two bodies, the smaller entered a creek, called Sungei Bedil, just above the Rajah's house, while the larger party continued its course to the landing-place of the fort, and sent out strong detachments to surprise the houses of Mr Crookshank, the magistrate, and Mr Middleton, the head constable, and a large force was told off to attack the stockades. Unaccountable as it may appear, none of these parties were noticed, so profound was the security felt; and everyone slept.

The Government House was situated on a little grassy hill, surrounded by small, neat cottages, in which visitors from the out-stations were lodged. The Chinese, landing on the banks of the Bedil stream, marched to the attack in a body of about a hundred, and passing by an upper cottage, made an assault on the front and back of the long Government House, the sole inhabitants of which were the Rajah and an English servant. They did not surround the house, for their trembling hearts made them fear to separate into small bodies, as the opinion was rife among them that the Rajah was a man brave, active, skilled in the use of weapons, and not to be overcome except by means of numbers.

Roused from his slumbers by the unusual sounds of shouts and yells at midnight, the Rajah looked out through the Venetian blinds, and immediately conjectured what had occurred. Several times he raised his revolver to fire at them, but convinced that he could not defend the house alone he determined to effect his escape. He supposed that men engaged in so desperate an enterprise would naturally take every precaution to ensure its success, and concluded that bodies of insurgents were silently watching the ends of the house; so, summoning his English servant, he led the way down to a bath-room on the ground floor which communicated with the lawn, and telling him to open the door quickly and follow close, the Rajah sprang forth, with sword drawn and revolver cocked, but found the coast clear. Had there been twenty Chinese there, he would have passed through them, as his quickness and practical skill in the use of weapons were unsurpassed. Reaching the banks of the stream above his house he paused, observing that it was full of Chinese boats; but presently, hearing his alarmed servant, who had lost him in the darkness, calling to him, he knew that the attention of the Chinese would be attracted that way, and dived under the bows of one of the barges and swam to the opposite shore unperceived. As he was then suffering from an attack of fever and ague, he fell utterly exhausted, and lay for some time on the muddy bank till, slightly recovering, he was able to reach the Government writer's house.

An amiable and promising young officer, Mr Nicoletts, who had but just arrived from an out-station on a visit to the Rajah, was lodged in a cottage near; startled by the sound of the attack, he rushed forth to reach the chief's house, but was intercepted and killed by the Chinese, who severed his head from his body, and bore it on a pike in triumph as that of the Rajah. Mr Steel, the Resident on the Rejang, and an experienced officer, quietly looked through the window of his cottage, and seeing what was passing, slipped out of the house, and soon found himself sheltered by the jungle; and the Rajah's servant, whose shouts had drawn the Chinese towards him, had to display very unwonted activity before he could reach the protecting forest and join Mr Steel.

The other attacks took place simultaneously. Mr

and Mrs Crookshank, rushing forth on hearing this midnight alarm, were cut down, the latter left for dead, the former seriously wounded. The constable's house was attacked; he and his wife escaped, but their two children and an English lodger were killed by the insurgents.

Here occurred a scene which showed how cruel were these Chinese. When the rebels burst into Mr Middleton's house he fled, and his wife, following, found herself in the bath-room, and by the shouts was soon convinced that her retreat had been cut off. In the meantime the Chinese had seized her two children, and brought the eldest down into the bath-room to show them the way by which the father had escaped. Mrs Middleton's sole refuge was a large water jar, which happened to be full, and she only raised her mouth above water to draw breath; there she heard the poor little boy questioned, pleading for his life, and heard his shriek, when the fatal sword was raised which severed his head from his body. With loud laughter these fiends kicked the little head from one to the other, and then rushed out in pursuit of Mr Middleton. Fortunately the bath-room was in darkness, so the mother escaped unseen. The Chinese then set fire to the house, and she distinctly heard the shrieks of her second child as they tossed him into the flames. Mrs Middleton remained in the jar till the falling embers forced her to leave it. She ran to a neighbouring pond and, fortunately, was thus sheltered from the savages who were rushing round the burning dwelling. Her escape was indeed extraordinary.

The stockades, however, were not surprised. The Chinese, waiting for the signal which was to be the attack on the houses, were at length perceived by a sentinel, and he immediately roused the Treasurer, Mr Crymble, who resided in the stockade which contained the arsenal and the prison. He endeavoured to make some preparation for defence, although he had but four Malays with him. He had scarcely time, however, to load a six-pounder field-piece, and get his own rifle ready, before the Chinese, with loud shouts, rushed to the assault. They were led by a man who bore in either hand a flaming torch. Mr Crymble waited until they were within forty yards; he then fired and killed the man who, by the lights he bore, made himself conspicuous, and before the crowd recovered from the confusion in which they were thrown by the fall of their leader, discharged among them the six-pounder loaded with grape, which made the assailants retire behind the neighbouring houses or hide in the outer ditches. But with four men little could be done; and some of the rebels, having crossed the inner ditch, began to remove the planks which constituted the sole defence. To add to the garrison's difficulties, they threw over into the inner court little iron tripods, with flaming torches attached, which rendered it as light as day, whilst they remained shrouded in darkness.

To increase the number of defenders Mr Crymble released the sole occupants of the prison—a fraudulent debtor and a Malay madman who had killed his wife in a fit of fury. The former quickly disappeared, whilst the latter, regardless of the shot flying around, stood to the post assigned him, opposite a plank the Chinese were trying to remove. He had orders to fire as soon as the first assailant appeared, and when the plank gave way and a man attempted to force his body through, he pulled the trigger of his carbine, without lowering the muzzle, and sent the ball through his own brains. Mr Crymble now found it useless to prolong the struggle. One of his four men was killed, and another, a brave Malay corporal, was shot down at his side. The wounded man begged Mr Crymble to fly and leave him to his fate, but asked him to shake hands with him first and tell him whether he had not done his duty. The brave Irishman seized him by the arm and endeavoured to drag him up the stairs leading to the dwelling over the gate ; but the Chinese had already gained the courtyard, and pursuing them, drove their spears through the wounded man. Mr Crymble was forced to let go his hold, and with a brave follower, Daud, swung himself down into the ditch below. Some of the rebels outside the fort, seeing their attempted escape, tried to stop the Treasurer, and a man stabbed at him, but the spear only glanced on his thick frieze coat, and the Chinese received in return a cut across the face from the Irishman's cutlass which was a remembrance to carry to the grave.

The other stockade, though it had but a corporal's watch of three Malays, did not surrender; but finding that every other place was in the hands of the Chinese, the brave defenders opened the gate, and, charging the crowd of rebels, sword in hand, made good their escape, though all were severely wounded.

The confusion which reigned throughout the rest of the town may be imagined, as, startled by the shouts and yells of the Chinese, the inhabitants rushed to the doors and windows and beheld night turned into day by the bright flames which rose in three directions—where the Rajah's, Crookshank's and Middleton's large houses were all burning at the same time.

It was at first very naturally thought that the Chinese contemplated a massacre of the Europeans, but messengers were soon despatched to them by the Kungsi to say that nothing was further from their intention than to interfere with those who were unconnected with the Government, which refinement of policy shows that the plan had been concocted by more subtle brains than those possessed by the gold workers of Bau.

The Rajah had, as soon as possible, proceeded to the Datu Bandhar's house, and being quickly joined by his English officers, endeavoured to organise a force with which to surprise the victorious Chinese;

but it was impossible. No sooner did he collect a few men than their wives and children surrounded them and refused to be left behind; and being without proper arms and ammunition, it was but a panic-stricken mob. So he instantly took his determination, with that decision which had been the foundation of his success, and, giving up the idea of an immediate attack, advised the removal of the women to the left-hand bank of the river, where they would be safe from a land attack of the Chinese, who could make their way along the right-hand bank of the river by a road which ran at the back of the town.

This removal was accomplished by the morning, when the small party of English under the Rajah walked over to the little river of Siol, which falls into the Santubong branch of the Sarawak river. At the mouth of the Siol the Rajah found the war boat of Abang Buyong, with sixty men, waiting for him, which was soon joined by six others and many canoes, for no sooner did the Malays of the neighbouring villages hear where the Rajah was than they began flocking to him. He now started for the Samarahan, intending to proceed to the Balang Lupar to organise an expedition from the well-supplied forts there. On their way they rested at the little village of Sabang, and to the honour of the Malay character I must add that never during the height of his power and prosperity did he receive so much sympathy, tender attention and delicate generosity as now, when a defeated fugitive. They vied with each other as to who should supply him and his party with clothes and food, since they had lost all; and if to know that he was enshrined in the hearts of the people was any consolation to him in his misfortunes, he then had ample proofs of it. No wonder that in reading these accounts the *Daily News*, hitherto so hostile to him, should say, 'We have sincere pleasure in proclaiming our unreserved admiration of the manner in which he must have exercised his power to have produced such fruits.'

When morning broke in Kuching, there was a scene of the wildest confusion. The six hundred rebels, joined by the Chinese vagabonds of the town, half-stupefied by opium, were wandering about in every direction, discharging their muskets loaded with ball cartridges. But at eight o'clock the chiefs of the Gold Company sent a message to the Bishop of Sarawak, requesting him to come down and attend the wounded. He did so, and found thirty-two stretched out, most of them from shot wounds; but among them he noticed a man with a gash across his face from the last blow Mr Crymble had struck at the rebels; and before the Bishop's arrival they had buried five of their companions.

Poor Mrs Crookshank had lain on the ground all night, desperately wounded, and with extraordinary coolness and courage had shammed death whilst the rebels tore the rings from her fingers, or cut at her head with their swords. Her life was saved by her mass of braided hair. Early in the morning her servant found her still living, and went and informed the Bishop, who had great difficulty in persuading the Kungsi to allow him to send for her. She arrived in the mission house in a dreadful state.

It was soon evident that, in the intoxication of victory, the Chinese aimed now, if not before, at the complete domination of the country, and summoned the Bishop, Mr Helms, agent for the Borneo Company, Mr Ruppell, an English resident, and the Datu Bandhar to appear at the Court House. The Europeans were obliged to attend the summons. The Malay chief also came, but with great reluctance, and contrary to the advice of the Datu Imaun, his more energetic brother; but he thought it expedient to gain time.

The Chinese chiefs, even in their most extravagant moments of exultation, were in great fear that on their return up the river the Malays might attack them in their crowded boats and destroy them, as on the water they felt their inferiority to their maritime enemies.

It must have been an offensive sight to the Europeans and the Malays to witness the arrangements in the Court House on that day of disaster. In the Rajah's chair sat the chief of the Gold Company, supported on either side by the writers or secretaries, while the representatives of the now apparently subdued sections took their places on the side benches. The Chinese chief then issued his orders, which were that Mr Helms and Mr Ruppell should undertake to rule the foreign portion of the town, and that the Datu Bandhar should manage the Malays, while the Gold Company, as supreme rulers, should superintend the whole and govern exclusively the up-country districts. During this time the Europeans could see the head of Mr Nicoletts carried about on a pole to reassure the Chinese that the dreaded Rajah had really been killed. The Chinese chiefs knew better, but they thought to impose upon their ignorant followers.

Everything now appeared to be arranged, when the Bishop remarked that perhaps Mr Charles Johnson might not quite approve of the conduct of the Chinese in killing his uncle and friends. At the mention of Johnson's name there was a pause. A blankness came over their countenances, and they looked at each other as they now remembered, apparently for the first time, that he, the Rajah's nephew, was the resolute and popular ruler of the Sakarangs, and could let loose at least ten thousand wild warriors upon them. At last it was suggested, after an animated discussion, that a letter should be sent to him requesting him to confine himself to his own government, and then they would not attempt to interfere with him.

They appeared also to have forgotten that there were Sadong, under Mr Fox, and Rejang, under Mr Steel, who, between them, could bring thousands into the field, and that Seribas also was panting for an opportunity to find fresh enemies. All this never seemed to have occurred to them before undertaking their insensate expedition.

The Chinese were very anxious to have matters settled at Kuching, as, with all their boasts, they were not feeling comfortable. They were not only anxious to secure the plunder they had obtained, but the leaders knew that the Rajah was not killed, and what he might be preparing was uncertain. They therefore called upon the European gentlemen and the Malay chiefs present to swear fidelity to the Gold Company, and under the fear of instant death they were obliged to go through the formula of taking oaths with the sacrifice of fowls.

Next day the rebels retired up-country unmolested by the Malays, and a meeting was at once held at the Datu Bandhar's house to discuss future proceedings. At first no one spoke. There was a gloom over the assembly, as the mass of the population was deserting the town, carrying off their women and children to the neighbouring district of Samarahan as a place of safety, when Abang Patah, son of the Datu Tumangong, addressed his countrymen. He was a sturdy man, with a pleasant, cheerful countenance, and a warm friend to English rule, and his first words were, 'Are we going to submit to be governed by Chinese chiefs, or are we to remain faithful to our Rajah? I am a man of few words, and I say I will never be governed by anyone but by him, and to-night I commence war to the knife against his enemies.'

The unanimous determination of the assembly was to remain faithful to the Rajah, but they were divided as to the course to be pursued. Patah, however, unfortunately, cut the knot of the difficulty by manning a light war boat with a dozen Malays, and proceeding at once up the river, attacked and captured a Chinese boat, killing five of its crew. In the meantime all the women and children had been removed from the town, and some trading prahus were manned and armed but imperfectly, as the Chinese had taken away the contents of the arsenal, and the chief portion of the crews of the war boats were engaged in conveying the fugitives to Samarahan.

Patah's bold act was no doubt well meaning, but was decidedly premature, as the Malays, being scattered, could not organise any resistance, and urgent entreaties were made to the Rajah to return and head this movement. He complied, as he could not even appear to abandon those who were fighting so bravely for him; but he knew it was useless, and arrived at Kuching to find the rest of the English flying, the town in the hands of the Chinese, and smoke rising in every direction from the burning Malay houses.

It appears that when the news reached the Chinese that the Malays were preparing to resist their rule, they determined to return immediately to Kuching, and attack them before their preparations could be completed. They divided their forces into two bodies, as they were now recruited by several hundreds of men from other gold workings, and had forced the agriculturists established at Sungei Tungah to join them; in fact, their great boats could not hold half their numbers, so one body marched by a new road which had been opened to the town, while the other came down by the river.

As soon as the Malays saw the Chinese barges rounding the point above the town they boldly dashed at them, forced them to the river banks, drove out the crews, and triumphantly captured ten of the largest cargo boats. The Chinese, better armed, kept up a hot fire from the rising ground, and killed several of the boldest Malays, among others Abang Gapoor, whose disbelief in his kinsman's story enabled the rebels to surprise the capital, and who to his last breath bewailed his fatal mistake; and one who was equally to be regretted, our faithful old follower, Kassim. The latter lingered long enough to see the Rajah again successful, and he said he died happy in knowing it. Notwithstanding their losses, the Malays towed away the barges, laden, fortunately, with some of the most valuable booty, and secured them to a large trading prahu, anchored in the centre of the river. Having thus captured some superior arms and ammunition they could better reply to the fire of their enemies who lined the banks.

In the meantime the Rajah arrived opposite the Chinese quarter, and found a complete panic prevailing, and all those Malays and Dyaks who had preceded him flying in every direction. Having in vain attempted to restore order, he drew up his boat on the opposite bank to cover the retreat, and after a sharp exchange of musketry fire he returned to Samarahan to carry out his original intention.

The Rajah joined the fugitives, and his first care was to see to the safety of the English ladies, the children, the non-combatants and wounded, and to send them off, under the charge of Bishop Macdougall and others, to the secure and well-armed fort of Linga. He now felt somewhat relieved, as he knew that there his charges would be in perfect safety, as they were surrounded by faithful and brave men, who could have defended the fort against any attack. There were no enemies at Linga, except such as existed in the imaginations of the terror-stricken runaways from Sarawak, who had not yet recovered from their panic.

The Rajah prepared on the following day to take the same route, in order to obtain a base of operations and a secure spot where he could rally the people and await a fresh supply of arms. It was sad, however, to think of the mischief which might happen during this period of enforced inaction, particularly as the Datu Bandhar and a chosen band were still in Kuching on board the large trading vessel, which was surrounded by lighter war prahus. Here was our gentle Bandhar, a man whom no one suspected of such energy, showing the courage of his father, Patingi Ali, who was killed during Keppel's Sakarang expedition, and directing attacks on the Chinese whenever an opportunity offered. Thus harassed, the rebels were dragging up heavy guns, and it was evident the Malays could not hold out for many days, particularly as there was now little to defend; the flames which reddened the horizon, and the increasing volumes of smoke, told the tale too well that the Malay town was being completely destroyed.

With feelings of the most acute distress the Rajah gave the order for departure, and the small flotilla fell down the river Samarahan, and arriving at its mouth put out to sea, when a cry arose among the men, 'Smoke! smoke! It is a steamer!' And sure enough there was a dark column rising in the air from a three-masted vessel. For a moment it was uncertain which course she was steering, but presently they distinguished her flag—she was the *Sir James Brooke*, the Borneo Company's steamer, standing in for the Muaratabas entrance of the Sarawak river. The crew of the Rajah's prahu, with shouts, gave way, and the boat was urged along with all the power of their oars, to find the vessel anchored just within the mouth.

'The great God be praised!' as the Rajah said. Here, indeed, was a base of operations. The native prahus were taken in tow, and the reinforcements of Dyaks, who were already arriving, followed up with eager speed. What were the feelings of the Chinese when they first saw the smoke, then the steamer, it is not necessary to conjecture. They fired one wild volley from every available gun and musket, but the balls fell harmlessly; and when the English guns opened on them, they fled panic-stricken, pursued by the rejoicing Malays and Dyaks.

Early that morning a large body of Chinese had proceeded from the right to the left bank to burn the half of the Malay town which had hitherto escaped destruction, but though they succeeded in destroying the greater portion, they signed their own death warrant, as the Malays, at the sight of the steamer, resumed the offensive, seized the boats in which their enemies had crossed the river, and the Dyaks followed them up in the forest. Not one of that party could have escaped. Some wandered long in the jungle and died of starvation; others were found hanging to the boughs of trees, having preferred suicide to the lingering torments of hunger. All these bodies were afterwards discovered, as they were eagerly sought for. The natives said that on every one of them were found from five to twenty pounds sterling in cash, from the pillage of the public treasury, besides silver spoons and forks, or other valuables—the plunder of the English houses.

The main body of the Chinese on the right bank

retired in some order by the jungle road, and reached a detachment of their boats which had been sent from the interior to its terminus, and from thence moved on to Balidah, opposite Siniawan, the fort famous in Sarawak history, which the Rajah had besieged on his first arrival, and which after the insurrection was over became the headquarters of Charles Grant, Resident of Upper Sarawak.

Thus was the capital recovered, all burnt, however, except the Chinese quarter of the town, and the Mission and Mr Helms's Borneo Company's premises. The Rajah established himself temporarily on board the *Sir James Brooke*, and the Government soon began to work again. The Land Dyaks, who had been faithful to a man, sent to request permission to attack the enemy. This being accorded, the chiefs led their assembled tribes, and rushed in every direction on the Chinese, driving them from their villages, and compelling them to defend two places only, Siniawan and Bau, with Tundong, the landing-place of the latter town. The smoke rising in every direction showed them that they were now being punished for the injuries they had inflicted on others. The Gold Company, in their blind confidence, had made no preparations in case of defeat, and it was well known that their stock of food was small, as everything had been destroyed at the above-named places except their own stores, and these were required to supply the people whom they had forced to join them from the town, and the whole agricultural population.

The harassing life they led must soon have worn them out without any attacks, for they could no longer pursue their ordinary occupations, or even fetch firewood or water without a strong-armed party, as the Dyaks hung about their houses, and infested every spot. It soon became a question of food, and they found they must either obtain it or retire across the frontier into Sambas. They therefore collected all their boats and made a foray eight miles down the river to Ledah Tanah, and there threw up a stockade in which they placed a garrison of two hundred and fifty picked men, under two of their most trusted leaders. They placed four guns in position to sweep the river, and, armed with the best of the Government's muskets and rifles, they not only commanded the right and left-hand branches, but felt secure from a direct attack by the main river. Parties were then sent out to plunder the Dyak farmhouses, and one bolder than the rest attempted to scale the mountain of Serambo to destroy the Rajah's country house; but the Dyaks barred the passage with stockades, and by rolling down rocks on the advancing party effectually defended their hill. These Chinese were very different from those we see in our British settlements. Many of them were half breeds, having Dyak mothers, and were as active in the jungle as the aborigines themselves.

To check the Chinese forays, and afford assistance to the Land Dyaks, the Rajah sent up the Datu Bandhar with a small but select force to await his arrival below the Chinese stockade; but the gallant Bandhar, on being joined by the Datu Tumangong and Abang Buyong, and a few Sakarang Dyaks, dashed at the fort, surprised the garrison at dinner, and carried it without the loss of a man. The Chinese threw away their arms and fled into the jungle, to be pursued and slain by the Sakarang Dyaks. Stockades, guns, stores and boats were all captured, and what was of equal importance, the principal instigators of the rebellion were killed.

As soon as the few that escaped from the fort reached Siniawan, a panic seized the Chinese there, and they fled to Bau, where they began hastily to make preparations to retire over the frontiers. The Rajah, who was hurrying up to the support of the Bandhar, hearing of his success, despatched Mr Johnson with his Dyaks to harass the enemy; these, together with the Sarawak Malays, to whom most of the credit is due, pressed on the discomfited Chinese, who, fearing to have their retreat cut off, started for Sambas. They were attacked at every step, but being supplied with the best arms, they were enabled to beat off the foremost parties of their assailants, and retire in fair order along the good road which led to the Dyak village of Gumbang on the Sambas frontier. Still, this road is very narrow, and every now and then the active Dyaks made a rush from the jungle that borders the path and spread confusion and dismay. But the Chinese had every motive to act a manly part; it was their only line of retreat, and they had to defend above a thousand of their women and children, who encumbered their disastrous flight.

At the foot of the steep hill of Gumbang they made a halt, for the usual path was found to be well stockaded, and a resolute body of Malays and Dyaks were there to dispute the way. It was a fearful position; behind them the pursuers were gathering in increasing strength, and unless they forced this passage within an hour, it must be death or surrender. At last someone, it is said a Sambas Malay, suggested that there was another path further along the range, which, though very steep, was practicable; this was undefended, and the fugitives made for it.

The Sarawak Malays and Dyaks, seeing too late their error in neglecting to fortify this path also, rushed along the brow of the hill, and drove back the foremost Chinese. Their danger was extreme; but at that moment, as if by inspiration, all the Chinese girls rushed to the front, and encouraged the men to advance. This they again did, and cheered by the voices of these brave girls, who followed close clapping their hands, and calling them by name to fight with courage, they won the brow of the hill, and cleared the path of their less numerous foes. While this was going on, another column of Chinese, in the absence of most of its defenders, surprised the village of Gumbang, burnt it to the ground and then crossed the frontier. They were but just in time, as the pursuers were pressing hotly on the rearguard, and the occasional volleys of musketry told them that the well-armed Malays were upon them; but they were now comparatively safe, as they were all clear of the Sarawak frontier, and although a few still pursued them, the main body of the Malays and Dyaks would not enter Dutch territory, and halted on the summit of the Gumbang range.

The miserable fugitives, reduced to two thousand, of whom above half were women and children, sat down among the houses of the village of Sidin, and many of them, it is said, wept not only for the loss of friends and goods, which they had suffered owing to the insensate ambition of the Gold Company, but also because they had to give up all hope of ever returning to their old peaceful homes.

That Company, which on the night of the surprise had numbered six hundred, was now reduced to a band of about one hundred, but these kept well together, and being better armed than the others, formed the principal guard of the Tai-pé-Kong, a sacred stone, which they had, through all their disasters, preserved from the profane hands of their enemies. Several times the assailants, who mistook it for the gold chest, were on the point of capturing it, but on the cry being raised that the Tai-pé-Kong was in peril, the men gathered round and carried it securely through all danger. At Sidin, however, all immediate apprehension being over, the discontent of those who had been forced to join the rebels burst forth without control, so that from words they soon came to blows, and the small band of the Company's men was again reduced by thirty or forty from the anger of their countrymen.

Continuing their disorderly retreat, they were met by the officers of the Dutch Government, who very properly took from them all their plunder and arms, and being uncertain which was their own property, erred on the safe side by stripping them of everything. The Dutch officers sent back to Sarawak all the loot the Chinese had taken either from the Government or from private individuals.

Thus terminated the most criminal and causeless rebellion that ever occurred, which during its continuance displayed every phase of Chinese character, arrogance, secrecy, combination, an utter incapability of looking to the consequences of events or actions, and a belief in their own power and courage which every event belied. The Chinese, under their native leaders, have never fought even decently, and yet up to the very moment of trial they act as if they were invincible.

This insurrection showed, in my belief, that though the Chinese always require watching, they are not in any way formidable as an enemy; and it also proved how firmly the Sarawak Government was rooted in the hearts of the people, since in the darkest hour there was no whisper of wavering. Had the Chinese been five times as numerous, there were forces in the background which would have destroyed them all. Before the Chinese had fled across the frontier, the Seribas and Sakarang Malays and Dyaks, under Mr Johnson, had arrived, and the people of Sadong were marching overland to attack them in rear, while the distant out-stations were mustering strong forces, which arrived to find all danger past.

I believe that it was almost worth the disaster to show how uniform justice and generous consideration are appreciated by the Malays and Dyaks, and how firmly they may become attached to a Government, which, besides having their true interests at heart, encourages and requires all its officers to treat them as equals. The conduct of the Malay fortmen, of Kasim and Gapoor, the generous enthusiasm of Abang Patah, the gallant rush at the Ledah Tanah stockade by the Bandhar and his followers, showed what the Rajah had effected during his tenure of power. He had raised the character of the Malay, and turned a race notorious for its lawlessness into some of the best-conducted people in the world.

I may add that the results of the Chinese insurrection were very curious in a financial point of view. Though about three thousand men were killed or driven from the country, yet as soon as quiet was thoroughly restored, the revenue from the Chinese soon rose, instead of falling, which proves what an extensive system of smuggling had been carried on. The breaking up of the Gold Company was felt by all the natives as a great relief. It is worthy of remark that while the Chinese were still unsubdued in the interior, boats full of their armed countrymen arrived from Sambas, fully believing that Kuching was now in the hands of the Kungsi, but on their proceeding up the river to join them, were met by the Malays, driven back and utterly defeated.

The Dutch authorities behaved with thorough neighbourly kindness on this occasion, for as soon as they heard of the rebellion of the Chinese, they sent round a steamer and a detachment of soldiers to the assistance of the Sarawak authorities. Fortunately by that time all danger was past, but the kindness of the action was not the less appreciated. H.M.S. *Spartan*, Captain Sir William Hoste, also came over to Sarawak, but I fear that his instructions were less generous: he could aid in protecting British subjects, but not the Government of Sarawak. The shadow of that baneful Commission still hung over the operations of our navy.

While the Rajah was struggling with all these difficulties, the *Sir James Brooke*, which had been sent to Singapore for supplies, now returned, bringing a large party to join him—his nephew, Captain Brooke, and Mrs Brooke, Mr Grant, Mr Hay, a new recruit, of whom the Rajah said: 'A gentlemanly man, young, of good family, and of the right stamp,' in truth, the only class of officer suitable for the work. There came also many people connected with the Borneo Company, including Mr Harvey, the managing director, Mr Duguid, the head of the Sarawak branch, and others. In giving me an account of the arrivals, the Rajah wrote: 'Our domestic intelligence is of the best and pleasantest. Brooke's wife is a sweet, sensible, but playful creature, charming in manners.'

When the news of the Chinese insurrection reached Seribas, all the chiefs were anxious to go to the help of the Government, and while many of them were away in Sarawak, our old Sakarang adversary, Rentab, of Lang Fort reputation, attacked the villages of our friends. The Rajah therefore determined to punish him, and started for Seribas himself to encourage the well intentioned, and Captain Brooke visited the Rejang, while Mr Charles Johnson was ordered to attack Sadok, the chief's mountain stronghold, with his Malays and Dyaks. The attack failed, however, though Charles Johnson exposed himself to every danger to secure success.

I went down to Sarawak by the first opportunity, and reached it in July, to find everything proceeding as if no insurrection had occurred. Though the Malay town had been burnt to the ground, yet the inhabitants had soon recovered their energy, and had rebuilt their houses, which, though not so substantial as the former ones, still looked very neat. Some things were missed in the landscape: the handsome Government House, with its magnificent library, had disappeared; and there were other gaps to be filled up, but fortunately the Chinese had had no time to destroy the church, the mission house, or the Borneo Company's premises.

I never saw a more perfect library than that destroyed by the Chinese, perfect in everything—the best historians and essayists, all the poets, the most celebrated voyages and travels, books of reference, and a whole library of theology and law, as well as a goodly array of the best novels. Besides losing his beloved library, the Rajah was at the same time deprived of all the records of his previous life, for he had collected his journals and papers, and these shared the fate of his books. He was, as I have said, a great reader, and had latterly devoted himself to the study of international law. He remembered the salient points of a question with great accuracy, and could explain clearly every subject he studied. He had a wonderful gift of language.

I found, as I had expected, that the loss of worldly wealth had had little effect on my old chief, who was as cheerful and contented in his little, comfortless cottage as he had ever been in Government House. His health, which before the insurrection had not been strong, had wonderfully improved through his great exertions in endeavouring to restore the country to its former prosperous state, and I never saw him more full of bodily energy and mental vigour than during the two months I spent in Sarawak in 1857. Everyone took the tone of the leader. There were no useless regrets over losses, and it was amusing to hear the congratulations of the Malay chiefs,—'Ah, Mr St John, you were born under a fortunate star to leave Sarawak just before the evil days came upon us.' Then they would recount the personal incidents which had occurred to themselves, and tell with great amusement the shifts to which they had been put for the want of every household necessary. There was a cheerfulness and a hope in the future which promised well for the country.

I found that the deserted gardens around the town had been in part reoccupied, for already Chinese were cultivating them. In order to avoid interrupting the narrative, I have not before noticed that during the height of the insurrection, when the rebels had only been driven from the town a few days, news came that several hundred Chinese, fugitives from the Dutch territories, had crossed the frontier near the sources of the left-hand branch of the Sarawak, and were seeking the protection of the Rajah's Government. Though harassed by incessant work, he did not neglect their appeal, but immediately despatched trustworthy men; and they were thus safely piloted through the excited Dyaks, who thought that every man that 'wore a tail' should now be put to death.

No incident could better illustrate the great influence possessed by the Rajah over Dyaks and Malays, or his thoughtful care for the true interests of his country, during even the most trying circumstances.

When the insurrection was completely over, the Rajah sent Sherif Moksain to Sambas with communications for the Dutch authorities. As the Sherif had been at one time in charge of the Chinese in the interior he knew them well, and he said it was distressing to see the unfortunate agriculturists, who had been made to join the rebels, lamenting their expulsion from the country. They begged for permission to return, and subsequently many did, and established themselves in their old quarters.

Thus ended the second plot against the Rajah's life and authority, the direct outcome of the loss of prestige and strength which followed the appointment of the commission sent to try him for high crimes and misdemeanours, the favourable findings of which had never been brought home to the native mind by any act of reparation made by the British Government.

CHAPTER VII

EVENTS IN THE SAGO RIVERS—THE RAJAH PROCEEDS TO ENGLAND—CORDIAL RECEPTION—FIRST PARALYTIC STROKE—BUYS BURRATOR—TROUBLES IN SARAWAK—LOYALTY OF THE POPULATION—THE RAJAH RETURNS TO BORNEO—SETTLES MUKA AFFAIRS WITH SULTAN—INSTALLS CAPTAIN BROOKE AS HEIR APPARENT—AGAIN LEAVES FOR ENGLAND—SARAWAK RECOGNISED BY ENGLAND—LIFE AT BURRATOR—SECOND AND THIRD ATTACKS OF PARALYSIS—HIS DEATH AND WILL

THE insurrection over, and all his absent officers returned from England, the Rajah had more time for the rest he required; but no sooner had a little calm been restored to him, than he was strongly moved by the news of the Mutiny in India. 'He turned clammy with agitation when he first heard of it'; and how true is the ring of the following—'I felt then, annoyed and disgraced though I have been, that I was an Englishman, and the ties and feelings which men have wantonly outraged are planted too deep to be torn up.'

Though it is highly probable that the many changes which had taken place in the management of the army in India had conduced to the Mutiny, by separating the officers from their men, and weakening the dependence of the soldiers on their superiors in order to concentrate everything in the hands of the War Department at Calcutta or elsewhere, yet one of its causes was the great increase in the number of married officers, who were completely out of touch with the native element, and heard nothing of what was going on among the men in the regiment.

A little later the Rajah wrote to his nephew, Captain Brooke: 'I have sometimes thought that since the earlier days the bonds of sympathy between the native and European have been slacker.' These words reflected the thoughts which had arisen in my own mind during the visit I paid to Sarawak in 1857. It was not so much that there was any outward sign of the mutual sympathy being less, but there was little of that old familiar intercourse which undoubtedly produced and fostered it. And this, ungallant as the opinion may seem, I put down to the presence of the ladies. After dinner they retired to the drawing-room, and we could hear music and singing going on, and most of the gentlemen were eager to join them. The native chiefs, and others who had continued their evening visits, soon became aware of this, and gradually they frequented Government House less and less, and finally ceased going except when business called them there. Under these conditions the same intimate friendship could not continue. I have been so long absent from Sarawak that I know but little of the present state of affairs there, but I fear that the former easy intercourse was never wholly re-established, and that those pleasant evenings with the best class of natives are things of the distant past, in fact, of the days of the old Rajah.

For these and many other reasons I think that gentlemen who govern native states should not marry, or if an exception be made in favour of the chief, certainly his subordinates, who are employed in out-stations where natives abound, should not be married. And this rule might well be applied to the officers sent to our North-Western frontier in India. Marriage immediately separates the governors from the governed. Ladies as a rule cannot be brought to understand that the natives can in any case be considered as equals, and are apt to despise them accordingly. With such ideas, how can bonds of sympathy exist between the rulers and the ruled?

At that time, 1857, the Sago Rivers, north-east of the Rejang, were very much disturbed. Though there were some extenuating circumstances, the action of Sarawak was not altogether free from blame. A quarrel had arisen between two native chiefs, one the governor of the district of Muka Pangeran, Nipa, and the other his cousin, Pangeran Matusin. The first act of the tragedy was that the latter dashed into the house of the former and murdered him and eleven of his women and children. The second was the driving out of Matusin and the slaughter of thirty-five of his friends and relations. Sarawak, then administered by the Rajah's nephew, unfortunately sided with Matusin, and interfered with arms in her hands within the Sultan's territory.

Before, however, these latter acts occurred, the Rajah had been to Brunei to try and induce the Sultan to let him settle matters in the Sago Rivers,[1] and although no formal documents were executed he was requested to see that right was done, but the Sultan would have nothing to do with that man of violence, Matusin. The Rajah went to Muka, and a period of calm followed this visit, but nothing was settled on a permanent basis.

Sir James now decided to proceed to England, as many important affairs required his presence there. On his arrival he found everyone disposed to treat him with distinction, and Lords Clarendon and Palmerston were especially cordial. They even offered a Protectorate, all that was really wanted to ensure the stability of Sarawak and its future progress. But that unfortunate Commission had made the Rajah suspicious of Ministers. He thought they might grant a Protectorate, and then thoroughly neglect Borneo affairs. This was, no doubt, an error, as under the Protectorate of England, Sarawak has

[1] The Sago Rivers or districts are Muka, Oya, Egan Bruit and Mato.

progressed to its present prosperous state without needing, or being required to submit to, the slightest interference on the part of Her Majesty's Government. The Rajah thought, however, that if England had a monetary interest in Sarawak she would be more apt to look after the nascent State. He therefore asked that they should repay him the money he had expended in bringing the country to its present condition. Another reason for this request was that after the Chinese insurrection he had been compelled to borrow £5000 from the Borneo Company, and he wished to repay it. Every penny of his own fortune had been spent, and his only assured income was the pension of £70 which had been granted to him on account of the wound received in Burmah. But this does not alter my opinion that he should have accepted the Protectorate without further question. The Government next offered to establish a naval station in one of the ports of Sarawak; why this was not accepted I never heard.

On February 21, 1858, Sir James Brooke went to a Drawing-Room, and Her Majesty spoke to him most graciously, and the Prince Consort shook him cordially by the hand; indeed, the Royal Family ever showed the greatest interest in his career; and his reception at the Prime Minister's greatly pleased him.

Then came a change of Ministry, as Lord Palmerston had been defeated on the Conspiracy Bill, and the Rajah instantly felt a difference in the tone adopted towards him by the Government. Lord Derby cared little for Borneo, though his son, then Lord Stanley, showed a very appreciative interest in Sarawak.

The Rajah's friends thought that by continually agitating, by dinners, meetings, and deputations, they might influence the Government, and they persuaded him to join in the movement, but upon a temperament so nervous as the Rajah's this wrought infinite mischief. His nephews also were wounding his feelings by writing from Sarawak that the Rajah desired to 'sell Sarawak into bondage.' No wonder he felt dreadfully 'hurt and humiliated,' and cried out that 'he was weary, weary of heart, without faith, without hope in man's honesty.'

On the 21st October 1858, after making a brief speech in the Free Trade Hall at Manchester, he says, 'I felt a creeping movement come over me. I soon knew what it was, and walked with Fairbairn[1] to the doctor's. Life, I thought, was gone, and I rejoiced in the hope that my death would do for Sarawak what my life had not been able to effect.' Thus the Rajah described his first attack of paralysis. This closed his active participation in the movement, though his friends did all they could, and a very strong effort was made to interest the commercial classes and induce the Government to do something in support of his position in Borneo.

[1] Afterwards Sir Thomas Fairbairn, and one of the most judicious and tried friends whom the Rajah ever had.

As soon as the Rajah could be moved with safety, he went to his cottage at Godstone to rest, but with little result, as his friends were then negotiating with the English Government respecting Sarawak. His views on the subject were quite clear and he was now strongly in favour of a Protectorate. Many wished the Government to take the country over as a Crown colony, but that would have proved an expensive failure, as the people were not sufficiently advanced to bear the necessary taxation.

A great deputation, one of the most influential that ever waited on a Minister, had an interview with Lord Derby, but all to no purpose. His lordship was as unsympathetic as he could well be. He failed to appreciate the noble conduct of the Rajah, and could only look upon his efforts in Sarawak as a sort of speculation—half commercial, half political. He had evidently not taken the trouble to study the subject, or he was incapable of appreciating a generous nature. But the Cabinet was not of the same opinion, and soon overtures were made by Lord Malmesbury with reference to a Protectorate being granted by England. Before anything could be settled, however, Lord Derby's Ministry resigned.

The Rajah was now again worried by his pecuniary embarrassments. The Borneo Company pressed for the repayment of the £5000 advanced after the Chinese insurrection, but a generous lady came forward and freed him from this claim. At the same time some of his friends raised a testimonial to mark the appreciation of his public work. Had there not been some underhand opposition by those who pretended to support it, it might have reached the amount expected, namely, £20,000, but it only realised £8800. With a portion of this he bought the small estate of Burrator on the skirts of Dartmoor, and here he ever felt truly at home. He became strongly attached to the place, and it was difficult to make him leave it even for a season. It was a charmingly wild spot, under the shadow of the great tors which render the country about them so wonderfully picturesque. The air is pure and bracing, and his sojourn there may be said to have relit the lamp of life which had been almost extinguished.

In Sarawak affairs were in a bad state. The unreasonable efforts made by its Government to support Pangeran Matusin in Muka, the savage instigator of the civil war, were the cause of much strife, and the illegal conduct of the officer administering the Government was deeply resented in Borneo. The Sarawak officials were possessed with the monomania that the Sultan of Borneo was always intriguing against them, which was a pure myth, as the Brunei Government had neither the energy nor the power to affect them.

The intriguers were within their own territories, for whilst they were watching for outside plots and hostile action, a dangerous conspiracy was being hatched by some discontented chiefs. The heads of this conspiracy were the ex-Datu Patingi Gapoor, now named Datu Haji, as he had made the pilgrimage to Mecca, who had been permitted to return to Sarawak after the Chinese insurrection, and Sherif Musahor, a chief of Arabian descent, established on the Rejang. The first evidence of this treachery was the surprise of the fort at Kanowit, and the murder of two Sarawak officers, Messrs Fox and Steele. Yet so ignorant of the real plotters were the English officials at the capital, that when an expedition was sent to punish the murderers, Tani, one of our best friends, was accused as an accomplice and was executed. As he was led forth to death he protested his innocence, but added, 'You will soon know who is the real culprit.' In the end not one of the actual murderers escaped, as they were tracked for years, and were all ultimately killed.

Sherif Musahor, however, was the real instigator of these murders, and the truth soon came out that the Datu Haji and he were the promoters of all the disturbances. The former was banished and the latter driven out of the country. He had practically no influence in Sarawak, and the Malay chiefs were as ready to follow Charles Johnson in his campaign against him as against any other enemy of the Government. All the stories about his mysterious influence were all nonsense, and had no effect on the minds of the Sarawak people.

Some of the biographers of Sir James Brooke have fallen into the error of supposing that Sarawak was abandoned by the English Government during these perilous years. This, as I have already shown, was not so, for immediately after the Chinese insurrection, both Lord Palmerston and Lord Clarendon offered a Protectorate, but this offer was refused, except under conditions difficult for the British Government to accept. A naval station placed within Sarawak territory was also proposed; this likewise was rejected. Therefore, it must be confessed, the charge of entirely abandoning Sarawak was not well founded, as the refusal to accept British protection tied the hands of Ministers. The British Government went as far as they thought they could safely go, but, as I have already remarked, the Rajah did not feel satisfied with a bare Protectorate, as he mistrusted their sincerity.

On my way home from Brunei to England, early in 1860, I stopped at Singapore, and falling in there with Charles Grant, who had come over to recruit an English crew for a small gunboat, I heard of all that had been going on in the Rajah's territories. I resolved to go over to Sarawak to judge of the situation for myself, so as to be able to carry home the latest news to Sir James Brooke. All real danger was now past. The energy and courage of the Rajah's nephew, Charles Johnson, the present Rajah, had triumphed over all difficulties, and the coast as far as the Rejang was completely tranquil. It is easy to be wise after the event, but I did not then believe, nor do I believe now, that the Sarawak Malays were in any way affected by the plottings of the Datu Haji or of Sherif Musahor. They were afraid of some assassinations of foreigners until the former chief was banished the country, but on my arrival, in March 1860, I found them as sound and as loyal as ever they had been. If they had not been so, there was nothing to prevent them expelling every European from the country. They were all unanimous in their praise of the manner in which Charles Johnson had met the danger and crushed it.

Things were indeed now about to assume a brighter aspect. The same generous lady who had paid off the debt due to the Borneo Company found the money to buy a steamer, and with a steamer the stability of Sarawak would be finally established. The Rajah visited Glasgow to look out for a suitable one, and soon selected the *Rainbow*, for so he christened her, as the emblem of hope. Arriving in England shortly after this purchase, I went down to Scotland with my old chief to see the steamer start. There was no more despondency. He would nail his colours to the mast. In fact, the presence of the steamer on the coast as the property of the Sarawak Government closed the period of alarms, of plots and troubles, and since then I do not believe there has been a single dangerous conspiracy to check the progress of this little kingdom. But before the *Rainbow* arrived on the coast there was to be one more difficulty.

When Johnson drove Sherif Musahor out of the districts subject to Sarawak, he first fled to Muka, and then proceeded to Brunei and Labuan. His stories did not influence the Sultan, who knew the man, and was well persuaded that he had instigated the murder of Fox and Steele. Indeed, before I left Brunei, he had confided to me his suspicions. But the Sultan was still angry with the action of Sarawak, which had treated his sovereign rights with great contempt, so he encouraged the fugitive to proceed to Labuan and lay his complaints before Governor Edwardes, who was known to be hostile both to Sir James Brooke and his rising raj. This led to an interchange of views between the Governor and the Sultan, in which I fear the former promised to use all his influence to lower the position of His Highness's great feudatory, and he sent for a ship of war to carry out his intentions. Unfortunately, he obtained an Indian steamer, the *Victoria*, instead of one of Her Majesty's navy. No naval officer would have countenanced his proceedings.

Early in 1860, Captain Brooke returned to Sarawak and took over the administration of the Government, and I am persuaded he had the firm intention of living at peace with his neighbours, but he found that the high-handed proceedings of the previous year had been so deeply resented that the Governor of Muka, Pangeran Dipa, son of the murdered chief, had ordered all the Sarawak trading vessels to leave his district, and having fortified the entrance to the Muka River, awaited the effect of Sherif Musahor's appeal to the Acting Consul-General.

Captain Brooke, thinking that he could settle these difficulties by negotiation, went with a small force to Muka to interview Pangeran Dipa, determined to try every method of conciliation, but no sooner did his vessels enter the Muka than the guns of the fort opened fire on them. Captain Brooke thereupon retired to the entrance of the river, built a stockade, and sent for reinforcements. These soon came pouring in, a brisk attack was opened upon the enemy, and success would soon have crowned their efforts, had not Governor Edwardes appeared in his steamer and commanded Captain Brooke on his allegiance to suspend his operations. He naturally protested against such interference, but prudently withdrew his forces, and retired to Sarawak. The Governor had brought down with him Sherif Musahor, the murderer of his fellow-countrymen.

Captain Brooke now appealed for justice to the British Government, and Lord John Russell, who was at the Foreign Office, thanked him for his conciliatory and prudent conduct, and then took Mr Edwardes in hand.

When I left Brunei early in 1860, I had requested Mr Edwardes to accept the acting appointment of Consul-General, which had enabled him to interfere on the coasts of the Sultan's dominions. But as soon as I heard of his violent proceedings I could not but offer to sacrifice my leave and return to Borneo to resume my official duties.

Sir James Brooke decided to go back to the East by the same mail in which I had taken my passage. From Singapore the Rajah went over to Sarawak in his own steamer, the *Rainbow*, and I followed in H.M.S. *Nimrod*, Captain Arthur. I called in at Kuching, and there addressed a letter to the Council of Sarawak, stating that Her Majesty's Government disapproved of Mr Edwardes's interference. I then went on to Labuan, relieved my substitute of his position as Consul-General, and proceeded to my post in Brunei. I found the Sultan very reserved, and rumours were rife that the Governor of Labuan had promised not only to interfere in Muka, but to remove all the English from Sarawak, and restore that country to the Sultan. This, I imagine, was but an invention of the Oriental mind, which jumped too hastily to conclusions. At all events the Sultan and all his high officers of State were still very angry, and naturally so, at the original armed interference of Sarawak within their territory. But when they found that the Rajah himself had arrived at Kuching, that he would pay over all the fines his nephews had raised within the Sultan's frontiers, and that he was prepared to make advantageous proposals to the Brunei Government, their brows cleared, and I found myself once more a welcome visitor in their Halls of Audience.

The Rajah arrived, and matters were soon explained and arranged. The Brunei Government decided to banish Sherif Musahor from their dominions, and to send for the Governor of Muka to explain his conduct. I was requested by both parties to act as mediator, and I went as soon as possible to Muka in Her Majesty's corvette *Charybdis*, Captain Keane. We entered the river with all the boats of the ship, and were soon behind the fortifications with two hundred marines and bluejackets. This judicious display of force awed these turbulent chiefs. No show of resistance was made, and both Sherif Musahor and Pangeran Dipa decided to obey the Sultan's mandate.

Little, therefore, remained to be done. The Rajah went up to Muka with a large squadron, and all the chiefs there kept their word and submitted. Dipa went off to Brunei, and Musahor was exiled to the Straits Settlements. With all his faults, nay, crimes, I could not but pity him. He had been such a good fellow in former years, and he had been so injudiciously treated by the local Sarawak officers with whom he had come in contact, men very inferior to him in every way, and totally unfitted to deal with a man of rank, a supposed descendant of the prophet Mahomed. He lived for many years in Singapore, but I do not know whether he is still alive.

The Rajah took up his residence for some weeks in the fort at Muka to endeavour to restore order in what might be called a regular chaos of misgovernment, and succeeded to a great extent. It was regretted by all that his stay was so short, as his magnetic influence over the natives was so remarkable that they all were ready to carry out his views and submit to his superior judgment. No one only accustomed to European countries could imagine the confused state of affairs, for no man among the lower classes appeared to know whether he was a free man or a slave, and if the latter, who was his master, as he had probably been sold half-a-dozen times by people who had no authority over him. However, in most cases, these sales were more nominal than real, as the self-created masters, unless chiefs, seldom attempted to enforce their fictitious rights.

We soon went to Brunei again, and then the Rajah gladdened the heart of the Sultan by taking over the Sago districts on a yearly payment of four thousand five hundred dollars, and giving him a year's revenue in advance. Past complaints were now put on one side, and all was peace.

I had been promoted to be *Chargé d'Affaires* in Hayti, so that as soon as I had introduced my successor to the Sultan, I prepared to proceed home; but as the Rajah had decided to leave for England also, we returned together to Sarawak, where he wished to arrange some affairs before bidding adieu to Borneo.

At his nephew, Captain Brooke's, request he publicly installed him as Rajah Muda or heir apparent, and left him in charge of the Government. To this ceremony Sir James Brooke summoned all the principal men of the country, and introducing Captain Brooke as the Rajah Muda, bade them all farewell; adding, however, that should his presence ever be necessary, he would return to resume the Government and to aid them in their difficulties. I never heard a better speech; many of the audience burst into tears, and all were deeply moved.

Definite explanations were exchanged between the uncle and his nephew, which gave the Rajah a free hand in all negotiations in England, and these arrangements were reduced to writing. I also had a distinct explanation with Captain Brooke as to his views, so that I might advance them as far as I could agree with them.

We started for Singapore in the *Rainbow*, and, as we were detained there by an accident to the mail steamer, the inhabitants of the settlement, to show that no unkind feeling remained in any section of society, gave the Rajah a ball. At supper his health was drunk with all the honours; some good speeches were made, and most of his friends then said farewell to him, thinking they should see his face no more. Though rejoiced at my removal from Brunei, I could not leave the Further East without regret, as I had spent many happy years there.

Among Sir James Brooke's most active friends and supporters was Mr John Abel Smith, who was very intimate with Lord John Russell, our Foreign Minister, and, in 1862, he opened negotiations with him and other Ministers for the recognition of Sarawak as an independent State. At first there was a proposal to make it a Crown Colony, but that was prudently discarded. Then a Protectorate was proposed, and at last all the negotiations centred on one point, the recognition of Sarawak. There was little or no opposition in the Ministry, when someone unfortunately suggested that Lord Elgin, the Governor-General of India, should send over an official to report on the actual condition of Sarawak. The Governor of the Straits Settlements, Colonel Cavanagh, was chosen to prosecute this enquiry. Instead of simply carrying out his instructions, he showed Captain Brooke the secret and confidential papers which had been entrusted to him. The latter thought that his rights were being tampered with, whereas, had he been fully informed, he would have found that recognition was the only question then under the consideration of the Ministry. But Captain Brooke was not quite himself at that time. He had just lost his second wife and his eldest son, and the inquisitiveness of the Governor probably chafed him. Whatever may have been the cause, he wrote to Lord John Russell to say that the country could not be handed over to England without his and the people's consent, and then sent a defiant letter to his uncle announcing that he had assumed the government of the country and would defend his rights by force.

The Rajah could not accept such a defiance. He returned to Sarawak, met his repentant nephew at Singapore, and sent him home on leave. Bad advisers in England induced him to withdraw his submission, and it ended in a complete estrangement between the uncle and nephew. He was deposed from his position as heir apparent, and thenceforth he ceased to have any interest in Sarawak. He had been my most intimate friend, and I regretted his action exceedingly, particularly as it was one of my own confidential memoranda to our Government which had incited his ire. This memorandum related to a different question from that which was before the Government, and had he been more patient he would have learnt that Lord John Russell fully recognised the inhabitants of Sarawak as a free people, whose consent would have been necessary to any transfer.

When the news reached England that the Rajah's authority was uncontested in Sarawak, and that Captain Brooke had retired from the scene, Lord John Russell determined to acknowledge its independence, and appointed a consul, who had to ask for his *exequatur* from the Sarawak Government. Thus this much vexed question closed to the satisfaction of all those who loved and admired the Rajah, but not to that of a group of false friends who had been working against him in all kinds of underhand ways. But as these are now turned to dust I will not refer to them again. It was a triumph for the Rajah, and was the reward of his constancy, of his high principle, his irreproachable character and devotion to his people. The evilly-disposed were now silenced, and left him at peace for the remainder of his life.

I was at that time in Hayti and did not see the Rajah during the years 1863, 1864 and 1865, but we kept up a constant correspondence. I could not rise superior to injuries as he did, and in one of my letters I slightly reproached him with appearing to forgive a person who had deeply injured him, and remained impenitent. His answer shows the kindly nature of the man. 'True it is he injured me, and deeply, and perhaps what you say is true, he will injure me again, but in Sarawak *I cannot quarrel* or feel resentment against anyone, however great the evil done to myself.'

Mr Ricketts was named consul at Sarawak, and he soon sent home highly interesting reports about the country. He stayed there two years, but as there was really nothing for a consul to do, a vice-consul succeeded him. At present Great Britain has a vice-consul at Brunei, who is accredited to the Rajah of Sarawak as well as to the Sultan.

The Rajah, during these years, really enjoyed life. His anxieties had almost ceased. The revenues of Sarawak were improving, thus ensuring increased stability. There was both peace and contentment there, and trade was rapidly extending throughout all its dependencies. His own health was remarkably good, and he could enjoy visits to country houses, and occasionally indulge in partridge shooting. He could now write, 'In spite of trials and anxieties, calumny and misrepresentation, *I have been a happy man*, and can pillow my head with the consciousness of a well-spent life of sacrifice and devotion to a good cause.'

I never knew a man so ready to help when he saw the strong oppress the weak. As an instance of this, he boldly threw the weight of his influence on the side of Bishop Colenso, when he saw the great Church dignitaries ready to condemn him.

The Rajah spent much of his time during the remaining years of his life at Burrator, and became as popular and as beloved among the small farmers and cottagers as ever he had been in the Far East during the height of his prosperity. He often took me to visit these rough but kindly people, and it was a pleasure to see how they all greeted him. I particularly noticed how the children would run out of the cottages to touch his hand, as if his gentle smile fascinated them. He did all he could for the parish, helped to restore the ruined church, and, in 1865, was cheered by the arrival of a clergyman and his wife, Mr and Mrs Dakyn, who remained his kind and tender friends to the day of his death.

In the autumn of 1866 he received a severe shock. His nephew wrote that he had sold the steamer *Rainbow* to pay off a debt due to their Singapore agent—a debt incurred through careless extravagance in carrying out too many public works at a time. For a moment it almost stupefied him, as this steamer had not yet been paid for. We soon proved to him, however, that there was but little cause for uneasiness, as the Sarawak revenue was ample to meet all disbursements, if more care were exercised in the expenditure on public works. But Sarawak without a steamer, he felt assured, would sink back into its old state of insecurity, and therefore a steamer must be had. By great exertion he succeeded in raising the necessary funds, and purchased a vessel which was christened the *Royalist*, after his famous yacht.

I stayed with the Rajah at Burrator during the autumn of 1866, and he appeared very much stronger. He took his daily rides and walks, but he was full of anxiety about Sarawak, which continued until the steamer was secured. When we were alone we would take our afternoon ride and then return to tea, and between that meal and dinner he enjoyed his reading. He liked to have someone with him, and every now and then would put down his book and talk of any question that was then interesting him. After a while he would resume his reading and we would both remain quiet for a time. I never knew anyone who understood better what has been called 'the luxury of silence.'

Two or three days before Christmas I left Burrator for London, and we went up together as far as Plymouth. I never saw the Rajah more gay or full of spirits, and he played whist with great enjoyment, but on his return home, the next day, he was struck down by a second attack of paralysis, and we were hastily summoned to his bedside. He partially recovered, but was never again able to write. His career was closed. He lived on, however, for about two years, when the final attack came at Burrator where, fortunately, he was surrounded by many of his nearest relatives. He died on the 11th June 1868. After his third attack he did not recover consciousness, but passed peacefully away. He was buried at Burrator under the yew tree in the churchyard, at the spot he had chosen himself. His death was felt by all his neighbours as a personal loss, as he was, in truth, the friend of everyone in his parish.

More than thirty years have passed since the Rajah's death, and yet the admiration for his character and his great qualities has but increased among those who knew him well or could appreciate the work he had done. I have endeavoured to portray him as he appeared to me, but there was a grandeur about his personality which it is difficult to describe. He could not enter a room without the impression being conveyed that you were in the presence of great superiority, and yet in manner he was ever simple and courteous.

The purity of his private life was such that it

could not but impress both natives and Europeans, and that magnetic influence, as it is called, which he undoubtedly possessed was but the result of a superior mind, ever influenced by a kindly heart. He was a *chevalier sans peur et sans reproche*, and it will be difficult to look upon his like again.

The Rajah bequeathed Sarawak to his nephew, the present Sir Charles Brooke, G.C.M.G. He had lived to see the country prosper, and died without anxiety as to its future. The public debt due to him by Sarawak, he passed on to his successor, and the only encumbrance remaining was for the money advanced to buy the steamers, and the warlike expenditure incurred during the Muka expedition. This was but a slight burden on the finances, and was soon paid off. I rather dwell on this subject, as an unfounded statement has been made that at the Rajah's death Sarawak was a bankrupt State. There is no ground for such an assertion. The paltry debt due was covered tenfold by the value of the ships, the buildings, the public works, and the rising revenue which had accrued principally from the security given by the presence on the coast of Borneo of the steamers in the service of Sarawak.

I will add a copy of the Rajah's will, as far as it relates to public matters:—

'The last will and testament of Sir James Brooke,

K.C.B., Rajah of Sarawak. I, James Brooke, Rajah of Sarawak, of Burrator, in the County of Devon, give, devise and bequeath all that my sovereignty of Sarawak, aforesaid, and all the rights and privileges whatsoever thereto belonging unto my nephew, Charles Johnson Brooke, Tuan Muda of Sarawak, son of the Rev. Francis Charles Johnson, and the heirs male of his body lawfully issuing; and in default of such issue unto my nephew, Stuart Johnson, another son of the said Francis Charles Johnson, and the heirs male of his body lawfully issuing; and in default of such issue I give, devise and bequeath the said sovereignty, its rights and privileges, unto Her Majesty, the Queen of England, her heirs and assigns for ever; and I appoint Miss Angela Georgina Burdett-Coutts of Stratton Street, Piccadilly, and Thomas Fairbairn, of the city of Manchester, Esquire, and John Abel Smith, of Chester Square, in the County of Middlesex, Esquire, M.P., trustees of this my will to see the purposes aforesaid carried into effect. I bequeath to my said nephew, Charles Johnson Brooke, his heirs, executors and administrators, all my real and personal estate in the Island of Borneo and England, and constitute him likewise my residuary legatee.' (After mentioning some private legacies which he wished paid, he added), 'I leave all my papers to the care of Spenser St John, Esq., H.B.M. *Chargé d'Affaires* at Hayti, whom I appoint as one of my executors, together with Alexander Knox, Esquire,' etc.

Sir Charles Brooke, the present Rajah, has three sons living, and his brother, Stuart Johnson, died, leaving one son.

CHAPTER VIII

PRESENT CONDITION OF SARAWAK — RAJAH AN IRRESPONSIBLE RULER — SARAWAK COUNCIL— GENERAL COUNCIL—RESIDENTS AND TRIBUNALS —EMPLOYMENT OF NATIVES—AGRICULTURE— TRADE RETURNS — THE GOLD REEFS — COAL DEPOSITS — VARIED POPULATION — IMPOLITIC SEIZURE OF LIMBANG — MISSIONS — EXTRAORDINARY PANICS—REVENUE—ADMINISTRATION OF JUSTICE — CIVIL SERVICE — ALLIGATORS— SATISFACTORY STATE OF SARAWAK

I HAVE found materials for writing this chapter in the numbers of the Sarawak *Gazette*, an official journal published once a month. I have read its contents with great interest, as every district to which it refers was once familiar to me, and I am able to trace clearly the changes which have taken place since I left Borneo. I might rather have used the word expansion, as in truth the changes have not been so great as might have been expected.

The Government is carried on as it was in the old days. The Rajah is *de facto* an irresponsible ruler, though he can summon the Sarawak

Council to meet and advise him as to any new law, or any modification to be made in the financial arrangements of the country; and I understand that the Rajah always consults them on such occasions. This Council is composed of the Rajah and two of the senior English officers, and four native chiefs of Sarawak Proper. It was the Earl Grey of 1855 who recommended its establishment to the old Rajah, and it has proved itself exceedingly useful. Its first meetings took place in 1856.

There is also a General Council composed of the chiefs of the various districts under the rule of the Rajah, with a due proportion of English officers. They assemble about once a year, to the number of from forty to fifty. Though it is not often that business is submitted to their deliberations, they are addressed by the Rajah on subjects of general interest, and are afterwards invited to dine at the Palace. It is a decided step in advance that this meeting of native and European officers should take place, as it tends to efface local prejudices, and to consolidate the Government. This General Council was not summoned during the lifetime of Sir James Brooke, though he often talked of doing so, and would have carried out his intention had he lived.

The country is divided into five chief districts under English Residents: Sarawak Proper, Batang Lupar, Rejang, Baram and Limbang. In each of these there are also several assistants to look after the management of the sub-districts. All these officers hold courts, but there is an appeal from the findings of the junior officers to the Resident of the district, and all very serious sentences are ultimately referred to the capital for the Rajah's decision or approval. From the reports in the *Gazette*, I gather that very substantial justice is administered. The notions of equity entertained by some of the junior officers may be rather crude; but the power of appeal enables anyone who is dissatisfied with a sentence to refer the matter to the Resident, and the natives often make use of this privilege with results satisfactory to themselves.

The Government of Sarawak is a kind of mild despotism, the only government suitable to Asiatics, who look to their chief as the sole depositary of supreme power. The influence of the old Rajah still pervades the whole system, and native and European work together in perfect harmony. Though the head of each district is an Englishman, every effort is made to employ the natives in responsible positions, as collectors of revenue, as judges with the Rajah or the Residents in the superior courts, as sole judges in the native tribunals, which try all cases where their religion or racial customs are affected, and as chiefs of the different tribes and local communities, and, on the whole, the results appear to be satisfactory.

The old Rajah used to write that the development of native states must be slow in order to be permanent, and the development of Sarawak has been very slow, slower than most people would have expected, as the introduction of steamers on the coast pointed to more rapid progress.

Agriculture is the mainstay of every Asiatic country. In the early years of the old Rajah's Government the natives only grew rice sufficient for their own consumption, and the Chinese confined themselves to a little gardening near their small settlements; but when, in 1850, the Chinese flocked from Sambas into Sarawak, Captain Brooke saw the necessity of encouraging as many as possible of those accustomed to agriculture to settle on the fertile soil near the river's banks, and began by establishing colonies of these industrious immigrants at places about eight miles above the capital, at Sungei Tungah and Batu Kawa. These flourished until the year 1857, when the Chinese insurrection interfered with their progress for a time.

The financial distress which followed this great upheaval prevented any further assistance being given to agriculturists, until, in 1875, the present Rajah, Sir Charles Brooke, determined to encourage gambier planting, and this he followed up by introducing the cultivation of pepper, coffee, including the Liberian variety, cocoa and the oil palm. Of these coffee appears the most popular among the Malays and Dyaks, who have carried its cultivation into most of the districts of Sarawak, on a small scale, it is true, but as the plants bear, and the returns come in, many more are now encouraged to cultivate this useful shrub.

Only one English Planting Company tried its fortune in the country, and this failed for want of capital to enable it to await results. In 1895, 500 cwts. of coffee were exported, whilst in 1896 the export rose to 1483 cwts., nearly treble the amount, and there is every probability that the annual produce will proportionally increase; gambier rose from 26,250 cwts. in 1895 to 29,285 cwts. in 1896; and pepper, a very valuable article, was exported in both years to the amount of over 18,000 cwts. These three important cultivations were introduced into the country by the present Rajah, and their products were valued in 1895 at £46,820, and in 1896 at £44,082.

The planting of sago, an indigenous palm, has been much encouraged, and the export of the manufactured flour in 1896 amounted to over 15,000 tons, of a value of about £70,000. A little tea is grown but is not exported. There is no doubt that the Sarawak Government has done much to encourage agriculture, but it has failed as yet to attract European capital. I notice that lately the Borneo Company has commenced to plant gambier. One of the causes of the failure above referred to is, that European capitalists are not tempted by the prospect of having their enterprises under the control of an irresponsible ruler, however just and capable he may be, as all might change on the advent of a successor. But they might reflect that the Borneo Company have been carrying on their business for the last forty years without any difficulties arising.

There are millions of acres in the Sarawak territory which are open to European capitalists; hundreds of thousands of acres on the great river of Rejang alone, where water carriage would be at their door, and produce could be shipped direct to Europe, and that is only one out of the many districts awaiting foreign enterprise.

It is curious that an agricultural population like that of Sarawak does not grow sufficient rice for its own consumption. In 1896 it had to import of this grain to the value of about £42,000. It is true that only a portion of the population is really industrious—the Chinese and the Seribas and Sakarang Dyaks. The former are otherwise employed, whilst the latter devote much of their energy to the collection of jungle produce. And yet in the district of Samarahan alone sufficient rice might be cultivated to supply the whole country.

If we compare the trade returns of Sarawak for the years 1876 and 1896, and take only the dollar value, the increase is striking, but if you turn the amounts into sterling the results are very disappointing. In 1876 the exchange value of the dollar was four shillings, whilst in 1896 it had fallen to two shillings only. This depreciation of silver certainly aids those countries where the dollar and rupee circulate by the great nominal augmentation of the value of their produce, whilst it enhances the price of European goods by a hundred per cent. when paid for in silver.

In 1876	Imports from Foreign Countries,	£169,000
„ 1896	„ „ .	227,000
„ 1876	Imports Coasting Trade, . .	94,000
„ 1896	„ „ . .	142,000
„ 1876	Exports to Foreign Countries, .	186,000
„ 1896	„ „ . .	242,000
„ 1876	Exports Coasting Trade, . .	98,000
„ 1896	„ „ . .	113,000

These figures may relate principally to the trade of Sarawak Proper, as each of the large districts has a small direct trade with Singapore, but the indications are to the contrary, as the coal exported from Sadong is included in these returns, and the sago flour from some at least of the out-stations.

The export of antimony has fallen off considerably, and cinnabar has been nearly worked out. Jungle produce continues to be found in large quantities, and gutta-percha, India rubber, rattans, beeswax and timber considerably swell the trade returns; but coal and gold are, I think, destined to develop Sarawak in a remarkable manner. The Borneo Company, which until lately had not been able to invest much capital in their operations on account of the difficulties attending the first working of coal in Sarawak, as a result of the scarcity of antimony and the gradual failure of the great deposits of cinnabar, has now entered on a new phase of activity.

Gold has been known to exist for many years. Even on the arrival of the first Rajah, the Chinese were working it on a small scale, but only in the alluvial deposits. I was with the late Dr MacDougall, Bishop of Sarawak, when, in 1854, he picked up a piece of quartz with specks of gold distinctly visible in it, but it was not until many years later that great reefs of gold-bearing quartz were discovered, and although good results were obtained in the laboratory, the industry could not then be worked on a commercial basis. Lately, however, the Borneo Company has found that by the cyanide process it can make the working of the stone pay, and it has now erected very extensive and elaborate machinery, which, when in full operation, will crush three hundred tons of quartz a day. This will be the salvation of Sarawak, for there is no reason, if the working of the present plant prove a mercantile success, why a dozen similar establishments should not be erected, as the stone is practically inexhaustible, the reefs having been traced for about thirty miles. The latest reports from Sarawak show that the machinery is doing well in the Company's establishment at Bauh, and so satisfied are the directors with the results that they are putting up a considerable plant at Bidi, where the quartz is richer in quality.

Both these places are in the interior of Sarawak Proper.

The benefit to Sarawak will be twofold, as the Government is to receive five per cent. of the gold produced, and large numbers of Chinese, whom the Company finds can alone be relied on for regular operations, must be imported to work the plant and quarry the stone. The 'farms' and the import duties will benefit by this influx of labour, and it may enable the Sarawak Government ultimately to abolish all export duties on agricultural produce. We used to reckon that each Chinaman on an average increased the revenue by two pounds sterling per annum.

The washing for gold by the Chinese in the alluvial soil has not for many years proved very productive; in fact, it has been thought that the discontent of the Chinese, before the great insurrection of 1857, arose partly from the fact that the gold workings did not pay, and the coolies began to look with suspicion on the integrity of their chiefs.

Coal, though worked for many years, produced at first no practical results, but in 1896 nearly 23,000 tons were exported, and the amount increased greatly during 1897 and 1898. This also must affect the revenue both directly and indirectly in a very satisfactory manner.

The only factories which have proved successful in Sarawak are those that produce sago flour. These will doubtless increase, as in many places the natives have for several years past augmented their plantations, and it is a cultivation which suits their indolent habits, for after tending the young plants during the first year, little or no care is subsequently given to the palm trees.

The population of Sarawak is very varied. In all its districts, with the exception of the Milanau rivers and Baram, there is an indigenous Malay population, who are born traders and fishermen, and only cultivate as it were under protest; but they do grow a little rice, a few rough vegetables, and lately some have made small coffee gardens. As a rule they neglect the last, or overcrowd the plants with other products.

In Sarawak, Samarahan and Sadong the interior is inhabited by Land Dyaks, a very primitive race, who are, however, slowly advancing, while some, as those in Samarahan, must be getting rich, as a Resident reports seeing the girls dancing in silks and brocades, with strings of silver dollars hanging round their waists. It was a pleasure to read of this advance, as many previous accounts had pointed to a great deterioration in their condition.

But the pride of Sarawak must always be the Sea Dyaks who live on the Batang Lupar, the Seribas and the right-hand branches of the Rejang. These were the destructive pirates of the coast, who put to sea in large fleets of fast vessels, and ravaged every district they could reach. When the expeditions of Captains

Keppel and Farquhar had put down their piracies at sea, and the land operations, principally conducted by the present Rajah, then chief Resident on the Batang Lupar, had subdued them in the interior, they began to look to other fields of activity. Even as early as 1853 I sent a report home about their energetic work in the antimony mines. Now, they are the most industrious of the collectors of jungle produce, and have spread wherever that is to be found, whether in the interior of the Rejang, Baram, or Limbang districts. One hears of them also in the territories of the British North Borneo Company, where they should be welcome immigrants, not only on account of their industry, but of their readiness to support the established Government. Owing to this last amiable trait in their character they have been recalled by the Sarawak Government under the penalty, in case of disobedience, of being declared outlaws. This was a mistake, as they would be equally useful to the North Borneo Company, which is combating lawlessness as much as the Sarawak Government, and among a far more dangerous population. In looking over my Sarawak correspondence I find that they were accused of acting against the regulations of the Company, particularly in the interior of Padas, but this appears to have arisen from the foolish restrictions placed on the Dyaks and others by the subordinate officers in that district, which were strongly condemned by the Resident at Labuan, the late Mr Maxwell, a man of remarkable intelligence and experience, the latter acquired when in the Sarawak service.

These Sea Dyaks even ventured across the China Sea, and sought for jungle produce throughout the Malay Peninsula, but I hear that they also have been recalled, why or wherefore it is difficult even to guess. In reading through these *Gazettes*, I have come across references to a Dyak selling gutta-percha in Singapore for $1200; to another having disposed of produce in the bazaar to the amount of $1500; and to a prahu being swamped with $2000 worth of goods or cash on board. These Dyaks are indeed a valuable population.

The next to be noticed are the Milanaus, who live at the mouths of the rivers Rejang, Oya and Muka, and are apparently a race apart. They are perhaps a little more industrious than the Malays, and devote themselves to planting and roughly manufacturing sago. A portion of this population has been converted to Mohammedanism, whilst the rest cannot bring themselves to abandon pork.

In the far interior of the Rejang, the Bintulu, and all through the Baram districts, are the numerous tattooed tribes, as the Kayans and the Kineahs; the mongrel villagers called Kanowits; and the wildest of wild tribes, the Punans and Pakatans. As yet none of these tribes have made their mark either in the field of battle or in any industry, except in the working of iron ores or their products, but it is comparatively lately that they have come under the influence of the English. The

Sarawak Government appears to have a very intelligent Resident in Baram, Mr Hose.

The Chinese will no doubt gradually fill up the different districts of Sarawak, but the progress is slow. They do not seem to take kindly to Borneo in general, probably because wages are low, the native seldom receiving more than twenty-five cents or sixpence a day, though the wages of the Chinese are doubtless considerably higher. In many villages, however, where they are permitted to settle, you will be sure to find Chinese shopkeepers, who carry on a thriving trade. They have the reputation of not being very honest dealers, as false weights are too often resorted to, in order to enable them to pay a price nominally higher than the market rate, which renders fair competition impossible. I could never understand why restrictions were so often placed on their settlement among the interior tribes, except where the Dyaks themselves objected to their presence. It is true they are not very honest, but in my time we found the natives a match for them in this line, as they used to insert stones into the large lumps of gutta-percha. As might be expected from the low class of Chinese who immigrate into Sarawak, the principal occupants of the prisons are found among their ranks.

Limbang and Trusan, to the north of the Sultan's capital, are the latest acquisitions of Sarawak. They contain a mixed population of Kadayans, Muruts and Bisayas, with no very marked characteristics.

I am loath to write anything which may appear as an adverse criticism of the conduct of the present Rajah, with whom I have been friends for over fifty years, but unless we are to adopt the principle that 'the end justifies the means,' it is difficult to approve the action of Sarawak in seizing by force any part of the Sultan's dominions. A little gentle, persevering diplomacy would have secured Limbang without violating any principle of international law. I am convinced, however, that the present Rajah was deceived by someone as to the political position of that district, as he wrote that, for four years previous to his action, Limbang was completely independent of the Sultan, which his officers subsequently found was not the case.

The Sultan is the Suzerain Lord of all the possessions of the present Rajah, with the doubtful exception of Sarawak Proper, and Great Britain is the Protector of Sarawak and Brunei alike, yet the Sarawak *Gazette*, the official organ of its Government, thus refers to the Brunei under British protection : 'Brunei has long been a disgrace, a blot on the map of Borneo. There murder and robbery thrive, and criminals from all around find a refuge from the punishment merited by their evil deeds, with the knowledge and sanction of the Sultan, and under the protection of the British flag.'

To use an expressive, but not very elegant, phrase, the writer has 'let the cat out of the bag.' It is probably true that the British Government would not permit Sarawak to seize Brunei and depose the Sultan, but there are other and more peaceful means of putting an end to Brunei, if it be the sink of iniquity described. Already the Kadayans are taking up their permanent residence in Baram under the Sarawak flag, and many Borneans and Kadayans are moving to Limbang; while a certain number have already established themselves in Padas under the flag of the North Borneo Company. By degrees the population of the capital will completely disperse and settle in the surrounding districts, and the capital will cease to exist as a centre of authority.

That the inhabitants of Limbang rejoiced to be placed under the protection of the Sarawak flag there can be no doubt. I knew them well, and how they suffered from the exactions of the Pangerans and their rapacious followers, and no one would have more rejoiced than myself to hear they had been put under Sarawak rule in a less forcible way. As poverty increased in Brunei, so had the exactions augmented, and Limbang, being near, suffered the most. Perhaps some of my readers may think that in this case 'the end *did* justify the means.' At all events, that appears to have been the view taken by our own Foreign Office.

As far as I can judge from the notices in the Sarawak *Gazette*, and from my private correspondence, neither the Missions nor education have made much progress, though there are schools at the capital, and both the Anglicans and the Roman Catholics have establishments in the country. The

Mission schools appear to educate from two to three hundred pupils, but little is evidently done at the out-stations, and the Dyaks in general are left to themselves, although at one time the field appeared most promising. I fear that the explanation is that the true missionary spirit is dead in our Church. It is no longer looked upon as a field for talent, and those who would not pass muster in an English parish are sent off to vegetate in a Bornean out-station, where their influence is *nil.*

I notice it reported in a private letter that the Catholic Mission is the more prosperous, as it appears to be well provided with money, erects substantial buildings, and has a very competent staff.

How little the influence of European rule touches the inner life and belief of the native, whatever may be his race! I remember being in Singapore at the time the Government was building a new church, when it was reported that the convicts were seizing people at night and murdering them in order to bury their heads under the foundations of the new building. A panic prevailed for a considerable time, and natives only ventured out in strong parties. And this occurred in a British settlement after our Government had been established there over thirty years. I discussed this unaccountable panic with my Chinese butler, who spoke English well, and had lived all his life in European families. His only answer to my repeated questions was that he hoped it was not true, that he did not know, but he understood it was generally believed. Our missionaries in China have the same experience.

Another intelligent native remarked that the English must have been a barbarous race, as formerly they sacrificed a human victim every time they prepared to take the sacrament, but that in more modern days they had become more civilised, as they now only sacrificed dogs, a reference to the periodical destruction in British settlements of all stray animals. What a perverse interpretation of missionary teaching!

After fifty years of English rule in Sarawak a similar panic occurred. I will quote the Sarawak *Gazette* of September 1, 1894: 'Some months back a most unaccountable scare took possession of the Asiatic population of Sarawak Proper—Malays, Chinese, Dyaks and others being similarly affected. It was at first rumoured that the Government required human heads to place under the foundations of the new high level reservoir at the waterworks, and that men were sent out at night to procure these. . . . Other equally absurd stories followed and were fully believed, many natives going so far as to assert that they had met with these head hunters about the native town at night. The people no longer ventured out after dark; coolies whose work would preclude their return to their own homes at night were unobtainable, not a boat could be obtained to cross the river after dark, and the majority of persons whose business took them further than the limits of the bazaar, carried arms.'

The entire article is too long to quote; the panic spread all along the coast, invaded the Dutch territories, and found its way to the furthest out-stations. Numerous murders were really committed, and at first the natives were afraid to report them. Gradually, however, people came to their senses, but only to fall into another panic, on the ground that robbers were wandering under the Malay houses, which are built on piles, and stabbing at the inmates from below. A few deaths from this cause did, in fact, occur, which gave an excuse for the alarm, and some ingenious thieves bored holes through boxes resting on the floor and extracted their contents. It must be remembered that these floors are not of planks, but of laths of the nibong palm with interstices between them, and are generally covered over with matting.

It is almost incredible that people who had been governed by the old Rajah and his successor, and governed in the most benevolent and generous manner for over fifty years, should have believed that their rulers could be capable of seeking their heads to bury under the foundations of the new waterworks. It appears as if there were no common ground on which the intellect of the white and coloured races can meet; they never understand us and we shall probably never fully understand them.

Finance has never been the strong point of the Sarawak Government.

The Revenue in 1876 (Exchange 4s.)	.	£36,636
" " " 1896 (" 2s.)	.	49,376

The treasurer's financial statement for the year, 1896, is too full of trivial details to be satisfactory, but the tables which are published in the same number of the *Gazette* enable one to form a very clear idea of the financial state of the country.

The 'farms' are the most important source of revenue, and those that are legitimate are the opium and spirit farms; the gambling farm is no doubt suitable to the Chinese, and discourages play among the Malays and Dyaks. But the objectionable farms are the pork, the fish and the pawnbroking. The pork farm was abolished in 1896, as it was found to restrict the supply of good meat, and raise its price to the industrious Chinese labourer, who could only obtain an inferior article, while it brought in but little to the revenue. The Government slaughter-houses are as profitable, and do not interfere so much with trade. The *Gazette* notices that after the abolition of this farm the supply of meat became more plentiful, and was of a much finer quality, with a reduction in price. The fish market is equally objectionable. The monopolists pay so poorly for the supply, that, according to the *Gazette*, the fishermen earned less than fourpence a day, whilst the price of fish was so raised that the Government imposed a maximum; but this paternal measure did not answer, and it was repealed. The fish farm should go the way of the pork farm. There are also obvious objections to a pawnbroking farm. A system of licenses would pay better, and be much less liable to abuse.

Though the export duties on agricultural produce are light, they are unsound in principle, interfere with trade, and lessen the profit of the industrious steady planter; and they only bring in about £2500 a year. It would be better to add to the list of imports subject to duty. The probate duties are quite unsuited to a half or quarter civilised people, and must render the Residents unpopular with the best of the population. No sooner is the news received of the death of a Dyak chief than the nearest English officer has to start off to the spot to see that the Government dues are not evaded, and the wages, or their equivalent, of the boat's crew must often exceed the amount received. There is another tax which checks what might become a considerable industry—the duty on salt. This prevents any real development of the extensive fisheries of the coast, as not only is a necessary product taxed, but a duty is also raised on the exported salted fish, which has thus to bear a double weight. A bounty might be granted equivalent to the amount of the duty on the salt used. The stamp duty has only lately been imposed, and may possibly be useful in the administration of justice, but it will have to be worked with very great caution.

If the Borneo Company succeed with their new gold working machinery, and there is no apparent reason why they should not do so, the increase in the revenues may enable the Rajah to do away with or modify those taxes and duties, which impede commerce and hinder the progress of the country. It must have been uphill work to carry on the Government with revenues so inelastic.

When I first arrived in Sarawak I do not think the cattle exceeded a dozen, and these were at a place about fourteen miles above the capital, and were very much neglected. At present we find cattle at every station, and English bulls are often imported to improve the breed. The natives also in several districts have cattle of their own, and under gentle pressure are paying more attention to them. I do not remember that during my long residence in Sarawak we had beef even once a year.

The Sarawak courts are not influenced by maudlin pity, and punish by heavy fines all those who by carelessness, or any action of their own, cause the death or wounding of any human being. Many casualties are said to occur from men supposing that a noise in the brushwood was caused by a wild beast, and firing at once and thus slaying a fellow hunter; these never escape deserved punishment. The setting of traps to kill pig or deer often caused the infliction of injuries or even death on the unwary, and the setter suffered in consequence. I wish this system of punishing wanton carelessness were introduced into English practice. We might then hear of fewer cases of criminally careless people presenting guns at their friends, and, when a fatal result follows, saying glibly that they thought the weapon was not loaded.

In outlying stations, the killing for the purpose of securing heads would have been a very constant practice had not the present Rajah sternly resolved to insist on the death penalty whenever the culprits belonged to tribes who thoroughly understood the law; whilst upon others who had but recently come under the sway of Sarawak, and were still almost in the savage state, he was content to impose heavy fines. This judicious administration of justice is having a very salutary effect, and will gradually extinguish the evil.

It sounds curious to read of both parties in a case being fined, but very often both are to blame in a greater or less degree, and are punished in proportion. But what must have taxed a Resident's gravity was the hearing a case of two privates in the Sarawak Rangers, accused of working a charm, in order to compass the death of an ex-comrade, and fining the victim as well as the culprits.

The Rajah is kept well informed as to what passes throughout his extensive territories, as he insists on the Residents and Assistant Residents sending monthly reports of all occurrences in each of their districts, and I understand that every one of them also keeps a diary of events. This methodical system must be very useful to the Government. The reports from Baram and Limbang are especially interesting, and I could have wished them fuller.

For the information of those who may desire to enter the Sarawak service, or are interested in the subject, I will mention the salaries which were fixed from January 1, 1898. I may premise by saying that I have taken the dollar to represent two shillings, the exchange value, but that by no means represents its local value, as prices and wages in dollars have not increased in anything like the proportion of the fall in the exchange. In some cases wages do not appear to have increased much since my time, when the dollar was always worth more than four shillings.

Maximum Salaries in Sterling.

Divisional Residents, . .	£540	per annum.
With allowances from £120 to	240	„
Treasurer, ...	480	„
Second-Class Resident, . .	360	„
Medical Officer in charge, . .	420	„
Assistant Residents, . . .	240	„
Cadets on joining, . . .	120	„
Do., of one year's standing, .	144	„
Postmaster, ...	360	„
Police Inspector, . . .	360	„

The treasurer, second-class Residents and medical officer have also allowances, the amount of which is not stated; military commandant, etc., according to respective agreements. Of course, to turn these salaries into dollars you have only to multiply by ten.

The terms for furlough pay are very liberal, leave being generally granted on full pay, and the dollar valued at four shillings. Pensions are given, after thirty years' service, at the same rate of exchange, half pay for life—furloughs in Europe not included.

I have remarked before how difficult it is to induce English ladies to associate with natives, but I have heard that the Ranee, Lady Brooke, has been in the habit of visiting the Malay ladies and receiving their visits in return, and I noticed in one of the *Gazettes* that Mrs Maxwell, the wife of the late chief Resident, gave an elaborate picnic to the daughters of the principal Malays. This is as it should be, and must have a good effect. It is interesting to read that cricket has been introduced among the native lads, and that some of them take to it with zest.

I have noticed an occasional remark in the *Gazette* on the hostility displayed by Singapore towards Sarawak. That there was in Sir James Brooke's time a great jealousy both of Sarawak and Labuan there can be no doubt. It was founded on a foolish idea that these two places might become centres of independent trade with Europe to the detriment of Singapore. The far-seeing knew that it would not be so, and that instead of being rivals they would become feeders of our great free-trade port, but it would seem that among a few of the narrow-minded this jealousy still exists.

Among the dangers to life in Sarawak are the crocodiles or alligators. Some naturalists declare that one of the two species—I believe the latter—is not found in Asia, but I think that those who have had the measurement of those reptiles, to estimate the amount of reward for their destruction, must have noticed that there are apparently two species—one very broad in the head, the other very long and narrow. It is true we never examined their teeth, by which we might have distinguished them. It is said on good authority that there is a third species only found in fresh water, living for preference in the deep pools of the far inland reaches of the rivers. Sir Hugh Low saw them in the interior of the Rejang, and I often heard of them in Sarawak. I remarked to a native chief that it was curious that this species should have fixed its habitat away from the deep water. 'Not more curious,' he answered, 'than seeing you white men in Borneo.'

Whatever the true name of these brutes may be, the destruction of life traceable to them is considerable. They seize people bathing on the banks of rivers, catch unwary children, and snatch people from their canoes. They will often swim on the surface of the water with their victims in their mouths, and the *Gazette* mentions one instance where the alligator appeared with the body on the second day. As they are called alligators in Borneo, I will not change their name.

Many a tale of quiet heroism may be told connected with these attacks. One day a mother and daughter were paddling up the Linga river, when the former was snatched from the boat by an alligator. It did not attempt to sink with its victim, which gave time to the daughter to spring on its neck, and, leaning forward, she gouged out the eyes of the reptile, which instantly let go the mother and dived to the bottom of the stream. I have known of several instances of these heroic attempts to save relations.

There was an alligator which created a panic among all those who had to pull by the entrance of the Siol stream on the Sarawak river, so many had been its victims. It was ultimately taken, and measured, it is said, over twenty-four feet in length.

When I was living in Brunei a similar panic occurred. So many people were snatched from their boats that there was talk of a crusade being undertaken against the alligator which caused it. But as that did not come off, I proposed to my six boatmen that we should attempt the destruction of the brute. I armed my men with muskets, and I took for my own use a Minié rifle. We arranged that I should have first shot, and if I missed, they were to fire a volley at the enemy. We pulled down quietly to the haunted spot, and then floated with the stream. We had not been there many minutes when my head man said, 'There he is.' I looked round, and all I could see were a pair of prominent eyes, a broad forehead and a streak of its back. It was coming at us with all its speed. I waited until it was within about twenty-five yards, and then fired. The heavy ball struck it between the eyes, then bounded off, and fell into the water many a yard away. There was great commotion as the alligator dived beneath the surface. My men, who had wonderfully sharp eyes, said that the bullet had torn the skin off the forehead, and that the beast must die, as the worms with which these waters swarm would get into the wound. A week or two subsequently, some fishermen told me they had seen an immense alligator, at least twenty feet in length, lying on the mud bank of a small stream. All the flesh on its head and neck was rotting away, and it was evidently nearly dead, as it scarcely moved on their approach. At all events, the man-eater never appeared again. The largest alligator which I ever measured myself was only seventeen feet six inches long, but Sir Hugh Low tells me that he has himself measured one which touched twenty-six feet in length.

I think it highly probable that hunger has driven the alligators to be as aggressive as they have been during the last few years. When the rinderpest was killing cattle in the Malay Peninsula, some similar disease attacked the wild pigs, and they died by hundreds. About the same time a like mortality occurred in Borneo. The principal food of the alligator is the wild pig, which is taken whilst swimming across the rivers in search of jungle fruits. When the pest occurred this supply of pork was much lessened, and the alligators became more voracious.

The wild animals in Sarawak must be rapidly disappearing as cultivation and population increase, and also as a ready market is found for venison. Wild pig and various species of deer are the only animals which were ever plentiful in Sarawak. In its last acquired districts, however, such as Baram and Limbang, there are large herds of wild cattle—splendid beasts.

This account of the present condition of Sarawak I feel to be very meagre, but I have been unable to obtain any information except from the *Gazette*, which, being written for a special purpose, only enters into the minor details required to keep the superior officers informed of what is passing in the interior and at the out-stations.

If the old Rajah could see the present state of his adopted country, he would have every reason to be proud of the results of his work, for although it has not become what he hoped—a second Java—it is progressing. As the present Rajah, Sir Charles

Brooke, was brought up to his work under the old influences, he has carried out the views and projects of his uncle in a very satisfactory manner, and it is only to be hoped that whenever his son may succeed him he may be thoroughly imbued with those traditions which have secured the success of one of the most striking enterprises of modern times.

The old Rajah relied entirely for his position in Borneo on the support of the natives themselves, and the present Rajah does nearly the same.[1] They both had a corps of English officers (civilians) to aid them in governing the country, but the military forces are purely native, and these also constitute the bulk of the civilian employés, from the Datus, those valued members of the Supreme Council, to the humblest policeman. The more one reflects on the subject the more one is disposed to admire the system which has produced a unique Government, the like of which has never been seen before. But whilst we admire the system introduced by the old Rajah, we must not forget those who have so admirably carried it out, at the head of whom is the present Rajah, with his staff of trustworthy assistants.

[1] There are now a few Sikh police.

CHAPTER IX

PRESENT CONDITION OF NORTH BORNEO — LOVELY COUNTRY—GOOD HARBOURS ON WEST COAST—FORMATION OF NORTH BORNEO COMPANY—PRINCIPAL SETTLEMENTS — TELEGRAPHIC LINES —THE RAILWAY FROM PADAS — POPULATION —TOBACCO CULTIVATION — GOLD — THE PUBLIC SERVICE — THE POLICE OF NORTH BORNEO — METHODS OF RAISING REVENUE—RECEIPTS AND EXPENDITURE—TRADE RETURNS—EXPORTS—INTERFERENCE WITH TRADERS—A GREAT FUTURE FOR NORTH BORNEO

To complete the survey of those countries, which, through the policy of Rajah Brooke, were ultimately brought under the influence and protection of England, I must devote a chapter to the British North Borneo Company.

There is nothing grander or more lovely than the country which lies between our colony of Labuan and Marudu Bay, on the extreme north of the great island. I have sailed many times along that beautiful coast, and have been lost in admiration at the variety of its scenery, from the soft outline of its well-wooded shores to the succession of ranges of undulating hills which form the background, until all are dwarfed by the magnificent mountain of Kina Balu, which towers above them.

In our journeys towards this lofty mountain, Sir Hugh Low and I passed through a great variety of country. Our first expedition took us from Abai Bay across a cultivated plain to the interior of the Tampasuk river, the low land extending for many miles on either side of the path we followed, and stretching for an indefinite distance ahead of us. Here the natives ride the water buffaloes, the oxen, the bulls and cows as they do horses in other countries. We took up our quarters for the night in the substantial house of a Bajau chief, an old friend of my fellow traveller, and next day we started inland, riding for many hours over a slightly undulating plain, which continued to the foot of the ranges of hills in front. We occasionally passed pretty villages, shaded by dense clumps of cocoanut palms and mango trees. The scene was magnificent. When we reached the first low range the path became stony and very rough, so that we had to give up our horses and trust to our own feet, and most enjoyable days they were, as we advanced along the banks of the Tampasuk, through fertile fields in full cultivation, the only inconvenience our having so constantly to ford the river. At length we turned from the stream, climbing a steepish hill to the extensive village of Kiau, which is built on a sloping buttress of Kina Balu, about three thousand feet above the level of the sea.

On our next visit to the mountain we started from Gaya Bay, then across the lake-like Mengkabong river, and after riding over a well-cultivated plain we climbed to the summit of the first range of hills, and then followed the ridges towards the mountain. Nothing could have been finer than the scenery. There was no forest, of which in Borneo one sometimes gets tired; all the land was either under cultivation or had been cultivated, ideal spots for coffee plantations if the soil be suitable. We continued on the high land until we reached the Tampasuk river, when we followed the same path as we had taken on our previous journey. The weeks we spent on the great mountain were weeks of pleasure, and we explored many of its buttresses, and at length climbed again to its summit. Mr Alfred Wallace used to say that it was worth the journey to Borneo in order to eat the fresh fruit of the Durian, but I think the fatigues of the long voyage would be amply repaid by a visit to this lovely coast and an excursion to its great mountain.

On one occasion we pitched our tents for a time on the western slope of Kina Balu, about five thousand feet above the sea, on a spot which was fairly level for half a mile in length by a quarter in breadth. There were but few trees, the ground being rocky, but the stony surface was covered by beautiful nepenthes plants, with purple pitchers, which held as much as two quarts of water. From this elevation we could see over the ranges of hills we had passed in our journeys, the reaches of many rivers, the Tampasuk plain to the China Sea beyond. It would be a perfect site for a sanatorium. Roads would have to be made, then invalids and others would come to enjoy the healthy breezes, and gain strength to make excursions over the mountain. Forty years ago I recommended the Government of India to send the least guilty of their mutineers to the north-west coast, where they would have opened up a splendid country, and our camping ground would have furnished space for the barracks required for a garrison of English troops.

In these days when mountaineers are seeking new worlds to conquer, it may interest them to read the following short discription of our first joint expedition to Kina Balu. To ascend this splendid peak has, no doubt, been the desire of all those who have looked upon its noble proportions. Seen from the north-west, no grander effect can be conceived, as it rises sheer out of the plain and sweeps aloft until it attains the towering height of nearly fourteen thousand feet. Its grand precipices, its polished granite surfaces, glittering under the bright tropical rays, the dashing cascades which fall from a height so great that they dissolve in spray before they are lost in the dark valleys below, have a magical effect on the imagination, and I felt a longing, scarcely to be conceived, to explore its unknown beauties. No amount of fatigue, no suffering, no opposition could stop us when once we started from the coast, and the first time I reached the summit, it was with bare feet that left a red tinge on the rocks at every step. But all this was unnoticed as I viewed the grandeur of the scene around, the lofty peaks of every varied form, the magnificent slopes of apparently polished granite, the broad terraces, the cyclopean walls fringing the giddy precipices, the chasms, whose depths the eye could not penetrate. There was nothing that stopped our onward march, and no rest was sought until we reached the solitary southern peak and I had climbed to its very pinnacle, and rested on a spot not a yard in breadth. Then, and only then, did the glow of triumph mantle in my cheeks as my eyes rested with satisfaction on the vast panorama spread out below. Unfortunately misty clouds swept round the mountain obscuring the splendour of the scene, but they lent a powerful aid to the imagination, as through the rents in the fleecy curtain, rivers, mountains and villages were now visible, now hidden. And there, looking south, in the distance high above all, with nothing but the thin air between, rose another peak, so lofty that it was impossible to estimate its distance.

In that rarefied air remote objects appear near, and the voice can be heard without an effort through a space which in the plains below it could not penetrate.

I had never before attained so great a height, and never before had I seen such flowers so brilliant and so numerous. There were rhododendrons of the brightest scarlet, or blood colour, or rosy pink, in bunches of forty blossoms, covering trees twenty feet in height. And not single trees, but masses of rhododendrons in sheltered nooks, literally bending beneath the weight of their flowers. And how marvellous were the shapes of the nepenthes, how beautiful in colour, how delicate in form!

Fourteen thousand feet does not appear very lofty for a mountain, but from the north-west you see the whole gigantic form without the intervention of other summits. In Bolivia I have looked at heights rising to over twenty-five thousand feet, but you observe them from plains twelve thousand feet above the sea; in Mexico, the highest volcano reaches to about nineteen thousand feet, but then it is usually seen from the capital, itself at seven thousand five hundred feet; and the same with the highest European mountains.

Sir Hugh Low and I were for many years the only real explorers of these mountains, and I feel a sort of paternal interest in the British North Borneo Company, as Sir Alfred Dent once informed me that it was my work, *Life in the Forests of the Far East*, which first suggested the idea of acquiring the north-west coast for a governing and developing company.

The north-west coast possesses two very important harbours. Gaya Bay has often been recommended as a naval station to command the China Seas. It certainly offers every facility, and would be a port of refuge in war time for our mercantile marine. In many respects, however, the Port of Labuan is more suitable for all purposes, as it not only has an excellent anchorage easily defended, but it is well supplied with coal from mines on the island itself, and is opposite the terminus of the trans-Bornean railway, now in course of construction, which would bring down full supplies of cattle and provisions from the fertile districts of Padas and Kalias. It has also the advantage of having the whole of Brunei Bay enclosed by territory under English protection, with the Sarawak Government coal mines at Muara, and the productive rivers of Limbang and Trusan to add to its supplies.

Labuan is administered, with the sanction of our Government, by the British North Borneo Company, and is likely to be one of the most flourishing of its possessions, as it is not only connected by telegraph lines with Singapore and Hong Kong, a through British line, but it must increase in consequence in these days of wars and rumours of wars.

Sir Alfred Dent acquired through an agent the concession of the north-west coast of Borneo from the Sultan of Brunei, though with some important exceptions, now in process of being handed over to the Company, as well as the north-east coast, which during the last century had been ceded to England by a Sultan of Sulu, but which we had left unoccupied ; all necessary arrangements were made with the government of those islands. These concessions were first worked by a Provisional Association, and were, in 1881, taken over by the newly-formed North Borneo Company on very onerous terms, which, at the present day, it would be useless to criticise, but which left the directors with insufficient working capital to push development with any vigour.

It is not necessary to trace in any detail the history of the Company during the last seventeen years. My object being rather to give a general view of its present condition. I may remark, however, to account for its still backward state, that its progress was much impeded by a want of knowledge, on the part of both the chairman and the directors, of the country they were chosen to administer. Within these last few years this defect has been rectified, and we may now confidently expect that progress will be more rapid.

The north-east coast of Borneo presents a great contrast to that of the north-west, as the land lies low, but is in general very fertile. As long ago as 1852 we marched through the district of Tungku on Darvel Bay, and could not but admire the splendid crops which covered the earth, and the vigour of the growth of the palms and fruit trees.

The principal settlements of the North Borneo Company are Labuan, Padas, Kalias and Sandakan. To Labuan I have already referred. As a centre of native trade it is likely to become important, and Victoria Harbour is often crowded with steamers anxious to secure coal. Its unhealthy stage appears to have passed away; in fact, the whole of North Borneo may be looked upon as fairly healthy, for although on the north-east coast there are many districts where fever is prevalent (an incident common to every tropical country when the jungle is first cut down), yet this malaria disperses in time.

Next to Labuan lie the districts of Padas and Kalias, well filled with an agricultural population, quiet and fairly industrious. Their principal industry is the cultivation of the sago palm and pepper. Padas had been chosen as the starting point of the telegraph line, which has been carried across the country to Sandakan Bay, a distance of three hundred miles. It does not appear to work very successfully, as it is liable to constant interruption from the wires being broken by falling trees. My experience of Bornean forests is that trees seldom fall even during the fiercest storms if their supports are left untouched. The finest forest trees, except the Tapang, have most of their roots running along the surface of the ground, and have a very poor hold, but they are supported in their positions by innumerable creepers, which vary in size from those resembling a ship's cable in diameter to the most delicate rattan. Cut these braces and the tree is liable to fall. This is so well known to the natives that, when clearing old forests, they only cut the principal trees partly through, except a line of the outermost ones, which are hacked until they give signs of falling. The whole line then comes down, dragging to the earth all the trees partially cut through, as if they were bound together by cords, instead of by Nature's cables. It is probably the cutting of the telegraphic line through the forest which has weakened the natural supports, and so the trees fall. If any other telegraph line be run it would be worth while trying to make the forest trees serve instead of poles, as these appear to have rotted within the first year.

From the occasional notices in the *Herald*, the North Borneo official paper, it would appear that the line was cut most of the way through primeval forest, thus opening out millions of acres of virgin land for agriculturists to develop. When the existence of this line is thoroughly understood, and its working can be ensured, it will no doubt induce those ships which trade between Australia and China to call in at Sandakan. Had the line been reliable, no doubt the Spaniards of the Philippines would have used it, in order to telegraph to their Government, instead of going all the way round to Labuan.

But the great experiment in Borneo is the railway. It starts from what may be termed the Padas district, at a point on the coast called Bukau, and the first section is to the Penotal Gorge, about fifty miles in the interior on the way to the east coast. Its course, as traced on the map, will take it well south of east, and it will have its terminus in Santa Lucia Bay. I have seen no reason given why it should not be taken to Sandakan, the headquarters of the Company, and a first-class harbour. It appears a mistake to lessen the importance of the capital, unless there are strong commercial reasons, depending on the tobacco plantations, for diverting its course through an unknown country, close to the Dutch frontiers.

If this railway succeed it will open a new era in Bornean development; and it should succeed, as, with liberal land laws, foreigners and natives will settle along the line and form plantations. But who are the inhabitants beyond the Penotal Gorge? They are mentioned once or twice in the course of the reports as Muruts or Dusuns, who will no doubt work jungle produce as soon as they find a profitable market; in fact, they are doing so now to a small extent. If the promises made to the Company be kept, and sawmills be erected near the western terminus, then the timber trade will give profitable employment to the railway. Neither timber nor jungle produce, however, will make a railway pay, and therefore the Company must be prepared to support cultivators and planters all along the line, and the money will be well and profitably employed. They have themselves started an experimental plantation at Sapong, where tobacco and other products are cultivated with very fair success, and this will encourage others. I shall watch the progress of this railway with the greatest interest, and though there will be many complaints at its slow progress, yet if capital can be found to finish it, it must prove of great benefit to the Company. It is satisfactory to learn, from the latest reports, that the natives are flocking to its neighbourhood, and that they have already cleared the land for a width of three miles on either side of the line.

Gaya Bay has so lately come under the direct control of the Company that nothing has been done yet for its development, but only some of its smaller harbours can be expected to be touched at first. Nearly all the districts in its neighbourhood are, however, fairly populated, and there is considerable cultivation on the rivers Patatan, Ananam and Kabatuan.

Kudat, on Marudu Bay, appears at one time to have been chosen for the Governor's headquarters, but it showed no promise of rapid development, and they have now been transferred to Sandakan. There is, however, a good deal of cultivation going on, and among the immigrants are several hundred Chinese Christians called Hakkas, who appear to have fled from the persecution of their heathen brethren. These are likely to be a permanent population and should be encouraged, as they are sure to support the Government.

The most important settlement on the mainland of Borneo, within the Company's grants, is Sandakan. It is a fine bay, fairly healthy, with excellent sites for a town, and is connected by a water passage with the important river of Kina Batangan, from which a short road leads to the gold workings of Sigama. Its inhabitants already muster, I understand, about three thousand, and it has the principal Government offices, a church, a club, an hotel and some rideable roads. It only wants coal to render it an important port of call, and this is said to have been found not far from the town, and is about to be worked.

The inhabitants of the districts under the sway of the Company are of many different races. The bulk of the population are Dusuns or Idaán, very much like the better class of the Land Dyaks of Sarawak. They are easily governed, and among them head hunting is a tradition rather than a practice, as only in one village that Sir Hugh Low and I visited did we find a head house, or any skulls hung up to the rafters, as is commonly the case in the communities south of the Baram. We stayed in their villages on several occasions, and formed a very favourable opinion of the people.

The above remarks are based upon our observations made in 1858, but, if Mr John Whitehead is not mistaken, these races must have greatly deteriorated, as he writes a good deal about the practice of head hunting among them in 1888. When we were there we heard like reports and met many parties of armed Dusuns, who were said to be on the war-path, but as at the same time we also met numerous parties of Dusun men, women and children carrying tobacco to the coast villages through what was said to be an enemy's country, we did not pay much attention to such statements. We saw also small parties of women and children working in the fields miles away from their villages, which could not occur if there were any real danger from hostile tribes. Either Mr Whitehead was deceived by similar stories to those which were constantly dinned into our ears, or the Dusuns have sadly deteriorated. These stories of enemies were fabricated chiefly with the object of preventing our visiting neighbouring villages.

I am afraid we should find great changes if we returned to Kina Balu, as Mr Whitehead mentions that the Company have found it necessary to send punitive expeditions against these Dusuns. I trust, however, that this is a mistake.

The next in importance to the Dusuns from their numbers are the Bajaus, who are still often called

Sea Gipsies from their wandering habits, but many thousands of them have abandoned their old custom of living in boats and have settled on the lake-like Mengkabong river and in many other places along the north-west coast, until you reach Tampasuk, where, a few miles inland, they are numerous. The Bajaus are also to be found on the north and east coasts, and are there deemed a very useful class, as fishermen and collectors of sea produce for export to the China market.

The Lanuns, of marauding celebrity, lived formerly on the Lower Tampasuk and Padasan rivers, but since their pirate settlements were routed out by Sir Thomas Cochrane in 1846, they have gradually abandoned the coast, and retired to their own country, the great island of Mindanau. Probably a few who have intermarried with the Bajaus may still be left. They were a gallant, courteous people, but too lawless for our times.

On the north-east coast there is a very mixed population of people from the Sulu Islands—some Malays, many Bajaus, and since the advent of the Company, several Chinese and a few Europeans and Madrasees.

In Padas and Kalias and on the rivers to the south of Patatan, there are many Malays from Brunei; Kadayans, who are probably aborigines converted to Islam; many descendants of the ancient Chinese colony, who can still speak their old language, but dress and live like other natives of the island. From these curious mixtures of races are derived the industrious agriculturists of those districts.

The native Borneans of whatever race have shown no power to augment the population. The deaths appear almost to equal the births, but that may arise from the great neglect of the children, and the inability of the natives to combat epidemics—smallpox and cholera sometimes sweeping them off by thousands. These causes of depopulation may lessen under the influence of civilisation, but not to a very great extent.

The Company will have therefore to depend on the Chinese, and perhaps on the Japanese, for the future population, as their industry is undoubted, and the teeming millions of the parent countries can supply endless recruits. But it would be dangerous to rely upon these hard-working but turbulent people alone, and therefore a mixture of Javanese, Boyans and Tamils would be very desirable.

The Company have very rightly based their prosperity on agriculture, and have done much to encourage subsidiary associations in their efforts to cultivate tobacco, and in some respects with very great success, as the produce has been of first-rate quality and fetches very high prices. In fact, the soil appears particularly adapted to this valuable plant, but, as always occurs when any new business is started, insufficient capital, and managers without any idea of economical working, nearly wrecked this promising industry. It now appears to have passed this trying stage and established itself on a firm basis, and its prospects are excellent.

The soil of the east coast, and many districts of the west, appears suited to every tropical cultivation. Coffee, both Liberian and Asiatic, grows with astonishing vigour, even yielding fruit in the third year. In other countries the best coffee is grown on hills at least three thousand feet above the sea level, and planters in Borneo may find it worth their while to attend to this. It is in favour of planters that all the products they have essayed have flourished for generations before the advent of the Company. Coffee is found in the hills round the capital. I sent home excellent specimens of cotton grown on the north-west coast as long ago as in the Fifties, and Saba tobacco was famous and much preferred to the Javanese by all the natives of Brunei. We noticed at Kiau, on Kina Balu, how carefully the Dusuns cultivated their tobacco, keeping the fields perfectly clean. Pepper was grown by the Chinese throughout the last century, so that none of these products are experiments. They have simply to be grown by experienced managers, instead of by the careless native methods.

As yet the search for minerals has not been successful. Gold has been found in many districts, but has not hitherto been worked so as to prove a mercantile success. As, however, alluvial gold has been collected in several streams, the quartz reefs will yet be found, as in Sarawak, where, after more than fifty years of expectation, machinery has heen erected to crush the stone. A small company has been formed in London to work the gold found in the sand and gravel banks in the Sigama river, which will be raised from its bed by a dredging machine. The latest accounts are that the dredger is already above the rapids, and had commenced working. There is nothing in the world like gold to attract population.

The geological formation of the great mountain of Kina Balu, and its surrounding ranges, would appear to offer a grand field for geologists, but it is a difficult country to explore, except where the sandstones check vegetation, but these last-named strata are never prolific in minerals.

Since the North Borneo Company has had a business man at their head, and there is a better knowledge of Borneo among the directors, it appears to be going the right way to work to develop the country. It has made some necessary roads ; the electric telegraph, though not at present very important in itself, has opened up the interior and shown what may be expected from pushing on the railway through this as yet undeveloped country.

The territory of the State of North Borneo is under the rule of a governor, Mr Beaufort, chosen by the Court of Directors, and under him are many

Residents and sub-officers who administer the affairs in the various districts. As the *Herald* appears to publish only *résumés* of the reports from the different stations, it is difficult to form any idea of the capacity of the officials or the manner in which they perform their work, but, on the whole, I should say it was satisfactory. However, there is nothing more difficult than to find men to manage natives so as to gain their confidence. As a rule the higher the class from which they are chosen, the greater chance there is of their success.

The State of North Borneo has an armed police, which only numbers four hundred, for their very extensive territory, and it proves how amenable the natives must be to authority that they can keep comparative order. The few outbreaks which have occurred have been easily suppressed, though as yet it is uncertain what will be the future conduct of the last rebel, Mat Sali, and his gang. If terms have been made with him which will in the future keep him quiet, so much the better for all. A portion of the North Borneo armed police consists of Sikhs. It is difficult to exaggerate the admirable conduct of these men during the difficult operations against Mat Sali. In the attacks on his fort their behaviour was simply splendid, and their English officers, both civil and military, were indeed well worthy to lead such men. It is to be regretted that their brave commandant, Jones, was killed. It is easy to criticise the desperate onslaught, and say it was foolhardy, but it is by such gallant contempt of odds that the Empire has been won, and that we can record with pride 'the Deeds which made the Empire.' And all this goes on in an almost forgotten part of the world, as a mere matter of duty, without any idea on the part of these brave fellows that their countrymen will ever hear of their noble conduct. Wherever the Sikhs and their English officers may be, we may feel assured of good work being done, as, for instance, in East Africa, with the late Lieutenant Alston and his dashing followers.

The revenue is raised in British North Borneo generally on the lines adopted in other Eastern possessions. The principal source of income is derived from 'farms.' The most important are those of opium and spirits. They are the easiest and best methods of raising revenue, as they only touch the weaknesses or the vices of the Chinese, and are generally highly productive; and, where the authorities are not amenable to the influence of ignorant but well-meaning fanatics, the gambling farm is not only productive but has a good moral effect, as experience has proved that the evil is lessened by being concentrated at spots under the surveillance of the police. The farms of pork and fish, and in a lesser degree, perhaps, the pawnbroking, are liable to great objections. The pork farm might be suppressed and public slaughter-houses established, as is done now in Sarawak; and pawnbroker's licenses might be substituted for that farm, which, in practice, proves so onerous to the poor. The fish farm should be suppressed and an open market substituted. As there is no clear financial statement published, I am aware that I may be criticising in the dark.

Duties on imports are often necessary, and export duties on timber and jungle produce are very defensible, as someone aptly remarked that the collectors only reap the harvest without having been put to the trouble or expense of sowing or planting, and someone must pay for the protection they all enjoy. As a rule, however, duties on agricultural products should be avoided. The tax on nibongs and attaps is something quite original, can produce but a trifle, and must be excessively annoying to the natives, as these are the building materials of their houses.

I will now give the receipts and expenditure in North Borneo for the five years 1893-7, as the receipts are now normal, and not affected by the speculative rush of planters and others, who disbursed money without a thought of the morrow :—

	Income.	Expenditure.
1893, .	£31,345	£30,338
1894, .	31,559	28,818
1895, .	37,075	33,266
1896, .	42,841	33,015
1897, .	43,778	...

As far as it goes this is a satisfactory increase in the

revenue, but is a mere bagatelle if we consider the vast territory from which it is produced. But no striking increase can take place until the Chinese feel thoroughly at home there. That North Borneo was once very popular with them is attested by all the accounts we gather from travellers and from native tradition. The very names show how they influenced the country. We have Kina Benua, the Chinese land; Kina Balu, the Chinese widow, the name of the great mountain; Kina Batañgan, the Chinese river (in the written annals of the Court of Brunei, it is mentioned that a Chinese kingdom was established on that river); then we have Kina Taki and Kina Bañgun, the names of small streams in the north. This shows how numerous the Chinese must have been in this territory. The causes of their disappearance are obscure, but may be readily imagined. Bad government in Brunei, the increase of piracy, the cutting off of the junks, the risings against oppression by this unwarlike race led to massacres; in fact, these causes are clear from the accounts of the natives. But where the Chinese have once been, they will come again.

It must be uphill work trying to extract taxes from natives, who, though they are accustomed to be robbed and plundered by their own rulers, are very unwilling to pay even the smallest regular impost. The Sarawak Malays do so readily with their capitation tax, as that payment frees them from the liability of being called out for military service, and the more civilised and industrious they become, the more they appreciate this freedom from liability. The capitation tax is a just one, though often it requires great caution in its collection to avoid discontent. As a rule it should not be collected in those districts in which the Company have no permanent officers located. Flying visits often do more harm than good. It is difficult to see how any addition can be made to the taxation. The State of Borneo must trust to the gradual development of the country and to the increase of its population, but all trammels on the free circulation of traders should be removed.

It is evident from the trade returns of North Borneo that the country is progressing. Take the statistics for the same five years :—

	Imports.	Exports.
1893, .	$1,116,714	$1,780,593
1894, .	1,329,066	1,698,543
1895, .	1,663,906	2,130,600
1896, .	1,882,188	2,473,753
1897, .	1,887,498	2,942,293

The dollar is now only worth two shillings. I do not know if these returns include those of our Colony of Labuan. I believe not, as no mention is made of the export of coal in the detailed lists.

Tobacco is the most important article of export.

There are several companies busily engaged in developing this industry, as the Bornean leaf has now taken a high position in the markets, and its quality is excellent. It not only furnishes the leaves used as wrappers, but as a smoking tobacco it has met with much favour. The principal plantations are in the north-eastern coast, near the river Kina Batañgan and Darvel Bay. The Government are also trying an experiment on the Sapong line, which will be followed by the railway. The tobacco which was so sought after by the natives in old days was, however, a product principally of the north-west coast. It would probably be advantageous to find out the exact spots where the Saba plants were grown. There is very little likelihood of there being a glut of tobacco on the market, as many of the old sources of supply are drying up, as in Cuba, and, to a lesser extent, in Manila, and the recent judicious reduction of duty in England will increase its consumption. I have no sympathy with those who would instead have lowered or abolished the duty on tea, as if tea drinkers should not contribute to the support of our navy, which secures the arrival of their favourite leaf.

The production of coffee, cotton, gambier and pepper are as yet on a very small scale, as most of the plantations are in their infancy. Pepper used to be grown to a considerable extent in the districts opposite, and a little north of Labuan, but here, as elsewhere, no doubt, the exceedingly low prices may have induced the natives to neglect the cultivation of this vine. Sarawak now produces about 15,000 tons of gambier, worth $700,000. This should encourage planters in North Borneo.

Cutch, manufactured from the bark of the mangrove tree, has became a very important export, and the development of this industry can only be limited by the demand. Gutta and rubber are of some importance, and rattans are taking an important place in the list of exports, and so are sago flour and timber. Although as a rule export duties on cultivated products are to be avoided, there are many good reasons why the Government should put a duty on tobacco, which, however, is so very light, only one per cent., as scarcely to affect its price, whilst the sum so raised is of importance to the Treasury. The police and other expenses connected with the protection of this industry are considerable.

In reading over the reports in the *North Borneo Herald*, I have noticed the tendency of the officers in charge of districts to interfere with the movements of traders. One will only allow certain men to go into the interior to collect jungle products, but they must not take with them merchandise to barter with the natives; another objects to traders going into the interior to buy produce there, as it prevents the aborigines coming down to have 'a glimpse of civilisation'; a third charges for permits, which induces people to get into the Company's interior districts from the Brunei territory, and to return that way, thus depriving the Government of its export duties (to this I notice Mr Maxwell objected); a fourth is afraid that the Chinaman will cheat the innocent Dusun, but after a very short time the latter becomes a very good match for the trader. I remember certain natives bringing hundreds of pikuls of worthless gutta, carefully coated over with the genuine article, to the bazaar in Sarawak. The Chinaman tested it, and finding no stones concealed inside the lumps, bought it at rather a high price, but was surprised to find on its being sent to Singapore that it was unsaleable. I do not think, therefore, that the officers of the State of North Borneo need trouble themselves about the trading incapacity of the Dusuns. But the scales and weights of the Chinese should be periodically tested, as this is their favourite method of cheating the unwary.

I have always objected to these restrictions on trade, and to the free movements of traders, as they existed in Sarawak. They owed their origin there, as in North Borneo, to the jealousy of the native chiefs, who do their utmost to monopolise the trade themselves, and therefore counsel the English officers not to allow Chinamen to penetrate into the interior. I would give perfect liberty to everyone, and this would not only increase the number of traders, but add considerably to the exports.

I have considered with great attention the negotiations which took place between the directors of the British North Borneo Company and the present Rajah of Sarawak, Sir Charles Brooke, and I have come to the conclusion that the shareholders were perfectly right not to part with their territory or resign its management. The Rajah would have found this great increase of dominion very burdensome, and I should be inclined to doubt whether Sarawak possesses either the capital or the staff to enable her thus to increase her responsibilities. Sarawak, as I have observed, has generally failed to attract English capital, and although the Rajah has governed his own territories with eminent success, it does not follow that he would have succeeded in so developing North Borneo as ever to have been able to pay the shareholders a dividend. They have already waited seventeen years, with an occasional trifling return, and probably they may have to wait some time yet, as the country has been but very partially opened out, but that there is a great future before North Borneo, I have full confidence.

When the State of North Borneo has advanced sufficiently, it might follow the example of the old East India Company—convert the capital of the association into stock at high interest to compensate for past losses, and then, under a Court of Directors, devote the whole of the revenue of the State to the advancement of the interests and welfare of the country. This solution would no doubt be satisfactory to everyone connected with the enterprise.

APPENDIX

Mr Brooke's Expedition to Borneo.[1]

Borneo (in the language of the natives Bruni), Celebes, Sulu, the Moluccas, and the islands of the Straits of Sunda and Banca, compose what is commonly called the Malayan group, and the Malays located on the sea shores of these and other islands may with certainty be classed as belonging to one nation.

It is well known, however, that the interior of these countries is inhabited by various tribes, differing from the Malays and each other, and presenting numerous gradations of imperfect civilisation.

The Dyaks of Borneo, the Arafuras of New Guinea, and others, besides the black race scattered over the islands (objects here, as elsewhere, of traffic), present an interesting field of inquiry; and it is surprising, whilst our acquaintance with every other portion of the globe, from the passage of the Pole

[1] This Appendix is reprinted from Vol. I. of *The Private Letters of Sir James Brooke, Rajah of Sarawak*, edited by J. C. Templer, Barrister-at-Law (Bentley, 1853), from the original MS. in his possession. A brief abstract of it was published in the *Journal of the Geographical Society* in 1838, Vol. VIII., p. 443.

to the navigation of the Euphrates, has greatly extended, we know scarcely anything of these varieties of the human race beyond the bare fact of their existence, and remain extremely ignorant of the geographical features of the countries they inhabit.

Countries which present an extended field for Christianity and commerce—which none surpass in fertility—rich beyond the Americas in mineral productions, and unrivalled in natural beauty, yet continue unexplored, and spite of the advantages which would probably result, have failed to attract the attention they so well deserve. The difficulty of the undertaking will scarcely account for its non-performance; if we consider the voluntary sacrifices made on the shrine of African research, or the energy displayed and the sufferings encountered by the explorers of the Polar regions, yet the necessity of prosecuting the voyage in an armed vessel, the wildness of the interior tribes, the lawless ferocity of the Malays, and the dangers to be apprehended from the jealousy of the Dutch, would prevent most individuals from fixing on this field for their exertions, and points it out as one which can only be fully accomplished by Government, or some influential body.

It is not my object to enter into any detail of the past history of the Malayan nations, but I may refer to the undoubted fact that they have been in a state of deterioration since we first became acquainted with them; and the records of our early voyagers, together with the remains of antiquity still visible in Java and Sumatra, prove that once flourishing nations have now ceased to exist, and countries once teeming with human life are now tenantless and deserted. The causes of such lamentable changes need only be alluded to, but it is fit to remark that whilst the clamour about education is loud, and extravagant dreams are entertained of the progressive advancement of the human race, a large tract of the globe has been gradually relapsing, and allowed to relapse, into barbarism.

Whether the early decay of the Malay states and their consequent demoralization arose from the introduction of Mohammedanism, or resulted from the intrigues of European ambition, it were useless to discuss; but we are very certain that the policy of the Dutch has, at the present day, reduced this 'Eden of the Eastern wave' to a state of anarchy and confusion, as repugnant to humanity as it is to commercial prosperity.

Enough is known of the harshness of this policy, and there is no need of here contrasting it with the energetic, successful, though ill-supported sway of Sir Stamford Raffles—but it is the indirect influence which it exerts that has proved so baneful to the Archipelago, under the assumed jurisdiction of this European power. Her unceasing interference in the concerns of the Malay Governments, and the watchful fomenting of their internal dissensions, have gradually and effectually destroyed all rightful authority, and given rise to a number of petty states, which thrive on piracy and fatten on the slave trade. The consequent disorganisation of society arising from these causes has placed a bar to commercial enterprise and personal adventure, and has probably acted on the interior tribes much in the same way as this fatal policy has affected the Malays. As far as can be ascertained, the financial and commercial concerns of the Dutch have not been prosperous ; it is easy to conceive such to be the case, as it will be conceded that oppression and prosperity cannot coexist. In short, with the smallest possible amount of advantage, the Dutch Government has all along endeavoured to perpetuate an exclusive system, aiming more at injury to others than any advantage to themselves, or to the nations under their sway ; for where an enlightened administration might have produced the most beneficial results, we are forced to deplore not only the mischief done, and the mass of good neglected, but the misery and suffering inflicted on unhappy races, capable, as has been proved, of favourable development under other circumstances.

The policy of the British in the Indian Archipelago has been marked by vacillation and weakness. The East India Company, with a strong desire to rival the Dutch, aimed at doing so by indirect and underhand means, and shrunk from the liberality of views and bold line of conduct which was perhaps inconsistent with their position and tenure of authority. It was in vain that Sir Stamford Raffles urged on them a line of conduct which, had it been pursued, must eventually have ensured the ascendency of the British over the space from Borneo to New Holland, and have linked her colonies in the East by a chain of posts from the northern part of India to the southern extremity of Van Diemen's Land. The timidity of the Company and the ignorance or indifference of the then existing Governments not only neglected to carry this bold project into execution, but sacrificed the advantages already acquired, and, without stipulation or reserve, yielded the improving Javanese to the tender mercies of their former masters. The consequences are well known; all the evils of Dutch rule have been re-established, and the British watchfully excluded, directly or indirectly, from the commerce of the islands.

It is true that the settlement of Singapore has attracted a large portion of the native trade to its free port, and has become, from its happy situation, in some measure an emporium for Straits' produce; but, with this single commercial exception, our loss of footing and political influence in the Archipelago is complete, and our intercourse with the natives has gradually become more restricted. We may sum up these remarks by taking a brief survey of the present position of the Archipelago. The Dutch are masters of a large tract of New Guinea at one extreme, and, at the other, have possessed themselves of the coast of Borneo, extending from the western boundary of Borneo proper to the southern limit of Matan. A glance at the chart will show that they have stations of more or less importance connecting these points, and that Java, and their settlement on Sumatra, give them exclusive command of the Straits of Sunda. It may likewise be here observed that their territorial extension is only limited by their desires, for as there is no check from European nations, a title to possession is too readily acquired from distracted and contending native Governments.

But the position of the Dutch nation in the 'Far East,' though apparently so imposing, is, in reality, far from strong, and their power would easily sink before the vigorous opposition of any European country.

Java, exhausted and rebellious, submits, but remembers the period of British possession. The wild Battas, of Sumatra, successfully repel the efforts of the Dutch to reduce them. The Chinese of the southern part of Borneo are eager to cast off the yoke of masters who debar them every advantage, and would fain, were it in their power, exact a heavy tribute. Their possessions in New Guinea are nominal rather than real, and their older settlement of the Moluccas, fallen in value, can scarcely be supposed to compensate for the sacrifice of men and money caused by their narrow-minded views and ill-directed efforts. The Dutch are strong enough to defy any native power directed against them, but their doubtful title and oppressive tenure would, as I have before said, render the downfall of their rule in the Archipelago certain and easy before the establishment of a liberal Government and conciliating policy.

Of the Malays, it is sufficient here to remark that they have ceased to be powerful, and that their distracted and disorganised state renders it dangerous for friends or strangers to trust themselves in their hands; but their hatred of the Dutch is unbounded, and there is no reason to think that any insuperable obstacle would be met with in the formation of a strong legitimate Government amongst them.

Our recent knowledge of the position of the native states is so circumscribed, however, that it is difficult to say much on this subject.

The Bugis, the traders of the islands, and their hardiest and most enterprising race, are checked and hampered by Dutch restrictions, and this remark, applying most forcibly to them, is true of the whole trading interests, and renders all alike inveterately hostile to the Dutch.

It may be fairly concluded from the foregoing remarks that the injury done to British interests by the cession of Java and the consequent loss of power has been greatly counterbalanced by the misrule of the Dutch since their undisputed re-establishment. The field is again open, therefore, to any nation desirous of rivalling Holland, and little doubt can be entertained of the success of such an effort, if carried on by a course of policy and conduct the reverse in every respect of that pursued by the present monopolists. The fact must be always borne in mind that the Dutch are masters of the Archipelago *only* because no other nation is willing to compete with them, and although any attempt by another power might, and would, doubtless, be watched with the greatest anxiety and distrust, and every opposition, direct and indirect, be levelled against it, yet it could not be considered any infringement of acknowledged right or actual possession.

A liberal system, indeed, recommended by mutual advantage, would assuredly triumph over any local opposition, if not obstructed by European interests; nor is there any great reason to apprehend such a probability, unless, going from one extreme to another, we should attempt hostility to regain what was foolishly thrown away.

Nevertheless, sooner or later, the time *must* arrive when we shall again be in possession of these islands, and we may accordingly look forward and prepare for the event in various ways.

The subject may be divided under two heads, viz., Territorial Possession, and Commercial Prosperity; and these appear so intimately blended, that the second is greatly dependent on the first, for it must be remembered that Sir Stamford Raffles, the highest authority on this point, has pronounced that no purely commercial settlement can succeed in the Archipelago, and has attributed the numerous failures which have occurred to a lack of knowledge of the country, and the non-possession of territory.

Many arguments might be urged, and many reasons given, to show the entire justice of this opinion, but it will be sufficient to state that where a native population exists, and is rightly governed, an influence is insensibly acquired and strengthened, not only over those immediately protected, but also over the neighbouring tribes, and that on the occasion of any disturbance or collision with other powers, the means of resistance or the punishment of aggression are at hand. A commercial post, on the contrary, though advantageously situated, is liable to the fluctuations and distractions of its neighbours, its means of attack or defence are necessarily limited, and whilst it fails to command respect, the natives are rather injured than benefited by its existence.

The chief consideration, however, seems to be that territorial power is constantly opening new sources of traffic, and extending those already established, by disembarrassing trade of the intermediate clogs which tend to limit exports, from the small amount of benefit to the original dealer—and to lessen the demand—from the increased price attendant on passing through various hands.

The insular situation of Singapore may be adduced as a proof of this, for all articles of Straits produce, before coming into the possession of the British merchant, afford profits to several classes of natives, in a very unequal degree; and little hope can be entertained of the favourable progress of a trade wherein the original producer or proprietor participates to so trifling an extent in its advantages. It may, indeed, be considered a monopoly by the natives inhabiting the coasts, as severe on the interior tribes as the Dutch restrictions on themselves.

For these and many other causes which readily occur, it would seem that territorial possession is the best, if not the only means, by which to aquire a direct and powerful influence in the Archipelago, but any government instituted for the purpose must be directed to the advancement of the native interests and the development of native resources rather than by a flood of European colonization, to aim at possession only, without reference to the indefeasible rights of the Aborigines.

On the second head, viz., the Commercial Prosperity, nothing need be added save that, being dependent on the right working of the first principle, it must unavoidably, in its progress, present a striking contrast to the commercial monopolies of the Dutch, and be the means of bringing the English merchant in contact with the original native dealer.

The advantages, political and commercial, accruing

from a well-managed territory need only be alluded to, as everyone in the slightest degree acquainted with the country is well aware of its vast capability.

In a political view, the contiguity of the islands to our possessions in New Holland and India, and the command over China, are sufficiently apparent; and commercially, it would only be necessary to quote their productions to prove their value. The difficulty of once more placing our interests on a footing worthy a great nation is no doubt considerable, but apt to be greatly overrated; as the unpopularity of the Dutch, and the weakness of the native states, would ensure success to an establishment aiming at sufficient results by slow but steady means. The question, indeed, is not one embracing the acquisition of territory, but its *occupation*: viz., whether England shall claim and improve lands she holds by as good a title as any the Dutch can show, and whether, doing so, she shall use the full ascendency of her national position to extend her commerce, and distribute her manufactures among a people who have always, when permitted, shown their craving for mercantile adventure?

A strong government established in Malludu[1] Bay, a British territory capable of extension, and possessing internal resources, having sufficient authority to cultivate a good understanding with the native governments, and spread inferior posts over the Archipelago,

[1] In the text of this volume the name is spelt 'Marudu.'

as opportunities offered, would effect this object, and, without infringing upon the claims of any foreign state, ensure a commercial footing on a scale never yet developed in this portion of the world. Malludu Bay, situated at the northern extremity of Borneo, has been mentioned as best adapted for the purpose in view on several accounts.

1st. It is a British possession.

2nd. There is no great Malay or Bugis settlement in its vicinity.

3rd. It is the place where, in all probability, a direct intercourse may be held with the Dyaks of the interior.

4th. The position relative to China is advantageous.

5th. It forms the western limit of the Archipelago, and our new settlement at Port Essington bounds it to the eastward. The climate and the soil are well spoken of: a river flows into the bay, and is reported to communicate with the lake of Keeny Balloo[1] and the mountains in the interior—one of very considerable elevation. Above all, however, the natives are reported to be docile and easily taught; the servants of the Company attached to their settlement of Balambangan were decided in opinion that this bay was far preferable in every respect to the station chosen and subsequently abandoned.

[1] Kina Balu.

Supposing these advantages to be as above stated, yet it would scarcely authorise any active steps being taken without a more accurate knowledge than we at present possess of the particular locality and of the States in its vicinity; it is to this point that I would direct attention, remarking, however, that although Malludu Bay should on inquiry be found to be unfit for the purposes of colonisation, yet the general view of our policy remains unaffected, as it would be only necessary to obtain a suitable place.

With a settlement at each extremity of the Archipelago, we could readily protect the trade of the natives, and obtain minor posts, and free-trade ports, whence the best principles of commerce and good government might be disseminated, and our interests best promoted, by the general prosperity of the countries under our sway, or in our own vicinity. It is scarcely necessary to say more on this subject, but before closing these remarks, I cannot help adverting to the colony at Port Essington.

The former settlement, which existed in the immediate neighbourhood of Port Essington, was after a trial (of a few years) abandoned as useless, and the same difficulties which checked the progress of the first will probably impede the present colony.

It was a striking feature of this settlement, that the natives, though frequenting the coasts to the northward of New Holland,[1] seldom if ever visited or offered to trade with the settlement. This has, I know, been attributed to the natives being ignorant of the existence of the place, but this reason appears to me improbable in the highest degree, and we may with more justice surmise the cause to be our utter disinclination and local inability to protect traders from the consequences attendant on a breach of Dutch regulations. This conjecture gathers confirmation from the facts that the inhabitants of the Eastern portion of the Archipelago are not addicted to maritime adventure, being supplied by the traders of the Western Islands with such articles of European or Chinese manufacture as are suited to their tastes. The Bugis vessels that frequent the north coast of New Holland chiefly carry on the trade with the Arafura group, and it is evident that going and returning from this voyage they are at the mercy of the Dutch cruisers. Is it probable, then, that the Dutch would allow an intercourse with a British settlement which it was in their power to prevent? And whilst the Bugis are the carriers, is it not in the power of the Dutch to restrict and harass, if not totally to prevent, their communication with us? The natives of the Archipelago cannot look to the British for protection, but they can and do look for Dutch vengeance, and dread it.

These considerations are not urged against advan-

[1] *I.e.*, Australia.

tages to be derived from the possession of Port Essington, but rather as a warning against the over-sanguine expectations of its having a trade of any considerable extent, whilst our relations with the Archipelago continue on their present eclipsed footing. The good to result from this colony must be looked for on the continent of New Holland, where it will probably extend and make the same progressive strides to importance as the sister colonies in the same country: but with reference to the Archipelago, its government will want authority to control the evil influence sufficiently to ameliorate the present system.

Not far distant to the westward of Port Essington is the large and fertile island of Timor, a portion of which there is no doubt the Government of Portugal would cede willingly for the smallest equivalent, as it has been long virtually abandoned, and is utterly useless to the mother country. The size and situation would render the possession of the Portuguese frontier of this island a desirable acquisition, and the favourable opportunity may not, if allowed to pass over, again recur.

The same, indeed, may be said of Leuconia, which, offering no real benefit to Spain, would, in the hands of the English, be a lever to rule both China and the Archipelago. Rich, fertile, and blessed with a fine climate, within a few days' sail of Canton, and commanding the China sea, it would be an unrivalled jewel in the colonial tiara of England. When our relations with China come to be settled, and settled they must shortly be, the importance of Manila can scarcely be overrated.

Spain, distracted and torn by internal factions, and pledged to England by treaty and obligation, would readily place Leuconia in our hands as a guarantee for the sums due, and would probably cede the possession in lieu of the claims we have on her exchequer.

For such an acquisition, the present is the time, the tide in our affairs which, taken at the flood, would lead on to fortune ; and as I have before stated, that in a political point of view it is only on an extended scale that any real advantage, national or local, is to be gained, I must re-urge my conviction that it is better to leave the Archipelago in its present state until the next general war, when it will again pass into our hands, than, by contenting ourselves with paltry and insignificant stations, convey false impressions of our national importance, not easily removed from the minds of the natives.[1]

Whatever difference of opinion may exist, or what-

[1] I may here add a brief summary of the Dutch trading regulations :—Death was inflicted on traders in spice and opium not first bought from the Company. It is forbidden, under heavy penalties, to export or import the following articles, viz., pepper, tin, copper, Surat silks, Indian cloths, cotton yarns of all sorts, unstamped gold, Samarang arrack, muskets, gunpowder, etc., etc. All vessels required a pass. No vessel to carry powder or shot in greater quantity than specified in the pass. No port was open to any vessel coming from the northward of the Moluccas, except Batavia. No navigation was allowed to be carried on by the vessels of Banka and Billiton, except to Palembang : no navigation from Celebes !

ever degree of credit may be due to the views here recommended, there can be no doubt of our future ascendency in the Archipelago, whether attempted at the present time, or delayed until the fortunes of war offer a fitting occasion. In either case a previous acquaintance will greatly facilitate the result, and must in all probability tend to a more just appreciation of these highly interesting countries; for when public attention is once aroused, and a stimulus given to inquiry, it cannot fail in fully developing the resources, and exhausting the knowledge of the mine, which has heretofore been left to the weak and casual efforts of individual exertion. It has been remarked by Mr Farquhar that the indifference of the British Government must have originated solely from the want of information, or its incorrectness, since it is not improbable that the riches of Sumatra and Borneo are equal to those of Brazil and New Spain. The lapse of years has by no means weakened the force of this observation, for Borneo, Celebes, and indeed the greater portion of these islands are still unknown, and the government is as indifferent now to these countries, equal in riches, and superior in commercial advantages to the new world. The apathy of two centuries still reign supreme with the enlightened people of England, as well as their Government, and whilst they willingly make the most expensive efforts favourable to science, commerce, or Christianity in other quarters, the locality which eminently combines these three objects is alone neglected and alone uncared for.

It has unfortunately been the fate of our Indian possessions to have laboured under the prejudice and contempt of a large portion of the well-bred community, for whilst the folly of fashion requires an acquaintance with the deserts of Africa, and a most ardent thirst for a knowledge of the usages of Timbuctoo, it at the same time justifies the most profound ignorance of all matters connected with the government and geography of our vast possessions in Hindostan. The Indian Archipelago has fully shared this neglect, for even the tender philanthropy of the present day, which originates such multifarious schemes for the amelioration of doubtful evils, and which shudders at the prolongation of apprenticeship in the West for a single year, is blind to the existence of slavery in its worst and most exaggerated form in the East. Not a single prospectus is spread abroad, not a single voice upraised in Exeter Hall, to relieve the darkness of paganism and the horrors ot the slave trade. Whilst the trumpet tongue of many an orator excites thousands to the rational and charitable object of converting the Jews and reclaiming the gipsies; whilst the admirable exertions of missionary enterprise in the Ausonian climes of the South Sea have invested them with worldly power as well as religious influence; whilst the benevolent plans of the New Zealand Association contemplate the protection of the natives by the acquisition of their territory: whilst we admire the torrent of devotional and philosophical exertion, we cannot help deploring that the zeal and attention of the leaders of these charitable crusades have never been directed to the countries under consideration. These unhappy countries have failed to rouse attention or excite commiseration, and as they sink lower and lower, they afford a striking proof how civilisation may be crushed, and how the fairest and richest lands under the sun may become degraded by a continuous course of oppression and misrule.

It is under these circumstances I have considered that individual exertions may be usefully applied to rouse the zeal of slumbering philanthropy, and lead the way to an increased knowledge of the Indian Archipelago.

Such an exertion will be made at some cost and some sacrifice, and I shall here quit the general topic, and confine myself to the specific objects of my intended voyage. It must be premised, however, that any plan previously decided on must always be subject, during its execution, to great modification, in countries where the population is always wild and often hostile, and where the influence of climate is sometimes fatally opposed to the progress of inquiry. Local information, likewise, frequently renders a change both advisable and advantageous, and circumstances, as they spring up, too often influence beyond the power of foresight, especially in my own case, where the utmost care will still leave the means very inadequate to the full accomplishment of the proposed undertaking.

With a small vessel properly equipped, and provided with the necessary instruments for observation, and the means for collecting specimens in Natural History, it is proposed, in the first place, to proceed to Singapore, which may be considered the headquarters for the necessary intervals of refreshment, and for keeping open a certain communication with Europe. Here, the best local information can be obtained, interpreters procured, the crew augmented for any particular service, and, if needful, a small vessel of native construction may be added to the expedition to facilitate the objects in view. An acquaintance may likewise be formed with the more respectable of the Bugis merchants, and their good-will conciliated in the usual mode, viz., by civility and presents, so as to remove any misconceived jealousy on the score of trading rivalry, and to induce a favourable report of our friendly intentions in their own country, and at the places where they may touch. The *Royalist*[1] will probably reach Singapore in the month of February or March 1839, at the latter end of the N.E. or rainy monsoon. The delay consequent on effecting the objects above mentioned, besides gaining a general acquaintance with

[1] The *Royalist*, a yacht of 142 tons burthen, belonging to the Royal Yacht Squadron, in which the enterprise was prosecuted.

the natural history and trade of the settlement, and some knowledge of the Malay language, will usefully occupy the time until the setting in of the S.W. or dry monsoon. It may be incidentally mentioned, however, that, in the vicinity of Singapore, there are many islands imperfectly known, and which, during the interval of the rainy season, will afford interesting occupation. I allude more especially to the space between the Straits of Rhio and those of the Durien, and likewise to the island of Bintang, which, although laid down as one large island, is probably composed of small ones, a better acquaintance with which might facilitate the voyage from Singapore to the eastward, by bringing to light other passages besides those of Rhio and Durien, and at any rate would add something to the knowledge of the country in the immediate vicinity of our settlement. On the commencement of the healthy season, I purpose sailing from Singapore, and proceeding without loss of time to Malludu Bay. This spot has been chosen for our first essay for reasons previously enumerated, and in a country every part of which is highly interesting, the mere fact of its being a British possession gives it a prior claim to attention. The objects in view may be briefly mentioned.

1st. A general knowlege of the bay, and the correct position of its various points, so as to determine its outline.

2nd. To make inquiries of the settlement of Cochin-Chinese, reported, on Earl's authority, to be fixed in the neighbourhood of Bankoka. (An intercourse will if possible be opened with this settlement.)

3rd. Carefully and minutely to explore the rivers which flow into the bay, and to penetrate, if practicable, as far as the lake and mountain of Keeny Balloo.

4th. Every endeavour will be used to open a communication with the aboriginal inhabitants, and to conciliate their good opinion. I speak with great diffidence about penetrating into the interior of this country, for I am well aware of the insurmountable difficulties which the hard reality often presents, previously overlooked, or easily overcome on the smoothness of paper, or in the luxury of a drawing-room. The two points chiefly to be relied on for this purpose are a friendly intercourse with the natives, and the existence of navigable rivers. It is mentioned by Sir Stamford Raffles, on native authority, that a land communication of not more than forty miles exists between Malludu Bay and Keeny Balloo, but neither this computation, nor any other derived from the natives, can be relied on, for the inhabitants of these countries are generally ignorant of any measure of distance, and their reckoning by time is so vague as to defy a moderately certain conclusion. The fact, however, of the vicinity of the lake to the bay is certain, and it follows as a reasonable inference that the river or rivers flowing into the bay communicate with the lake. The existence of such rivers, which were from the locality to be expected, are mentioned by Captain Forrest.

Most of this north part of Borneo (he says), granted to the East India Company by the Sulus, is watered by noble rivers; those that discharge themselves into Malludu Bay are not barred. It is by one or the other of these rivers that I shall hope to penetrate as far as the lake and mountain of Keeny Balloo, and into the country of the Idaan. I have not been able to learn that any Malay towns of importance are situated in the bight of the bay, and their absence will render a friendly communication with the aborigines a matter of comparative ease. The advantages likely to result from such friendly relations are so evident, that I need not dwell upon them, though the mode of effecting such an intercourse must be left to the thousand contingencies which govern all, and act so capriciously on the tempers of savage races. The utmost forbearance and liberality, guided by prudence, so as not to excite cupidity, appear the fundamental rules for managing men in a low state of civilisation.

The results of an amicable understanding are uncertain at its commencement, for they depend on the enterprise of the individual and the power of the native tribe into whose hands he may chance to fall. I will therefore not enter into a visionary field of discovery, but it appears to me certain that, without the assistance of the natives, no small party can expect to penetrate far into a country populous by report, and in many parts thickly wooded. Without entertaining exaggerated expectations, I trust that something may be added to our geographical knowledge of the sea-coast of this bay; its leading features, productions, river anchorages and inhabitants; the prospects of trade and the means of navigation; and although my wishes lead me strongly to penetrate as far as the lake, yet the obstacles which may be found to exist will induce me to rest satisfied with the more moderate and reasonable result. It may not be superfluous to notice here that a foregone conclusion appears to be spread abroad regarding the aboriginal (so-called) inhabitants of Borneo, and that they are usually considered and mentioned under the somewhat vague appellation of Dyaks. They are likewise commonly pronounced as originating from the same stock as the Arafuras of Celebes and New Guinea, and radically identical with the Polynesian race. The conclusion is not in itself highly improbable, but certainly premature, as the facts upon which it is built are so scanty and doubtful as to warrant no such structure. On an island so vast as Borneo, races radically distinct might exist, and at any rate the opposite conclusion is hardly justifiable from the specimens of language, or the physical appearance of the tribes of the southern portion of the country. We have Malay authorities for believing that there are many large tribes in the interior, differing greatly in their degree of civilisation, though all alike removed from the vicinity of a superior people. We have the Dyaks of the south, the Idaan of the north, the Kayan warriors and the Punan, a race little better than monkeys, who live in trees, eat without cooking, are hunted by the other tribes, and would seem to exist in the lowest conceivable grade of humanity. If we can trust these accounts, the latter people resemble in many particulars the Orang Benua, or aborigines of the Peninsula, but the Dyaks and Idaans are far superior, living in villages, cultivating the ground and possessing cattle; besides these, we have the names of several other tribes and people, and in all probability many exist in the interior with whom we are yet unacquainted.

There are strong reasons for believing that the Hindoo religion, which obtained so extensively in Java and Sumatra, and yet survives in Balli and Lombok, was likewise extended to Borneo, and some authors have conceived grounds for supposing a religion anterior even to this. If only a portion of these floating opinions should be true, and the truth can only be tested by inquiry, we may fairly look for the descendants of the Hindoo dynasty as well as an aboriginal people. It never seems to have occurred to anyone to compare the Dyaks with the people of Balli and Lombok; we know indeed little of the former, but both races are fair, good-looking and gentle. Again, respecting the concluded identity of the Dyaks and Arafuras; it is clear we have a very limited knowledge of the former, and, I may ask, what do we know of the Arafuras? In short, I feel as reluctant to embrace any preconceived theory as I am to adopt the prevailing notion on this subject, for it requires a mass of facts, with which we are lamentably deficient, to arrive at anything approaching to a reasonable conclusion. To return, however, from the above digression to the proceedings of the *Royalist*, I would remark that it depends greatly on the time passed in Malludu Bay whether our next endeavour be prosecuted at Abai on the western, or Trusan Abai on the eastern coast. The object in visiting Abai would be chiefly to penetrate to the lake, which, on the authority of Dalrymple and Barton, is not very far distant thence by a water communication; but should any success have attended similar efforts from Malludu Bay, this project will be needless, as the enterprise will be prosecuted to the westward, and reach the vicinity of Abai. As Kimanis is the limit of the British territory to the westward, so Point Kenabantongen, situated to the southward of the bay of Londakua (Sandakan?), forms the eastern boundary, and a line drawn from coast to coast between these points is represented as including our possessions. A reference to the chart will show the extent to be considerable, and the eastern coast from Malludu Bay to Point Kenabantongen is so little known, that it is desirable to become acquainted with its general features and conformation, and to seek thence the means of gaining an inlet into the interior should it be denied at Malludu Bay. The reported proximity of Keeny Balloo to Malludu Bay, and likewise to Abai, would (supposing it to be anything like the size it is affirmed) lead us to expect that it cannot be far distant from the eastern coast, and it is reasonable to conclude that some rivers or streams discharge themselves into the sea, in the numerous indentations that abound on this shore. However this may be, the coast, with its bays, islands, and bold headlands, is one of great interest, the careful inspection of which as far as Point Keneonjon will add to our knowledge. The longitude of Point Unsong and Point Keneonjon will likewise determine the eastern extremity of Borneo, as the latitude of Point San Paniange will give the northern extreme of the island.

Much might be added on this topic, especially on the reputed communication by a line of lakes from Malludu Bay to Benjar Massin, which, if true, would in all probability place some of these lakes near particular points of the eastern coast, as the whole line from the relative position of the two extremes must be on the eastern side of the island. These reports, and the various surmises which arise from them, are matters rather of confirmation than discussion, and I will therefore only add that, tempted by success, I shall not devote less than a year and a half to this object; but in case of finding a sickly climate, or meeting with a decidedly hostile population, I shall more easily abandon the field, and turn to others of not less interest, and perhaps less risk.

Equal to Borneo in riches, and superior in picturesque beauty to any part of the Archipelago, is the large and eccentric country of the Bugis, called Celebes; so deep are the indentations of its coast, that the island may be pronounced as composed of a succession of peninsulas, nearly uniting in a common centre in the district of Palos, and thus, by the proximity of every part to the sea, offering great facilities for brief and decisive inland excursions.

The Dutch hold possession of Macassar, and formerly had settlements on the north-west coast and in the Bay of Sawa; their power appears never to have been very extensively acknowledged, and at present I have not been able to find any account of the condition of their factories. This information will probably be gained at Singapore, and at all events, I am by no means ambitious of frequenting their ports further than necessity obliges, and expect but little information from them respecting the internal regulations of their colonial Government, or the trade or productions of the territory under their sway. I propose, therefore, limiting my inquiries to the northern and north-eastern portion of the island, more especially the great Bay of Gunong Tella. It is impossible to state here the direction of these inquiries, or any definitive object to which they should be turned, as I am acquainted with no author who speaks of the country save in a general and vague manner. It is reported as rich, mountainous, strikingly beautiful, and possessed of rivers abounding in birds, and, like Borneo, inhabited by wild tribes in the interior, and by the Bugis on the seashores and entrances of rivers. The character of the Bugis, so variously represented, gives me strong hopes of rendering them, by care and kindness, useful instruments in the prosecution of these researches, for all writers agree that they are hardy, active, enterprising and commercial, and it is seldom that a people possessing such characteristics are deaf to the suggestions of self-interest and kindly feeling.

The arrogance and especially the indolence of the Malays counteract the influence of these strong incentives, and the impulse which governs such wild tribes as the Dyaks and Arafuras is a dangerous weapon which cuts all ways, and often when least anticipated. The Bajoos (Bajaus), or sea gipsies, are another race on whom some dependence may be placed, particularly if they be freed from the trammels of debt, swindled upon them by the Malays. Mr Earl, who had a personal acquaintance with this tribe, and could speak their language, always expressed to me a degree of confidence in their good faith which must have had some grounds.

I may here conclude the first stage of the expedition, during the progress of which the headquarters will be fixed at Singapore. During some of the intervals I hope to see Manila, and to acquire a cursory knowledge of the unexplored tract at the southern extemity of Manila, called in Norries' general chart the Tiger Islands. The time devoted to the objects above mentioned must, as I have before said, be regulated by the degree of fortune which attends them; for, cheered by success, I should not readily abandon the field; yet, if persecuted by climate or other serious detriments, I shall frequently shift the ground to remove myself beyond such evil influence. It is scarcely needful to continue a detail of projects so distant, having already carved out for myself a work which I should be proud to perform, and which is already as extended as the chances of human life and human resolves will warrant.

The continuation of the voyage would lead me to take the *Royalist* to Timor or Port Essington, thence making excursions to the Aru Isles, Timor Laut, and the southern shores of North Guinea. That part of the coast contiguous to Torres Straits I am particularly desirous of visiting, as it has been suggested to me by Mr Earl, and I think with reason, that a better channel than the one we are at present acquainted with may be found there. That such a channel exists, and will be discovered when the coast is surveyed, I entertain but little doubt, but the navigation is hazardous, and from the westward must be attempted with great caution. My own proceedings must of course be regulated by the discoveries previously made by Captain Wickham and others, and as this gentleman has orders to survey Torres Straits, the field may be well trodden before I reach it. The rest of the voyage I shall consider as one merely of pleasure, combining such utility as circumstances will permit. It is probable that I shall visit our Australian settlements, glance at the Islands of the Pacific, and return to Europe round the Horn.

Before concluding this long paper, I may observe that there are points of inquiry which may be useful to the studies of the learned, which, provided the process may be moderately simple, I shall be willing to make, and I shall always be happy to receive any directions or suggestions regarding them. I allude to observations of the tides, to geology, natural history, etc., etc., for the general observer often overlooks highly interesting facts from his attention not being called to them. The specimens of natural history will be forwarded from time to time, and information will be sent to the Geographical Society which may always, if it be of any value, be used as freely as it is communicated. In like manner, the objects of natural history will be open to any person who is interested in such pursuits. I cannot but express my regret that, from pecuniary considerations as well as the small size of the vessel, and the limited quantity of provisions she carries, I am unable to take a naturalist and draughtsman, but I should always hail with pleasure any scientific person who happened to be in the countries at the time; and I may venture to promise him every encouragement and facility in the prosecution of his pursuits.

I embark upon the expedition with great cheerfulness, with a strong vessel, a good crew, and the ingredients of success, as far as the limited scale of the undertaking will permit; and I cast myself on the waters, like Southey's little book; but whether the world will know me after many days is a question which, hoping the best, I cannot answer with any degree of assurance.

ERRATA

For 'on' *read* 'in,' page 99, line 9.
For 'Governor' *read* 'Government,' page 109, line 13.
For '*Weeraff*' *read* '*Weraff*,' page 120, line 9.
For 'Pangeran, Nipa' *read* 'Pangeran Nipa,' page 179, line 27.
For 'Imaun' *read* 'Imaum,' page 126, line 8.
" " " " " 157, " 15.

INDEX

C

L

M

N

O

P

R

S

T

THE END

Colston & Coy. Limited, Printers, Edinburgh.

www.ingramcontent.com/pod-product-compliance
Lightning Source LLC
Chambersburg PA
CBHW060528030726
47498CB00004B/1111